SMOKE SCREEN

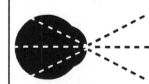

This Large Print Book carries the
Seal of Approval of N.A.V.H.

SMOKE SCREEN

TERRI BLACKSTOCK

THORNDIKE PRESS
A part of Gale, a Cengage Company

GALE
A Cengage Company

**LIBRARY OF CONGRESS CIP DATA ON FILE.
CATALOGUING IN PUBLICATION FOR THIS BOOK
IS AVAILABLE FROM THE LIBRARY OF CONGRESS**

ISBN-13: 978-1-4328-7169-7 (hardcover alk. paper)

Published in 2019 by arrangement with Thomas Nelson, Inc., a division
of HarperCollins Christian Publishing, Inc.

Printed in Mexico
1 2 3 4 5 6 7 23 22 21 20 19

*This book is lovingly dedicated
to the Nazarene.*

CHAPTER 1

BRENNA

He left me for a size-two selfie star and didn't want me to make a scene. My husband — who'd remarried as soon as our divorce was final — overestimated the preacher's kid in me and underestimated my maternal grit. I wasn't going to be blotted out of my children's lives. I couldn't be erased, and I planned to show him. I just had to figure out how.

"He's here," my sister, Georgi, said, looking out the front window. "It's not right that he's doing this, Brenna. It's not his day yet."

"He's announcing his candidacy for mayor tonight, so he wanted the kids with him." I turned to the hallway. "Sophia! Noah! Your dad's here."

The doorbell rang as my eight-year-old, Sophia, came out of her room, barefoot and wearing shorts and a My Little Pony T-shirt. Her corkscrew curls fell in front of her eyes.

She'd taken the bow out.

"Where's your dress? Why did you change?"

"I don't want to wear it," she said. "It itches."

"That's my girl," Georgi said.

I sent her a sharp look, then turned back to my daughter. "Honey, he's going to make you put it on."

"I want to stay home. It's not his day."

"I know, honey, but it's an unusual night with the campaign starting, so I'm trying to work with him."

The doorbell rang again, and I took a deep breath and opened the door. The man I once loved stood there under the light, his character so clear to me now. "They're not ready," I said.

"Why not?" He came in as if he belonged, though he'd never lived here. He looked at Sophia, then back at me. "Why can't you do the least little thing I ask, Brenna? I wanted her to wear the dress Rayne bought her."

"She hates it."

"I don't care. She's wearing it. This is an important event."

"Hi, Daddy," Sophia said meekly.

"Hey, baby." He shot me another look. "You couldn't even do her hair?"

"She undid everything. That's how much she doesn't want to go."

"Sophia, go to your room and put on that dress. Rayne will fix your hair in the car since your mother can't seem to do it."

"Don't start on her, Jack," Georgi said.

"Georgi, stop," I said. Neither of them had a problem brawling in front of the kids, but I wouldn't let it happen. "Noah!" I called.

Four-year-old Noah came out, thankfully still wearing the little suit I'd put on him. "I'm sweaty," he said, looking up at his dad with round, pleading eyes.

"You'll be okay, little man. You look really snappy."

"I hate snappy."

"I have gummies in the car."

Noah sucked in a breath. "Really?"

"Only for kids who keep their nice clothes on."

"I'm not sure gummies and nice clothes go together," I pointed out. "You might want to rethink that."

"There's no time. I'll feed them to him one at a time."

"No!" Noah said. "I want to hold them."

Jack ignored him and looked up the hall. "Sophia!" She came out with her dress on, and she had stuck the bow back in her hair.

It was crooked and hanging halfway over her forehead. I took it out and clipped it in right, hoping it would keep Rayne from torturing her. I bent over and kissed her. "Be sweet, okay? It'll be over before you know it."

I got the little backpack that went with Noah. "His inhaler is in here. Just keep it close. You never know who's going to smoke or wear perfume or . . . whatever."

"He's tougher than you think," Jack said.

"He has to be able to breathe to be tough. Please. If Rayne's going to be watching him, tell her where it is."

"Daddy, do I get gummies too?" Sophia asked.

"Maybe a few, if you don't complain about that dress. It'll hurt Rayne's feelings."

"Really, Jack?" Georgi set her hands on her hips. "You're saying that in this house?"

"I wasn't talking to you," Jack snapped. "What are you even doing here?"

"Visiting my sister," she said defiantly. "Remember those kids are not little tin soldiers bred to make you look good for the mayoral race."

"Georgi!" I said again.

Sophia looked up at me but wisely kept her thoughts to herself. I kissed both kids and watched as Jack took them away. "I'll see you tomorrow, munchkins," I called down the sidewalk.

No one answered. The light came on in the car, illuminating my nemesis in her gold lamé top that looked more sorority sister than stepmother. But then, she'd been barely out of her teens when he married her.

I restrained myself from slamming the door. When I turned back, my sister was standing right behind me.

"Did you see what that woman is wearing?" she asked.

"How could I not?"

"You should get angry, Brenna. You should get fighting mad."

I couldn't believe her. "You think I'm not mad? You think I like having to move out of my home, struggle for money, hand my kids over when it's not even his day? Trust me, I'm mad. I just don't want the kids to hear your smart-aleck comments. I don't want to make this harder for them."

"You think that if you give him the kids on demand, he'll change his mind about the custody suit. But he won't. He has to get the kids so he can play the part of the perfect family man and make people forget he cheated on his wife."

"I don't think that. *His father* is driving that suit, so there's no way Jack will drop it.

But I do want to look reasonable to the judge."

"Brenna, don't be reasonable. Be angry. Channel that anger and don't let him walk all over you. He has a lot of gall even looking you in the eye when he's suing you. You have to handle this, Brenna. Your head has to be clear."

I didn't respond. I knew what she meant.

I went back to the den and picked up the toys, tossed them into their basket. "No right-minded judge would take those kids away from their mother," Georgi muttered.

"Unless Jack's father has paid the judge off," I said. "And we both know that's possible."

"Then we have to make it harder for him to do that." She got her phone out of her purse on the couch's end table and thumbed it. "I'm going to stalk her on social media. Get pictures of her in that outfit. You can show that to the judge as evidence that she shouldn't even be around those kids, let alone making decisions about them. And we both know Jack's going to stick them with nannies if he gets them. It's not like he really wants them. He just doesn't want you to have them."

I went into the bathroom and closed the door as she started her cyberstalking. I knelt, reached under the sink to the far back of the vanity cabinet, and pulled out the little airline-size bottle I had stashed there.

I opened it and swallowed the whole thing in two gulps, then put the empty bottle back where it had been. I sat on the floor, my head against the wall, and waited for my pulse to slow.

"Brenna, your phone is ringing," Georgi called through the door. "Want me to answer it?"

"Yeah," I yelled back.

When I came out, she had my phone on speaker. Our mother's voice sounded higher pitched than normal.

"Calm down," Georgi was saying. "I can't understand you. What happened?"

"He's getting out," my mother yelled. "He got pardoned. Roy Beckett is coming home this week!"

Georgi's mouth fell open, and she gaped up at me. "How did that happen?"

"He asked the governor to pardon him. My lawyer said he laid out a whole case about how he was innocent and wrongly convicted, and apparently convinced the governor. Forget the jury. That man is pardoning people left and right."

Was I hearing right? I grabbed the phone out of Georgi's hand. "Wait. So he can just pardon a convicted murderer and let him walk? Shouldn't we have had a chance to weigh in on that? Don't they talk to the victim's family?"

"I guess he didn't care how we felt. The governor said that even if Beckett did it, it was a crime of passion and not likely to happen again."

"Unless he drinks and gets in a fight."

"Your father didn't fight with him. He walked away."

"I know. Still . . ." I was sweating now, feeling a little sick. "When will he be home?"

"They said probably tomorrow."

My heart was pounding again, and I could see that Georgi was struggling too. She got her purse and dabbed at the tears in her eyes. "I have to go."

"Georgi . . . ," my mother said.

"Mom, I'll call you back," I said. I clicked off the phone and went to my sister, but she shook me off.

"The world has gone completely bonkers. Roy Beckett back on the streets, and your husband suing the best mom in the world to take away custody. I can't stand it."

"Ex-husband," I whispered.

"I'm going. I have to tell people this is happening. Warn them."

"Yeah."

She swept her blonde hair back and then let it fall into her face. She turned to me before she went out the door. "Try to sleep tonight. Seriously. Don't do what you do, okay?"

I lied. "I'll be okay."

"Call me if you need me."

"I will."

"And if you don't sleep, write."

I nodded and watched her leave. Writing would be a good escape, if I could motivate myself tonight. But I'd had writer's block for a full decade when the rest of my life had to be rewritten. I didn't yet know how my own plot should go.

When I closed the door, the house, which was about two thousand square feet smaller than my previous one, felt enormous and empty.

I went to the kitchen and got a big bottle of wine. Wine wasn't so awful, was it? It wasn't as bad as straight vodka. All I needed was a little numbness. Just enough to survive.

I poured a tall glass of wine, called my mother back, and let her rant as I drank.

I felt a little more numb, but it wasn't enough. When I got off the phone, I stared at the empty glass, hating myself. What was I doing?

I wasn't going to let Jack Hertzog or Roy Beckett send me into the abyss. But I felt like a kid walking on top of a narrow wall. I was going to fall all by myself.

I went to the couch and opened my laptop. Instead of going to Word where my piecemeal fiction efforts were parked in promising folders, I clicked on Snapchat and saw that Rayne had already posted. She was sitting in the backseat between my brooding children, doing one of her clichéd duck-lip poses. Noah and Sophia wore their forced "say cheese" smiles. "Me and my sweetie pies," Rayne had written.

Three dozen of her closest friends had commented already.

I slammed the computer shut and took my glass back to the kitchen. I thought better of pouring another glass and set it in the sink. I got the cork, intending to put it back into the bottle. But before I'd even made the decision to, I was pouring it again.

I would drink until I fell asleep. Then in the morning I would guzzle Pedialyte and try to get myself to Georgi's boutique to work. Georgi couldn't suspect what I'd done to cope. She'd have me in some kind of rehab within the hour.

If my father had lived, he would have died all over again to learn that one of his daughters drank any alcohol at all, much less as much as I did. The preacher's daughters were supposed to be above reproach. Georgi had been the problem child, with her bad-boy relationships and a five-week marriage. But she was an entrepreneur now, doing well in spite of the bad choices of her youth, and I was the one who drank to survive. I was glad he couldn't see it.

And what would he think about the man who'd killed him being back on the streets?

I went to my bedroom that still didn't feel like home. I hadn't completely unpacked all the boxes yet. I'd focused more on the kids' rooms and the den and kitchen, so Noah and Sophia would feel at home. I stood in front of the mirror and looked at myself. Failure, victimhood, and hatred weren't a good look. But I didn't know how to change it. Somehow I had to channel my anger into a legal strategy.

I drank some more and crawled onto my bed. It wasn't going to get better anytime soon. The best I could do was hang on and pray like mad.

But I doubted God was listening to me anymore.

CHAPTER 2

NATE

From the sky, the fire was beautiful, burning in a neon arc down the side of the mountain, moving with rapid grace. But the grace was only visual. I knew it was really a monster, creeping down the slope to devour everything in its path.

That lethal wind whipped against my ears as I stood at the open hatch of the plane, trying to make the target our spotter had decided on. The darkness would make it a tough battle, but this type of challenge only pumped my adrenaline more. I glanced at the houses just a few miles downhill from the fire. The lights I could see from the air twinkled with hominess and ironic calm. It could have been my hometown of Carlisle, its residents distracted by homework and sitcoms, football games and dancing lessons, bedtimes and prayers. Few headlights were on the roads. From here, nothing in the town suggested a sense of urgency.

This fire had been burning in a fairly contained area for three days, but because the other teams of smokejumpers and heli-tacks had been tied up in a battle with some fires farther north until yesterday, it had been considered low priority. It had been a longer-than-normal fire season that had stretched us all thin, but with the drought continuing, it didn't seem close to ending. Now the wind had whipped up and the fire had taken a turn. We wouldn't get any sleep tonight, and the work wouldn't be pleasant. We would spend the night chainsawing trees to create a fire line, a gap where the fire would stop because there was nothing there to burn. I wished for sunlight to aid in our fight, but it would come soon enough.

I checked my parachute as the pilot flew toward the target, several miles south of the moving arc of flames. "All right!" I shouted to my team of Hotshots behind me. "See you in the furnace!"

I hurled myself out the door of the plane as adrenaline and dopamine rushed through my body like the beating wind. It never got old. Over the sound of the air rushing around my ears, I heard the whoop of the teammate who'd jumped next to me. I counted off seconds as I fell through the

19

sky, letting gravity have its way . . . then pulled the cord. The parachute walloped out into a mushroom, jerking me out of gravity's pull as the wind took over.

Around me, one by one, other parachutes opened, and with expert aim, they all floated down toward the target. A second plane moved overhead and another team jumped out.

I came down within feet of my target, the chute pulling as I ran to a stop. As others dropped around me, I gathered my chute and put it back into its case. I'd repack it later when I had room to do it right. The box with our supplies, chainsaws and all, floated down on a separate chute, and the designated guys caught it and got it to the right spot.

Spreading out in a line across the mountain with our chainsaws and Pulaskis, we began clearing brush and cutting down trees so the fire would die a natural death before it ever threatened the town below. The noise was deafening, with the buzz of saws all around me and the waffling sound of the flames moving across the landscape. I glanced up the mountain and saw the yellow-orange glow of flames creeping toward us. At its current rate, and if nothing went wrong, the fire would take hours to reach where my team and I worked.

But in a matter of minutes, the wind changed direction, billowing through the trees we were targeting for our fire line. Fed by the new blast of wind, the fire exploded as if a bomb had been dropped into the center of it. Flames shot out over us and behind us, spreading wildly with unbridled fury.

"I need help!" Bull yelled a few yards above me.

Saws dropped and tools were abandoned as my teammates closest to Bull tried to get him out of the flames caging him in.

"Take cover, Cap!" Hill shouted to me. Adrenaline pumped through me as I pulled out my survival shelter, a thin cover I could throw over myself if I couldn't get out. I saw a dozen or more men trying to outrun the blaze below me, and I shouted for those above me to follow. Wrapping the shelter around myself like a blanket, I tried to make it down the hill, out of the reach of the fire.

The team that had come in before us was already down there and had started digging a trench to be used to set the controlled backfires that would consume everything between the firebreak and the rushing conflagration. But these backfires would threaten the men now left behind.

"There's no more time!" T-Bird, the captain for the backfire team, shouted. "We have to set it. It's our only hope."

"Not until all my men are out!" I shouted back.

"There's a town down there, and I'm not gonna be responsible for letting it go up in flames!" He turned back and gave the order, and my stomach sank as they started the controlled fire that had trouble catching because of the direction of the wind.

I stood still, straining to see the rest of my men on the other side, then frantically I turned around and tried to count the ones who'd made it. Half of them were still in there. Wiping my perspiring brow with the back of my sleeve, I bolted toward them.

I was almost to the fire line, but T-bird grabbed me and wrestled me back. "Where do you think you're going?"

"To get my team!" I shouted and jerked free. Darting through a narrow space between the flames, I headed toward the eastern side of the fire, dodging the small circles of flames spreading around me.

I waved off the flames with my metallic cover and saw that my men had found a clearing and were frantically digging another fire line perpendicular to the one already set. "Are you guys crazy?" I yelled over the

22

sounds of burning brush. "Get out of here!"

"There's a house, Cap!" Gator yelled back to me, his face glowing in the firelight. He kept digging urgently. "I saw a light! There are people inside!"

I strained to see past the men and made out the house about a thousand yards up through the trees, visible only because of a dim light in one of the upstairs windows. I turned back to evaluate the fire, which was moving swiftly closer, and finally shouted, "I'm going in! You men get out of here! Now! That's an order!" The flames grew closer, drenching me in sweat as I ran uphill, my hundred pounds of gear feeling like five hundred. By the time I reached the house, I was gasping for breath and my spine shot with pain, but I pushed on, through the pines surrounding the house, pines that would explode with flames when the fire reached them. I banged on the door, then used the ax tucked into my belt to beat it in.

I broke through the door and stumbled in. "Fire!" I hollered, bolting toward the stairs. "Everybody out!"

I took the stairs in a few steps and yelled for everyone to wake up. I turned into the bedroom with the light on and saw two children crying. I had scared them to death.

"Come on, guys," I shouted. "There's a fire outside, and we have to get out of here. Let's go!"

One of them screamed, but I grabbed up both of them, took the corner of a blanket and dragged it off the bed to throw over them, then headed back out.

"Daddeeeee!" one of the kids screamed as we got to the door.

The two adults in the house ran out of their room on the downstairs level.

"Fire! Evacuate now!" I yelled. "Come on! Follow me."

A dog started barking. The woman saw the flames through the door and screamed, "Why didn't they tell us before?"

"Stay together!" I yelled, tossing them my survival shelter. "Put this over you and follow me."

The dad grabbed the dog, and I led them outside. The fire had reached the first pine, and flames shot up like rockets. "This way!" I led them toward the least dangerous part of the fire.

"There's no way out!" the man cried.

I found a breach and kept moving toward it. "Just follow me." I led them through the break in the fire, down the slope toward the haphazard ditch my men were digging.

"Run that way!" I shouted. I handed one

of the children to his dad, and he let the dog down and grabbed his child, while the mother grabbed the other child.

They started down the slope, but the flames were already speeding across the mountain as fast as they sped down. They halted, confused. I looked around, seeking an escape, but it seemed they were boxed in. I thought of throwing them all facedown on the small charred places on the ground, hoping the fire would pass right around them as it sped by, but there was no telling how long they'd have to lie there, surrounded by flames, with nothing but smoke to breathe . . . and there was no guarantee the foil blankets would keep their clothes and flesh from igniting as the flames flapped past.

I heard voices to my left and guessed I was close to the fire line where the backfires had been started. Heat baked through my gear and made my skin slick with sweat.

"We have to get through there," I yelled to the father. "The fire line is thin here. If we run through it, we might suffer a few burns, but at least we'll have a chance."

The mother screamed again as flames danced closer. I grabbed the aluminized cover out of her hands and threw it over her head, wrapping it around the child. She

25

screamed because she couldn't see, but I ran her through the flames.

One leg of my pants caught fire, but I got the mother and child to the other side and let them go, then turned back to her husband. He was mimicking what we had done with the blanket from the kids' bed and was pushing through the flames like we had. I hit the ground and rolled to put out the flames on my leg. By the time I got back to my feet, my men were rushing up to us. "Take care of them!" I shouted.

One of the men handed me another survival blanket, and wrapping it around myself, I went back into the inferno and picked up the barking dog. "Come on, dude, it's you and me now."

The dog went from barking to whimpering. One of my men had followed me. He covered the dog and me with another metallic survival cover and led us through the flames. The dog leaped out of my arms and joined his family as my men ushered them through.

I realized my right arm was on fire, and flames licked my side. I collapsed to the ground and tried to catch my breath as I rolled, but only smoke filled my lungs. I looked around, counting heads and trying to determine if all my men were accounted for. I counted fourteen silhouettes but wasn't sure they were all on my team. They were still digging and clearing brush as the fire line did its job of starving the fire before it reached the town below.

"Get a medevac up here!" I heard someone shout as my vision grew spotty. "Nate, hold on, buddy!"

"I'm fine," I choked, but the words came out in a coughing fit. I felt them slapping my legs, my ribs, my arm, cutting off my fire gear, opening my clothes. As I heard the blades of a helicopter overhead, the world seemed to melt and blend into the particles of smoke around me, pulling me into the abyss of my mind.

CHAPTER 3

NATE

I woke up in a blindingly bright room, my clothes off and something clamped to my face. I tried to reach it, but I couldn't bend my right arm, and my hand stung. An IV was taped to my other hand, but I moved carefully and touched the thing over my face.

An oxygen mask. I tried to sit up. "What happened?"

T-bird came to my bedside, a sheen of smoky sweat still soiling his face. "Nate, lie back, man."

"The fire," I said. "Need to get back. My men."

"They're still there. Making progress. But you're not going anywhere near a fire for a month or so."

I took off the mask and coughed a little, but managed to catch my breath. "A month?"

"Yep. Second-degree burns on 20 percent of your body. Some of the burns are deep."

It came back to me, the event that had gotten me here. "The family. Were they injured?"

"Not a scratch or burn. Turns out it was a US senator from Kansas. He says you're a hero."

"You know I had no choice. They were in the path —"

"Take the praise where you can get it, man. We don't get that much."

I looked at my right side. My right arm was bandaged, and so was my side and down my right leg to the point where my boots had stopped the flames. Second degree wasn't so bad, I told myself. Third degree would have been brutal. I'd be able to leave the hospital soon. I'd heal.

"I won't need a month," I said.

"Yes, you will. They can't let you go back. Doctor's orders. You're grounded until he releases you."

I managed to sit up, but it was a bad idea. The burns pulling on my skin reminded me why I shouldn't. "I can't be grounded during fire season. Are you crazy? I need to be there. You don't have enough men as it is."

"Sorry, Nate. It is what it is. Why don't

you go home to Carlisle for a while? Take it easy."

Go home? Pop had just been pardoned, and he and my mom were trying to navigate the reunion. Though she would love to have me home, I didn't know if I was up to it. My father could be challenging, and fourteen years of prison hadn't done him any favors.

I could just stay in my one-bedroom apartment here, stuck on the sidelines for a month, but that would be grueling. I couldn't take just sitting on the bench while my team was on the field. It felt like failure.

Yes, I would need the distraction of Carlisle. Maybe my hometown could heal more than just my burns — if it didn't cause newer, deeper wounds instead.

Saturday when they released me from the hospital, I drove to Carlisle. The last place I wanted to go was the bar my brother owned called Flannigan's, which was full of landmine memories, but I had no choice. I'd called ahead and told the family I was coming, but I hadn't mentioned my injuries. I would bunk with my brother, who'd recently bought a house. There was no way I was going to spend nights at my parents' house. Drew had told me to come to Flannigan's to pick up the key.

For my mother's sake, I was glad Pop hadn't gone back to the bottle since he'd gotten home a couple of days ago. She had been a trooper for years, enduring the shame of being the wife of the man convicted of killing the preacher. She'd stood by his claim that he wasn't the real killer, and she truly believed him.

But I figured the most obvious scenario was usually the right one.

I dreaded the thought of having Pop back in Carlisle. It wouldn't be easy. Would he eventually go back to his drunken ways? Would he treat my mother with respect this time?

I would have to go by there later, but for now, I just wanted to get settled. The freshly bandaged burns on most of my right side would send my mother into a panic.

Leaving my bag on the seat, I got out of the car and limped between vehicles. Though the fire raged on just an hour and a half north, it had rained here for about fifteen minutes earlier in the day, easing the drought that had lasted for months. But I knew it hadn't been enough rain to fireproof the vegetation. The cracked asphalt parking lot was still pocked with puddles. Pop had stumbled over these same potholes fourteen years ago, before his drinking days came to an end.

I pulled the door open, and music blasted me. It was too loud, or I was too much older. Little had changed. Griff Bently still sat in his usual place at the bar, though his shoulders looked more stooped and his hair had turned white. A few stools down sat Dooley, one of Pop's old cohorts. I wondered if he'd been by yet to see my dad.

"Son of a gun, if it ain't Nate Beckett."

I leaned across the counter and shook the bartender's hand. "How's it goin', Duke? I was just looking for my brother. Is he here?"

"Somewhere around here." Duke pointed his washrag to his left. "Last time I seen him he was that way."

I scanned the crowd, searching for my brother, who was no doubt partying with some of his customers. Buying the bar had been his dream so he could have a nightlife and still make a living.

"Welcome back to Carlisle, man," Duke said.

My chuckle was forced. "Not everybody will feel that way."

"They like Drew."

"Yeah, but he's their drinking buddy. I was practically run out of town."

"No, you weren't. You up and disappeared."

I looked back at the crowd and remembered the accusations that had prompted me to leave. After Pop had been convicted, I'd known that defending myself from arson rumors wouldn't go over well.

My phone vibrated. I pulled it out and saw a text from T-Bird: You all right?

With my thumb, I typed back, Yeah, I busted out. I'm in Carlisle.

Take care of yourself, he wrote.

A pair of arms grabbed me from behind, and I winced at the sudden pain ripping through the burns on my ribs.

"When did you get here?" Drew asked, taking the stool next to me. "I've been waiting, man. I thought you would be here two days ago, when Dad got home. Why haven't you answered your phone? Did you have to go back to the fire?"

My brother's brown beard and mustache never changed, but his hair was shorter than it had been the last time I'd seen him, when he'd driven Mom to visit. I gave him a half hug. "I didn't want everybody to get all concerned, but I had a little accident. Had to spend the last couple of nights in the hospital."

"What?" Only then did he notice the only bandage that was exposed. The one on my hand. "What's this?"

"Just a minor brush with death," I joked, reaching for some pretzels in the bowl a couple of feet away. "Nothing serious."

"Burns?"

"Yeah. Occupational hazard."

"Why didn't you tell me?" He motioned for the bartender as he turned on his stool. His foot hit my shin, and I recoiled again.

"Come on — your leg too?"

"Just take it easy."

"Where all were you burned, man?"

"My right arm, down my side, my leg."

"Nate!"

"I didn't want to distract from Pop's homecoming. He was the man of the hour."

"I thought you guys had training to stay out of the fires."

"We try."

Drew reached down and pulled up my pant leg. "Dude, you were in no condition for a road trip. You should have stayed home. Let us come to you."

"I'm fine. How's Pop?"

Drew shook his head. "He's okay. Claims he's a changed man."

"We'll see, won't we?" I slid off my stool. "Can I get the key? I want to chill a little bit before I go over to Mom's."

Drew fished his keys out of his pocket and

pulled off his house key. "Hey, before you go over to my house, I should tell you who just moved in across the street."

"Who?" I asked, taking the key.

"Brenna Strickland. Well, Brenna Hertzog. I don't know if she's going back to her maiden name or not."

I tried not to look interested. "Brenna moved?"

"Yeah. I saw her outside when the moving truck was there. She said she couldn't afford where she lived after the divorce, so she and the kids downsized. She looked good, though. I just didn't want you to be broadsided. I'm sure she didn't realize there was a Beckett pulling the real estate values down when she signed the papers."

He was kidding, but it didn't feel funny. "Okay, thanks for the heads-up."

"Hey, come say hello to everybody. Some of the old gang is here."

Drew turned back to the crowd, and for an uncomfortable moment, I thought he might yell out, "Hey, everybody, get a load of my brother!"

I knew that look in Drew's eye, so I grabbed his arm and stopped him. "I really don't feel great. I need to put this leg up for a few minutes."

"Yeah, right. I won't drag you through the

crowd tonight, then."

I waved goodbye to Duke, then opened the door. Drew stepped out behind me. "I think there are sheets on the extra bed. Take it easy, man. You need anything for those burns?"

"I have what I need. When will you get home?"

"Probably around three."

"Okay, so I'll see you when you wake up tomorrow afternoon."

"Good luck with the folks."

Drew lived five minutes away, in a neighborhood I knew well from my high school years. I'd never been to his house, since I hadn't been back to town in years, so I had to drive slowly, letting my headlights shine on the mailboxes to see the street addresses. Just as I found Drew's house, I saw the house across the street with empty boxes piled up at the curb.

Brenna's house.

I pulled into Drew's driveway and sat in the truck for a minute, looking at her house in my rearview mirror.

Should I go over? I hadn't seen her in fourteen years. She should have been a vague memory by now, a memory that started with childlike yearning and ended with grief. I shouldn't be fazed by her being so close.

As badly as my burns needed tending to, I wanted to go knock on her door and say hi. Maybe I could reassure her about my dad being home. She couldn't have taken his pardon well. Didn't I owe her that?

I got out of the truck, closed the door, and limped toward her house.

CHAPTER 4

BRENNA

I sat with my laptop open on my lap, staring at the few paragraphs I'd managed to write since Jack picked up the kids again last night, but nothing would come today.

The sound of the cable news on TV didn't help. Fires were spreading across the upper part of the state, and the winds were picking up, making things worse.

As always, when I thought of the fires, I thought of Nate Beckett. Was he one of those silhouettes on-screen fighting back the fires? Would he come to town to welcome his father home?

I took another swallow of my whiskey and waited, hoping, praying it would numb the memories, or at least give me a buzz that would make me forget them. But as the half-empty bottle on my table attested, it wasn't working.

Tears crested under my eyes, and I wiped

them away. My hands still trembled. Too much to drink, or too little?

What would the church people think if they knew I was drinking, the preacher's kid who hadn't made a wrong turn since that one tragic night in her teens?

What about that marriage of yours? that annoying, alcohol-fueled voice in my head asked me. *You don't consider that a wrong turn?*

True. That had been like making a rubber-burning 180, then slamming into a brick wall.

I should have known. Jack had it in him from the first day, but I was too good at pretending I didn't see what was there. All it took was some college blonde with longer legs to come along and erase ten years of commitment.

But did I really not know that going in? Was the money the thing that made me put blinders on about his character?

If it was, I loathed myself. Now I was stuck with him for the rest of my life because of my children.

I checked my watch, wondering where Sophia and Noah were right now. I wasn't even sure what they did with him each Saturday, especially since his mayoral race was ramping up. Were they at their father's fund-raiser, hobnobbing with judges and politicians and financial gurus? Had Rayne had the foresight to feed them something so they wouldn't starve before their eight or nine o'clock meal — which probably consisted of something that Sophia would be more likely to throw up than enjoy? Was the room filled with cigar and pipe smoke, which was sure to aggravate Noah's asthma? Would all of it please Jack's father — the billionaire who owned Hertzog Industries, Carlisle's biggest employer?

After all, everything was about pleasing him, wasn't it?

I took another swallow, praying for peace, for numbness, but God wasn't listening anymore. He was punishing me for so many things, and Jack was the perfect tool.

Though the hoped-for buzz never came, the self-indictments did. I wouldn't be divorced if I'd been a better wife. I should have dieted more, bleached my brown hair, dressed younger, and made wittier banter. If I hadn't spent so much time taking care of my children, I might not be losing them now. If I hadn't been so concerned with keeping the perfect home, being the perfect mother, living the perfect life, maybe I would have seen that my husband was looking elsewhere for the things I was so inadequate at giving him.

Wasn't it always the wife's fault?

Yes, God was punishing me for all those things, though I wasn't quite clear on the reason God wasn't punishing Jack. But that wasn't how it worked. It was only me who got punished, and not just for the divorce. If the truth were known — and the whiskey got down to the truth every time — God's punishment reached back to a time before I'd even met Jack. A time when I was sixteen. A time when my judgment had destroyed my family and killed my father — the ripples of which were still being felt by everyone involved.

The doorbell rang, and I jumped as if I'd been caught at something and quickly swallowed what was left in my glass. It was probably my mother, or Georgi coming by to check up on me. I couldn't let them see the alcohol.

I sprang up and ran to the kitchen, put the bottle under the sink, turned on the faucet, and took a drink from the streaming liquid to wash the smell out of my mouth. I should have chosen vodka.

When the bell rang again, I hurried to the door and threw it open.

Nate Beckett stood there, as if I had conjured him. For a moment, I just gaped

41

at him. "Nate?"

He looked like a wiser, more weathered version of the boy he'd been when we were teens, and that grin that involved his whole face made me smile too. "Brenna, hi. I was just coming to Drew's, and I saw your last name on the mailbox. I hope you don't mind my walking over."

I touched my hair, wishing I'd known he was coming. How did I look? Had I cried my makeup off? Was it dripping down my face like mud? "How long have you been in town?" I asked as if that made a difference in anything.

"About half an hour," he said. "I should have called first, but I didn't know your number."

He was taller than he'd been at sixteen, with the same sable-colored hair and a day's growth of beard on his jaw, broad lumber-jack shoulders and arms that looked as if he worked out for hours a day.

"You look great," I said.

"So do you."

I wiped my face, checked my fingerprints for mascara. "No, I don't. I was just . . . My kids are with their dad, and I was just . . . watching TV. Come in."

He stepped in and glanced at the tele-vision. "Watching the fires?"

42

"Um . . ." I looked toward the TV. "Yeah. I thought of you. Wondered if you were there."

"I was until a couple of days ago."

"Did you come home because of your dad?"

"Sort of." He looked down for a second, then met my eyes again. "I'd still be at the fire, but . . . well, it's complicated."

Nate's smile was shaky, tentative, but it started in the tired eyes that reminded me of another time, when love was still innocent and threatened no peril. "I lost track of you."

The words shot that innocence to death and reminded me of the peril that had followed anyway. The demons closed in on me, reminding me of my punishment, my guilt, my part in the tragic drama that had ended my father's life. "Yeah, my mom and sister and I went to live with my grandmother after . . . after Dad died. Then we came back a couple of years later. You were gone by then."

"Yeah. Call of the wild."

As I led him into the living room, I noticed his bandaged arm.

"What happened?" I asked, touching his wrist.

"Nothing," he said. "I was fighting that

43

fire. Had a little burn."

I touched his arm and felt more bandage through his shirtsleeve. "That doesn't seem little."

"It's just second degree. It'll keep me off the field for a couple of weeks."

I lowered to the couch, and he sat down next to me. I saw how careful he was with his right leg. Under his jeans, I saw that his ankle was bandaged too. "Nate! Where were you burned?"

"It's no big deal. Just on my right side."

"Down your whole right side? Your ribs? Hip? Thigh?"

"Yeah, pretty much."

"Nate, you *drove* here?"

"It's only an hour and a half."

"But you need to have that leg up." I put a pillow on the coffee table. "Come on. Put it up. It's just me."

He grinned and did what I said.

"You want something to drink?"

"No, I'm fine. I really just wanted to see how you are."

"I'm okay. I just get a little bummed when my kids are gone. Divorce. It's not for sissies."

"Guess not." He inclined his head a little until I met his eyes. "I'm sorry it didn't work out."

44

"Yeah, thanks. Never pictured myself divorced, fighting for custody. But life doesn't ever really work out like you think it will."

"No, it sure doesn't."

I folded my arms and locked in on him. "I didn't think you'd ever come back here." I could see that my words delivered a hard blow, but he didn't recoil from them. He'd survived words before.

"Well, I had to recuperate, and it seemed like a good time to spend some time with the family. How are you feeling about the pardon?"

"Honestly? I can't believe they let him out."

"He served fourteen years."

"You gotta love the governor's pardoning powers. That's the way our beloved justice system works, isn't it?"

"He still says he didn't do it."

I rolled my eyes. "Of course he did it. You know that, don't you?"

Nate sighed. "It sure looked like it. But they never investigated his story."

"Because it was ludicrous. They were fighting in the bar. They went outside to finish. We're supposed to believe that someone else came from out of nowhere, followed my father, and shot him for no reason?"

"I know. It was a lot to swallow." Nate was rarely at a loss for words, but I could see he didn't know what I wanted him to say. "I didn't come here to relitigate all that. The outcome is the same, no matter what."

That was the truth.

"Do you drink now?" Nate asked out of the blue.

I flinched as if he'd raised his hand to strike me. "What? No. Why would you ask that?"

"I thought I smelled it," he said. "I'm not judging. I just wondered . . ."

"I told you. Life has me a little shaky right now."

He looked at me as if considering that. "Custody battle sounds brutal."

I sighed. "I don't want to talk about that. Let's talk about something else."

"Like what?" He grinned, and I felt the heat radiating off his body. "Old times?"

I wished for another drink. "The old times are all recorded in the newspaper archives, if you want to reminisce."

"Yeah, I guess they are. I meant before that."

I deliberately looked away and locked onto the TV screen.

"Are these your children?"

I glanced back at him and saw that he was looking at a picture on my end table. My face softened. "Yeah. Sophia and Noah."

He smiled, the crow's feet next to his eyes deeper than they'd been before. I liked the way they looked on him.

"They look just like you. Two little brunettes. The little girl — Sophia, you say? — she has your eyes. And look at Noah's face. Are those freckles?"

I felt the despair seeping out of me and a tentative joy seeping in. "Yeah. All over his nose."

He laughed, as though he was as smitten as me. "You're lucky," he said. "Real lucky."

I stared down at the framed photo, part of me wishing I could open the floodgate and tell him just how unlucky I was.

"Oh, but I forgot. You don't believe in luck, do you?" he asked.

I smiled. "What do you mean?"

"You always said there was no such thing as luck. There was good fortune and there were blessings. But not luck."

My smile died a silent death again, and I got up and went to the kitchen, putting the counter between us. "That was a long time ago."

"Yeah, but it was real faith. I envied it,

47

because I didn't believe in anything back then. You taught me differently."

The very acknowledgment of that faith was like an indictment, and I felt my insides shrinking from the kind of faith I had now. I wasn't sure when it had fled from me, when things had changed, when I'd realized I hadn't survived my latest trial.

"I was naive then, Nate," I said. "Nothing bad had ever happened to me at that point. I had the perfect life. It was easy to be spiritual."

"But you weren't faking it."

"No, of course not. I never would have faked it. I just didn't know the flip side of all those blessings."

I felt his gaze on me, his eyes searching mine the way they used to, seeing into me, to the things I didn't want to say or reveal, the things I didn't want to share.

I didn't have the energy to put on a front any longer. I wasn't looking for a relationship, especially with him, so what did it matter if he thought badly of me? I sighed and pulled the whiskey out of its hiding place under the sink. "I lied. You did smell it. Want some?"

"No, thanks," he said quietly.

I poured some in a coffee mug for myself, more than I hoped he would notice, but as

I took a drink, I practically dared him to say a word.

"So tell me about your kids," he said in a softer voice that pulled my mind out of the darkness.

I brought my cup back around and sat next to him. "I miss them."

"Do they live with him?"

"Not yet."

The two short words were all I could manage in explanation, but Nate wasn't going to let it die.

"You sure you don't want to talk about it?"

I looked out the back window and saw my vague reflection there. I almost didn't recognize myself. "He gets them on weekends, generally, and I get them on weekdays. Of course, I have to work on weekdays, which leaves me about three hours a night with them before bedtime, but hey, you can't have everything."

"Every weekend? You never get a Saturday or Sunday with them?"

"No. The judge thought he was being fair, giving us joint custody and splitting it up that way. Now Jack's decided he should have them full-time."

"Is he remarried?"

"Of course. They tied the knot five minutes after our papers were signed. Literally. The justice of the peace was waiting."

"I'm so sorry."

"Ironic, isn't it?" I flashed him a bitter smile, shaking my head. "Wouldn't it be nice if people could just rearrange their lives when they didn't like them anymore? Just erase this person, plug this one in? That's how Jack's life works. Everyone else just adjusts around him."

My mind fogged, drawing me into the injustice of my life, caught between what might have been and what had become.

"You don't deserve that," he said. "You really don't." He glanced at my open laptop. "You still write?"

I smiled. "I'm trying to. I didn't write the whole time I was married. But it's kind of coming back. It's therapy, you know."

"It's more than that. You had talent."

I grinned and hid behind the mug. "You're about the only one in the world who thought that."

"I might have been the only one in the world who read your stories."

"True. Not that I didn't try. Jack was never interested. And why would he be, when I put it all aside so easily?" I tried to get up, but stumbled and had to catch myself.

"You okay?" he asked again.

"Yes. Don't look at me like that. The liquor doesn't even work. I don't get a buzz. I don't even get numb."

He didn't say anything. "When we started hanging out," I said, "you told me you drank because you couldn't find any good reason not to."

"But then I found one."

I stumbled as I started to get up, and he reached out to steady me. I pulled my hand away. "What? Me? I didn't change you, Nate."

"You have no idea how much you changed me. A lot of it I didn't even realize until later." He paused. "You want me to make you some coffee?" he asked.

"Do you want some?"

"No, it's for you."

"To sober me up? Don't worry. I'm not driving. No kids to take care of. I don't need coffee. And please . . . don't leave here and tell anyone you caught me drinking. I don't want that judgment on top of everything else."

"I wouldn't do that." He kept his gaze on me, and I felt as if he could see right through me, to just how much I'd already had to drink.

"I should go, let you get to bed. How

about if I call you tomorrow . . . when you feel better?"

My eyes filled with tears before I could stop them. "If I thought there was a chance I'd feel better tomorrow . . ." I let the sentence die. "What's the point?"

"Does there have to be a point?"

The question seemed to drain me of what was left of my energy, and I wiped my eyes with trembling fingertips. "I don't know," I said. "I can't think right now."

I got up again, this time steadying myself, and led him to the front door. He limped as he came toward me. I felt bad that he was trying to take care of me when he was the one who needed care.

I opened the door. He stepped out, but turned around before leaving. "I'll be here for a few days while I'm recovering. I'd like to see you again. When I call tomorrow, will you answer?"

I thought about it for a long moment, then said, "I don't know."

"Come on, Brenna. It's just me."

Just him. I dragged in a long breath and felt the early dawn of courage. "Okay," I said, finally. "I'll answer. Give me your phone."

He swiped the screen and handed it to me, and I typed in my phone number. I handed it back to him.

With a soft smile, he stepped off my porch, and I watched him limp across the street.

I closed the door and leaned back against it. I peered in the mirror just inside the door, wiped the tears from under my eyes, and tried to decide if I looked utterly repulsive, broken and old — the way my ex-husband saw me. My cream-colored blouse was youthful, but thirty still felt ancient when you encountered your first love after almost a decade and a half.

But what did I care? He was nothing to me except the son of the man who killed my father. And now that man sat in his recliner at home. That was justice, they said.

I couldn't let myself sink into those old feelings. I had too much going on, too many other things to think about. It had been nice to see him again, but I wouldn't answer if he called.

CHAPTER 5

NATE

When I finally made it to my parents' house that night, I pulled into the driveway and sat for a moment. The small blue frame house I'd grown up in had been well maintained, in spite of the fact that my mother had been alone for so long. She had blossomed while Pop was in prison, and her own personality had been allowed to shine. I liked seeing her like that every time she came to visit. I hoped he didn't put the kibosh on it now that he was back.

The impatiens in the little bed out front added a sweet hominess to the small yard. But the broken-down home next door was a stark contrast to the Beckett house, and I wished the neighbor could be convinced to haul off the rusty car and old stove in the front yard. But even if that house were cleaned up, there was still the house on the other side to contend with. With its peeling paint, foot-high grass, and grease stains on the driveway, it never let us forget we were from the side of town where property was something that deteriorated and pride rarely had a chance to shine.

I parked my truck on the street in front of the house so I wouldn't block in the small Toyota Drew and I had bought our mother a few years ago.

I didn't know whether to knock or just go in, because I didn't know what might ignite my father's wrath. Would he be sober and contrite, or angry and defiant? Had he already started drinking to make up for lost time?

The truth was, I didn't even know who he'd become in the last fourteen years.

I rapped softly on the door, then pushed it open. Pop was sitting in the recliner that had been unchanged since he left. "Pop," I said with a laugh. "Welcome back, man!"

The footrest snapped down, and Pop got up, looking a lot older and thinner than he had when he went in. I couldn't really shake his hand without him seeing my bandage, so I pulled him into a half hug with my left arm. He looked and smelled sober, and his eyes glistened like he was genuinely glad to see me.

"Nate!" Mama was at the door in a flash,

her white hair cut in a sleek bob. I suspected she had done a makeover so she'd look nice for Pop, who'd convinced her over the years from a ten-by-twelve cell that he was a changed man.

"I didn't know you were coming today! I thought you were fighting the fire."

As I kissed her, Pop said, "Your mama's been worried sick about that."

"I was fighting it until a couple of days ago. Had to get home to see the old man, right?"

My mother looked at me as if she knew something was off. I'd never been able to get anything past her. "You'd never leave a fire." She looked me over and saw the bandage. She lifted my hand. "Nate, what happened?"

"A little injury. Second-degree burns. No big deal."

She ushered me to the couch and instructed me to put my feet up. That's when she noticed the bandage on my leg. "You should have told me!" she said. "Nate, I'm your mother!"

"I didn't want you to know until you could look me in the eye and see that I'm fine."

"You're not fine! What can I get you? Tylenol? Should we do anything with those

56

bandages?"

"No, Mama. I'm absolutely fine. The dressing doesn't have to be changed for a while. So, Pop, how does it feel to be out?"

As we talked, my mother fussed around me, bringing me a drink and a plate of fresh-cut pineapple. When she was satisfied I wasn't going to collapse on the floor, she finally went back to the kitchen, humming a hymn I vaguely recognized. She came out with a pie, set it on the table, and began to cut us pieces. "Mama, I'm not hungry. But you and Pop go ahead."

"Are you sure? It's good."

"Yes, I'm sure."

"Well, now that you're here, we can have a family dinner tomorrow, to welcome your daddy home and celebrate our whole family being back together."

I looked down awkwardly. We'd never been the kind of family that basked in the joy of being together.

"Can't you eat something? Your body needs energy. You're healing."

"No, but I'll sit with you." I brought my iced tea to the table. Pulling out a chair across from Pop, in my traditional spot, I sat down.

My mother set my dad's pie in front of him.

"A far cry from the food in the joint, huh, Pop?"

Pop smiled. "If everybody there had a cook like your mama waiting when they got out, there'd be some incentive for rehabilitation."

"Did you ever think the governor would actually pardon you?"

"I have your mama to thank for that," he said. "She worked night and day on it. Put together everything in a nice little package for the governor to see, showed up at every public event any of his staff were at, had dozens of people write letters vouching for me."

"Dozens, huh?" I wondered who in the world would have done that.

"Your pop has good friends who believe in him."

I thought of all those drinking buddies who'd kept him on that broken path. They weren't the type to write letters. I wondered if Mama had written them herself and had them sign them. I wouldn't put it past her.

I looked around to see the house through Pop's eyes. The couch had been covered with a slipcover for the past twelve years so that it would be exactly as he remembered when he came home. My father's old easy chair had been cleaned. That hole in the

58

arm brought back memories. I'm sure it was all a great comfort to him.

I couldn't forget what my mother had told me a few nights ago when she called to tell me Pop was coming home, after I warned her there was a lot of water under the bridge. "That old bridge flooded over years ago," she said with the wisdom that always surprised me. "But we can build new bridges."

"No one really expected you to wait for him. You could've divorced him. Gone on with your life. Remarried. You're a beautiful woman, and surely there was someone out there who could treat you better than Pop did."

"Sweetie, you don't understand a thing," she said. "I love your father. I haven't always understood him or approved of him or been happy with him, but he's my husband. I made a vow to him before God."

"He made the same vow to you. Your marriage was never what it should be. Maybe it was a mistake from the beginning."

"Don't ever say that, Nate. I chose him for my husband, and right or wrong, blessed or cursed, I've chosen to live with that decision. You don't break vows just because things don't turn out like you want."

"I guess that's why I haven't married," I

said. "Life has too many bad surprises that you wind up being stuck with for the rest of your life."

"But life has a lot of good surprises too."

I couldn't believe how positive my mother's outlook was, despite years of enduring the drunkenness of her husband, the alienation when he'd killed the preacher, the heartache when we suffered because of it, the injustice of my getting blamed for a fire I hadn't set just because I was my father's son.

But Mama ran on a power I found foreign, a power that gave her a peace I couldn't fathom. Somehow, that power had gotten her through those bad times.

Now, as she sat down to eat, Pop cleared his throat. "You want to say grace, Sue?"

Praying over dessert? This was a first for Pop.

"Of course." Mama covered our hands with her own.

As she prayed and gave thanks for what they were about to eat and asked for blessings on our family tonight, I prayed a silent prayer of my own. I asked that this season wouldn't end in another broken heart for her.

When we finished praying and Pop began to eat his pie, I watched Mama flit from the table to the kitchen for coffee, more iced tea, and a thousand other little things she thought of that neither Pop nor I had requested.

"How long can you stay, angel?" she asked me.

"Until I heal, I guess. They won't let me work until the doctor clears me."

"Whoever would've thought you'd jump out of airplanes into fires for a living? Doesn't that just scare you to death, Roy?"

Pop set down his fork and crossed his arms on the table. "Tell me why you decided to do that. Who in their right mind would do a thing like that?"

"I always wanted to be a firefighter, since I was a little kid."

"I thought you wanted to play for the NFL."

I laughed. "That was your dream, not mine."

"Roy, you remember how he used to wear that fireman costume when he was in preschool? I could barely get it off of him."

I could see that my father didn't remember that at all. The truth was he'd never been home to see it. He'd worked all day and gone to the bar every night.

"I remember that backward baseball cap you always wore."

"That was Drew."

I should have provided him a graceful exit out of this conversation, but it was too late. I could see Pop stiffening defensively. "So . . . what you're saying is you basically came out of the womb as a firebug."

I glanced at my mother and saw her discomfort. I tried to chuckle it away. "Not a firebug, Pop. It's not like I went around starting fires."

"Just the church, huh?"

There it was. I swallowed hard, but I didn't speak. Silence fell over the room.

After a moment, my mother spoke up. "Roy, that wasn't Nate."

"Then why'd you run?" Pop asked, pinning me with his hard eyes.

I told myself not to let my voice rise. My mother needed me to stay calm. "I didn't run. I left. I started my career. I didn't think it would be a fair fight if I stayed."

"What I know is that I taught my boys to face their problems, not to run from them. You didn't see me running, even after I was falsely accused. I stuck around and took the heat. Fourteen years' worth."

I saw the tears in Mama's eyes as she said, "It was a long time ago, Roy. Let's not point fingers, okay? We all have to support each other. You're both innocent. The police never even questioned Nate about that fire."

Pop didn't follow her lead. "Support each other, huh? I never saw his face the last fourteen years."

Now I was angry. "Because you told me you didn't want me to come." Tired of this, I slid back my chair. "I'm just gonna go on back to Drew's place."

Mama jumped to her feet as I got up. "Honey, please. Your father didn't mean any of that, did you, Roy?"

Pop just shoved more pie into his mouth.

"Sit down, son," Mama insisted.

"If he wants to go, let him go," Pop snapped. "You can't force a thirty-year-old man to eat if he doesn't want to."

I got up. "I'll be back tomorrow, Mama."

She followed me out to the truck, apologizing all the way. "Honey, it's like he's two people right now, and he can't decide which one he wants to be. The humble, sweet man he turned into in prison, or the one he used to be. Just be patient with him."

"I will. I just . . . don't want to be patient tonight."

She looked down at my bandaged arm again. "Are you sure you're all right?"

"Yes. It's not the first time. I heal fast."

I kissed her good night, then drove back to the part of town where Drew lived across from Brenna. On the way, I drove past the church where an old acquaintance, Bo Levin, now preached — the church that stood on the property where the old Baptist church had stood before it burned down. If it hadn't been for that event, I might have left Carlisle with a little pride, a few friends, a reason to come back home every now and then. But as it was, I saw the writing on the wall and heard the rumors that someone claimed to have seen me setting the fire, and I didn't think a soul in town, except for my mother and brother, would believe in my innocence.

Maybe I should've tried to clear my name so people wouldn't think of me as a vengeful arsonist irreverent enough to burn down the house of God.

I turned onto Drew's street and glanced at Brenna's house as I pulled into Drew's driveway. Her light was off. I hoped she was sleeping well.

I limped into Drew's house, flicked on the lights, and dropped onto his twin-size guest bed in a tiny extra bedroom. I'd unpack tomorrow.

CHAPTER 6

BRENNA

Despite my resolve to put Nate's visit out of my mind, I couldn't make my heart fall into line. But what was wrong with me? After all I'd been through in the last year, I should have been able to banish that feeling. Love never ended well. It was traitorous and brutal, and it left you empty and alone.

Nothing about it was fair.

Even though Jack had been the one to have the affair and finally the one to leave me and the kids, he'd also been the one with all the money and the big-shot father and the friends who were lawyers and judges. In fact, as president of Hertzog Industries, Jack had employed the son of the judge on their case, played golf with him, and seen to it that his grandson was given the company's scholarship to the college of his choice.

All those things might be enough for the judge to find Jack a more fit and loving parent to our kids, and now that he was suing me for full custody, I had no faith in the system to protect me. All I had on my side were years of fidelity and love and patience, and total devotion to the two beautiful children who were my life.

The rage that kept me awake nights merged with the fear in my heart over the approaching custody battle. What lies would broadside me this time?

I padded across the floor and turned off the television, casting the house in total silence.

The phone rang, and I jumped. I picked it up. "Hi, Mom."

"Are you okay?" my mother asked. "Are you as upset as I am?"

I frowned, trying to get my bearings. "About what?"

"Roy Beckett being home! I can't sleep. It's all I can think about."

"Of course. I'm sorry. I was thinking you were talking about Jack having the kids."

"Have you found out anything about Roy? Has he been drinking? Going out?"

"No. But I saw Nate a little while ago."

"You did? Where?"

I floundered. I couldn't tell her he was staying with his brother across the street. She'd call the police in no time. I crafted a quick lie. "Uh . . . he stopped by Walgreens on his way to his mother's. I was buying milk."

Milk? The explanation, which had been unnecessarily thrown in, seemed ludicrous now. Did the drugstore even have milk? Mom would see right through it.

"They ought to arrest him," she said.

"For what?"

"For arson, that's what! If he hadn't disappeared after he burned the church down, they would've arrested him twelve years ago."

I didn't know why my mother always put me on the defensive. "Mom, no one ever proved Nate had anything to do with that."

"Oh no? Then what do you call his sudden disappearance from town? You know it was an admission of guilt."

"Maybe it was just an admission of defeat."

Mom hesitated for a moment, and when she spoke again, her voice cracked. "How can you defend him? Have you forgotten his father murdered yours?"

Once again, I felt slapped down. "Of course I haven't forgotten."

"Well, I hope you don't fall back into his trap again. Neither of those boys are any better than their father. It's genetic."

I sank onto the couch, suddenly too weary to go on with this. "Meanness doesn't run in families. Nate was probably as affected by Daddy's death as I was. His life changed too."

"I can't believe what I'm hearing. You've been drinking, haven't you?"

My eyes strayed to the mug on my table. "No."

But she knew. She had found some empty whiskey bottles in my bedroom when she was helping me pack. "Brenna, you're under a lot of stress, but you've got to get hold of yourself. Drinking isn't the answer, and neither is Nate Beckett."

"There are no answers," I said. "I've even forgotten the questions."

"Aren't the kids coming home today?"

"No," I said. "He has a donor dinner tonight. He demanded to keep them one more night."

"Trying to rehabilitate his image?"

"No doubt."

"Well, you shouldn't play along. If he wants to play hardball, you should too."

"Maybe. I have to go, Mom. I'm really tired."

I clicked off the phone when she hung up and stared at it, my mind wandering back to the days when Nate Beckett had seemed like the answer. But it was so long ago.

I picked up my laptop and started to type.

I never expected falling in love to result in my father's murder.

We were kids, just sixteen, and he was my first love. Dad said the Beckett brothers were bad news, because the apple didn't fall far from the tree. Their father, Roy, was a drunk and a menace. That was the worst thing I'd ever heard my father say about another man. He usually showed grace, as the preacher of the biggest Baptist church in our area.

But to me, Nate wasn't like my father said. Instead of the wild and reckless spirit the Beckett brothers were reputed to have, Nate Beckett had a sweet, affectionate, loyal spirit. He understood my conviction to wait for intimacy until I was married, and he promised never to compromise that. And he didn't. He never pushed me beyond the limits I'd set for us.

But Daddy didn't believe that. He went to his death thinking badly of me. He would have called it reckless to sneak out with the boy he had warned me not to see. And I guess you can't get more reckless than causing a death.

I told my dad I was sleeping over at my

friend Janie's house, which was going to be true after my date with Nate, but we stayed out past curfew. Georgi found out I wasn't with Janie, and she did her proper sisterly duty. She told our parents.

Dad thought the worst about me and panicked. What would I be doing with Nate if I was lying to him about where I was?

When I finally got to Janie's house, she told me what a mess I was in. My dad was looking for me, and he wasn't happy. I hurried home.

When I got there, my dad's car wasn't in the driveway. I ran in and found my mother in her robe, pacing in the living room. "Mom? Where's Dad?"

"What were you doing with Nate Beckett? Where were you?"

"We just went out. We were talking. Where did he go?"

"He's going to find Roy Beckett and make sure that boy never ever lays a finger on you again!"

I was horrified. We hadn't done more than kiss. "He didn't! We just wanted to see each other. We weren't doing anything wrong."

"You lied and defied us. What is he supposed to think?"

I got the rest of the details of that night

secondhand, after the fact.

My dad found Roy Beckett propped on a stool in a drunken stupor at Flannigan's Bar. Witnesses later testified in court that my father's face was red with fury and that he'd been shaking as he'd turned Roy around on his stool to face him. In a quiet, seething voice, he told Roy to keep his son away from his daughter.

According to the witnesses who testified at the trial, Roy looked at him with his bloodshot eyes and asked, "My boy and the preacher's kid?" Letting out a delighted laugh, he'd gotten up, staggering. "My boy and the preacher's kid! Whassa matter, Preacher? You afraid my boy's gonna make her forget all them fire-and-brimstone sermons of yours?"

It happened so fast that the accounts differed, but one thing all the witnesses agreed on was that my father grabbed Roy and shook him. Roy hurled himself at my dad, and a raging barroom brawl ensued.

Eugene, the bartender that night, tried to break up the fight, but only succeeded in moving it outside.

I found it hard to picture my sweet, loving father so angry he would confront another man like that, but accounts said the two men had gone outside, screaming threats at each other all the way to Roy's truck.

Several people spilled out of the bar to watch the fight that consisted mostly of yelling, and before it came to blows again, my father reined in his emotions and walked away. He got into his car and drove past Roy on the way out of the parking lot. "Keep him away from her!" he yelled out the window.

Roy got into his truck and pulled out behind him.

No one saw what happened after that, but a little while later, someone found Dad's car on the side of the road, about two miles up from the bar. Someone had run him off the road and shot him.

Roy claimed he had gone straight home and gone to bed. Someone else had followed the preacher and ended his life, he insisted. But everyone was sure Roy was the killer.

I stopped typing, unable to write more of that tonight. The pain of that time was still fresh. The funeral had been a horror, and afterward my mom, Georgi, and I went to my grandmother's house in Denver, where I finished high school.

I never heard from Nate again.

A couple of years later, when the church burned down, people buzzed about the possibility that Nate had done it to get even for his father's incarceration. But I was sure he hadn't done it. I couldn't blame him for leaving town. He'd had his father's act hanging over his head, just as I had my father's death hanging over mine. He was the only one who could understand the extent of that guilt.

I got up and forced myself to go to my bedroom. I kicked off my shoes and dropped on top of the bedspread.

Loneliness overwhelmed me like a cold, uncommitted lover. It made me long for that feeling I had had with Nate years ago. It had seemed so simple, the clean, pure love between us. But love had a way of igniting and burning out, especially when guilt was there to douse the flames.

So why did he rekindle my sense of myself? Why did he make me feel like I was more than just what Jack saw? More than the refuse of a broken covenant.

I wanted to pray, but I was still too mad at God. I closed my eyes and tried to sleep, but I couldn't escape my homesickness. My refuge was gone if I couldn't go to him. I'd lost everything, no matter what I'd done. Teenage defiance ended in death. But trying as hard as I could as a wife had ended in betrayal. What did God want from me?

I got up to get another drink, but I hated myself for it. Eventually I fell into a shallow, headachy sleep that did nothing to calm my raging thoughts.

CHAPTER 7

NATE

"I googled burns," my mother said when she called to check on me Monday. "It said they have to be debrided. It sounds terrible. Shouldn't you be in a hospital?"

I smiled. "No, Mama. That's for third-degree burns. I'm good."

"It said you need antibiotics. Did they give you any? If not, I want you to go see my doctor—"

"They did. I just took one."

"Well, all right, then."

"So how's Pop?"

"The first night he was home, he slept like a baby. But the last couple of nights, he's hardly slept at all. Don't tell him I said so." She lowered her voice even more. "I'm sorry about what he said the other night, Nate. You two can't go on believing the worst about each other."

"I know. I'm sorry. He just really knows

how to push my buttons."

"Well, I'm glad you're both home, and that he's not in prison and you're not in some fire. It looks really bad this morning. Did you see the news?"

"Yeah." My buddies were still out there, right in the worst of it, and most of them hadn't had a night's sleep in days. They ate what was dropped from the plane in their cargo trunks or what they had stuffed into their jumpsuit pockets.

I would have given anything to be there with them. I'd asked to be a spotter or to work in dispatch or help with logistics, but I wasn't cleared to go anywhere near the fire. Bureau of Land Management policy required that I not be involved in any way. It didn't matter how much they needed me.

I went into Drew's garage, where he kept his dusty weight bench. The dumbbells were lined up on the floor, and I grabbed the ones that were ten pounds less than I'd curled before my injuries.

With the first curl, my right arm and side pulled, and I set the weight down quickly. I had to be able to run uphill with a hundred pounds of gear, so sitting around while I recovered was not going to work for me. I set the dumbbells down and grabbed the barbell, tried to lift it over my head, gritting my teeth through the pain. I counted to ten, then dropped it back on the concrete floor.

"Are you supposed to be doing that?"

I turned and saw my brother standing at the door with a cup of coffee in his hand.

"Yeah, it's no problem."

"You've still got a lot of swelling, and your skin needs to heal."

"What are you? A doctor?"

"No, but I played football long enough to know that you have to take care of your body. Weightlifting isn't considered part of burn rehab."

I sat on the bench and wiped the sweat off my face with my sleeve. "You're up early for a guy who worked all night."

"I slept enough." He came into the garage and sat down on a lawn chair. His hair was disheveled like a little kid's. "So how did it go with the old man last night?"

"About what I expected."

"You didn't see any change?"

"Well, he wasn't drunk. But he's still himself. To tell you the truth, Drew, I don't really know how I feel. I guess I'm not all that anxious to start exhuming all those memories. Pop's blaming me for not visiting him in prison, even though it was because he took us both off the visitors' list."

"He'll learn to respect you. Remember,

we were kids when he left. He doesn't know us as adults."

"I'm not used to being treated like a kid. Where I live, people respect me. They know they can count on me. But the minute I drive into Carlisle, it's like nothing I've ever done matters. All of a sudden I'm Roy Beckett's no-account son, and I feel like I have to hang my head again and prove to everybody — especially him — that I'm not who they think I am."

"You need closure about that church fire."

"If there was one iota of evidence that I started that fire, they would have arrested me. They could have gotten my address from Mama or you in two minutes. But they didn't, because I didn't do it. But the rumors don't die." I bent and grabbed the weights again. I didn't want to admit it, but my brother was right. I shouldn't be doing this.

"Then prove who did it," he said.

I dropped the weights again.

"Pop called me the other night after you left and asked if we would take him around today," Drew said. "You don't have to come if you don't want."

"What for?"

"He's on this kick now. Says he wants to figure out who killed the preacher, since it wasn't him."

I blew out a long breath that was half pain and half frustration. "Why would he do that?"

"Maybe because it really *wasn't* him."

I shook my head at my brother. "You don't believe that, do you?"

He sipped his coffee and chuckled. "No, but he seems to."

"You think he's convinced himself over the years that he's innocent?"

"He's not crazy. He's cantankerous. But he's always insisted he was innocent. Never pled guilty, even though it would've taken years off his sentence."

I wiped my face again. "I'll go with you. But if he starts in on me, I'll let you drop me off and I'll get an Uber home."

"Seems to me you both have something to prove. Maybe you could prove it together."

"First we have to convince each other we're innocent."

After I showered, we loaded into Drew's truck. "Let me ask you something," I said. "You've been in Carlisle all these years. What do you know about Brenna Strickland?"

"You mean Hertzog?"

"Yeah."

"Just that her ex-husband's a jerk and she hasn't handled her divorce very well." He glanced at me as he drove. "So what are you up to? You going to see her?"

"Already did."

Drew's eyebrows shot up. "Seriously?"

"Saturday night. Saw that her light was on, so I walked over."

"Well, you've got guts, I'll say that."

"It was good to see her. But I agree with you. She's having a hard time."

"Jack Hertzog. I couldn't believe she married that guy."

"I guess she loved him."

"She loved his money."

I frowned and looked out the window. Brenna wasn't the type to choose a guy for money. If she had been, she never would have gone out with me. But maybe after she, her sister, and her mom struggled for money after her father's death, the prospect of stability had seemed attractive.

"He's torturing her," Drew said. "He has this new wife who was in college a year ago. She's the selfie queen of Carlisle."

"What are his grounds for suing Brenna for full custody?"

"His mayoral candidacy."

I frowned and looked at him, thinking he was joking. "Seriously."

"I am serious. The current mayor's retiring next year, so Jack's already decided he's the best fit. It's no holds barred. He's determined to win. And to combat his reputation as a dude who left his wife for a sorority girl, he's going for the narrative that he had no choice but to leave Brenna. And see? The judge is giving him custody of his children, because family comes first, don't you know."

I mulled that over for a few minutes, but as we turned onto my mother's street, I said, "Wonder if she'd have dinner with me."

Drew groaned. "Are you sure you want to open this Pandora's box again?" He turned into our parents' driveway. "Do me a favor and don't bring this up to them."

I shrugged. "It just feels like unfinished business. Maybe I need to finish it."

CHAPTER 8

BRENNA

Though my head ached and I felt as if I'd only slept for a couple of hours, I made it to work on time. But as I tried to organize my thoughts and get the store's computer to cooperate, my mind kept wandering back to Nate Saturday night.

It was obvious to me now, though it hadn't been then, that I'd had too much to drink. I'd looked awful. The thought of Nate seeing me like that after all these years was mortifying, but then I chastised myself for caring at all. I had no business daydreaming about Nate Beckett. He had called last night, but I'd let it ring to voice mail because I feared I would sound too slurred. He didn't leave a message, and he didn't try again.

Hadn't my father's death taught me anything? Hadn't I learned?

If life hadn't taught me the lessons I

needed to learn, Jack sure had. My thoughts strayed to my children, and I wondered if Jack remembered to make them brush their teeth or if anyone had said prayers with them. They'd dressed them up well for the selfies and photo opps, but after that, had Jack paid any atttention to them?

My sister came out of the back room with a box. "I got a new shipment of these bath bombs." She set it on the counter. "Are you all right?"

"Yeah. Just thinking about the kids."

"Call the school. Make sure they're okay."

Picking up the phone, I dialed the number of the private school they attended. Marilyn, the secretary, answered, and I could hear the noise of children in the background. "Marilyn?" I said loudly. "This is Brenna Hertzog. I just wanted to make sure Sophia and Noah got there this morning."

Marilyn hesitated. "I'm sorry, Brenna, but Jack never brought them."

I closed my eyes. "Sophia has a test today. Did he call?"

"No. Maybe they're sick."

I clicked the phone off without saying goodbye, then immediately dialed his number at work.

"Jack Hertzog's office. May I help you?"

"Can I speak to Jack, please?"

I knew the secretary recognized my voice since I'd called there so many times before, but the woman played dumb. "May I tell him who's calling?"

"The mother of his children," I bit out. "It's an emergency."

I held for an eternity, seething more with each passing moment, until finally he answered.

"What do you want, Brenna? I'm busy."

"Where are my children?"

"They're with Rayne, of course."

"So she didn't want to get up early enough to get them to school?"

"Relax, Brenna. Noah's four."

"Sophia's eight and she has a test today."

"She can make it up."

"Jack, you insisted on keeping them last night so you could parade them around when they should have been home. I would have gotten them to school." I sighed, realizing this was going nowhere. "So I'm picking them up at your house?"

"Yes."

"At what time?"

"Five o'clock."

"Jack, this isn't how it's supposed to work. I'm not supposed to have to knock on your door and get my children from your adolescent wife. You're supposed to bring them to me."

"Fine," he said. "But you'll have to wait. Dad called a meeting for tonight, and I have to be there. If you're waiting for me, they may wind up spending the night again."

Tears pushed to my eyes, and I glanced around and saw Georgi staring at me. "All right, I'll pick them up. But please warn her that I'm not in the mood for her drama."

"You know, Brenna, you should really see a doctor. You're starting to go off the deep end. You're the one who creates drama."

"You can't just blow off school, Jack, and that woman is practically a child herself."

"That woman is my wife," he said with great pleasure. "And when they're with her, they don't have to stay in day care after school."

"I don't think I have to remind you that my preference is to stay home with them as we agreed before we ever had them, and as I did before you had your midlife crisis. I'm working because of you, Jack! I'm between a rock and a hard place, and my children have had to suffer because of it."

"Well, you won't have to worry about them much longer. Court isn't that far off."

I slammed down the phone with a loudly ringing clank, and Georgi leaned over the counter to me. "That man is an animal."

Shaking my head, I covered my face and tried to get a grip on myself, but it seemed futile. I wanted to die. I wanted to kill. I wanted a drink.

But it was only a few hours until I'd get off work and could have Sophia and Noah with me again. I could get through the day without a drink, and once the kids were with me, I wouldn't need one anymore.

Boxing my arms on the sales counter, I dropped my head on them and prayed with all my heart to the God I still believed in, the one I'd strayed from but not forgotten, to protect my children while they were away from me. As long as the kids were okay, I would survive.

CHAPTER 9

NATE

Pop was in a good mood when Drew and I picked him up, and he got into the backseat of the truck, stuck his arm out the window, and tapped on the roof.

"Where we going, Pop?" Drew asked.

"Let's go to the bar," he said.

The bar? I rolled my eyes. "Pop, are you sure you want to go back to where you were before?"

"Get over yourself," he shot back. "I told you we were going to reconstruct the crime. We have to go where it started. If I'm going to prove my innocence, then first I need to prove it to you guys. Just take me to the bar. I don't intend to drink. I told you I'm staying dry."

We were quiet as we drove to the bar. At this time of morning no one was there, so Drew unlocked it and let us in. He flipped on the lights, and I saw the place with new eyes. I'd never seen it without the ambient lighting, people's faces in shadow and candlelight. I glanced back at Pop as he stood at the door. His eyes took in the sight like it was an old friend. "So you own this place now?"

"Yep, I do," Drew said.

My dad studied Drew for a moment. "I was sitting in this bar the night it happened. Our whole life changed. It started right here." He walked over to the barstool he was sitting on that night. "I was sitting right here when the preacher came storming in, probably the first time he'd ever darkened the door of the place. I wound up in prison for something I didn't do, and your whole lives changed." He looked at Drew. "Why on earth would you want to buy this place? I would think it had nothing but terrible memories."

Drew went behind the bar and poured us each a glass of seltzer water. "It had good memories for me. I spent a lot of time here after you went to jail, Pop. Nate was gone and Mama was busy with who knows what, and this was where my buddies hung out. It was family. The clientele has changed over the years, but not me. I'm still here. I wanted to make sure the place didn't go under, so when Ivan was going to sell it or close it down, I did what I could to keep it open."

"Is it making any money?"

"I'm breaking even. Paying bills. Some months I make a profit."

Pop slid onto the barstool he was on that night and leaned on the bar. "I was drinking a vodka tonic," he said. "It was probably my sixth. I should've stopped after the second or third, but I kept going like I always did. Could barely walk by the time Strickland came storming in."

I took a stool a couple down from him and sipped my water. It was terrible. "Why do we have to dredge up these memories? Can't you just be happy that you're pardoned now and it's all over? Just leave it alone and get on with your life."

Pop slammed his fist on the counter, shaking the bowls that usually held peanuts. "Because I didn't do it!"

"What does it even matter?" I asked. "Why do you care what anybody in this town believes?"

"It's a matter of personal honor. I'm not a killer. I may have been a drunk, but I didn't murder anybody."

"So what do you want to do here?" Drew asked in a less irritated voice than mine.

"We're going to reconstruct."

I opened my mouth to protest, but Drew speared me with a look and shut me up.

"So . . . I'm sitting here drinking, minding my own business. Drinking way too much. We've established that. They were playing that song, that 'Whipping Post' song. It was loud, way too loud. And the place was about half full."

"Who was here that night, Pop?" Drew asked as though he was taking this seriously.

Pop looked around, remembering. "Ed Jenkins was right here, two seats down to my right. And next to him I think was that kid, Jacob Ferrell. And over there on the corner, Leon had his usual seat. And Danny Brown was next to him."

He turned to his left, and I could see him studying his mental photo. "I think Wilma was sitting right there. She was with Bobby Thornton. They didn't usually sit at the bar, but their favorite table was taken, so they came up here and ordered. Guess they were waiting for somebody to leave. And down on the end there, I'm pretty sure was George Belmont. Hertzog was sitting next to him."

"Jack?" I asked, suddenly interested.

"No, William. I liked to call him Willy because he hated that."

We all chuckled. "He usually sat there so

he could see everybody who came in. Pre-tentious blowhard."

"What about at the tables?" Drew asked. "You remember any of the people at the tables?"

Pop turned his stool and looked back over the tables. "You've changed it. Painted the place."

"Yeah, a little upkeep. Tried to give it a fresher look. I bought new tables about three years ago. The old ones were looking bad."

Pop closed his eyes. "I don't really remember who else was here. I was facing the bar. The bartender was Eugene that night."

"So when Strickland came in, did he come straight to you?" Drew asked.

Pop chuckled. "When he walked in, it was like there was this audible gasp in the room. Even with all the voices and the noise, you could hear it. It wasn't often the Baptist preacher showed up in the bar on a Saturday night. Or any night, for that matter. I looked over and saw him scanning the faces, and his eyes were livid, like he was about to call fire and brimstone down on somebody. And then he saw me and cut through the crowd. Got right up in my face."

I felt my muscles tense, my burns pulling. "What did he say?"

"He told me to get on the phone and find you. Said you had his daughter and he wanted her back at home within ten minutes or he was calling the cops."

I looked down at my hands.

"If I'd had a clear mind, I probably would've just done it. Got you on the phone, told you to get his daughter back home. I've relived it a thousand times, tried to replay it in my mind. How things would've been different if I had. But I wasn't thinking clearly. Instead, I stood up and said, 'What's the matter, Preacher? My son isn't good enough for you?' "

I rubbed my jaw and sighed. "It didn't have to be a thing."

"What did he say?" Drew asked, but I was pretty sure I didn't want to know.

"He said, 'The apple doesn't fall far from the tree. Get him on the phone!' He grabbed me by my shoulders and shook me. What am I gonna do? Just sit there? I reacted. I brought my arms up and knocked his arms aside, and then I lunged at him."

I hated this. "Were you fighting for me, or for you?" I asked.

My dad looked at me and shook his head. "You make a good point, son. I think I was fighting for both of us. But mostly I was embarrassed." His face turned red, and he looked down at the bar. "I didn't like the preacher confronting me in front of a bunch of people. No man would."

"So you lunged at him," Drew prompted. "Did you hit him?"

"No, I knocked the stool over and a couple of glasses got knocked over and broke. I was clumsy so I didn't get a punch in, but I tried. Next thing I knew, Eugene came around the counter. He grabbed both of us and walked us hard toward the door. 'Take it to the parking lot!' So we stumbled out the door."

Pop slid off his stool and stepped toward the door. We followed him out. "When we got out here I lunged at him again, but this time he moved out of the way. I was so drunk I fell. I scrambled back up. I was only a few steps from my truck, so I opened the door, and Strickland came at me again, yelling, 'Call your son! Call him right now! Tell him what I said.' "

"And you still didn't," I said.

"I told him if he wanted his daughter, he should call her himself. He started toward me again, his arms in the air like he was about to grab my head and slam it against my truck, but then something happened and he stopped himself. His hands dropped to his sides. It was the darndest thing. I was

93

bracing, ready to go at him again. And then he just walked away. I watched him as he opened his car door. He turned back to me. 'Call your boy,' he said. 'Find him!' And he drove away. I stood there yelling after him, cussing him, like that dude in *Monty Python* who'd had his arms and legs chopped off but kept yelling, 'Come back and get what's comin' to ya!' "

It wasn't funny to any of us.

"What did you do then, Pop?" Drew asked.

"I started to go back in the bar. Wish I had, because then I would've had an alibi. People who saw me. Instead, I drove home. It's a wonder I didn't go into a ditch, but I made it there and then I collapsed into bed."

"Are you sure you didn't black out?" I asked. "Do something you just don't remember?"

His voice went up several decibels. "No, I didn't black out. I remember it in detail. Why would I lie about that, now that I've served fourteen years and I'm pardoned? Why would it be so important to me to clear my name?"

I really couldn't say. It didn't make much sense.

We followed Pop as he walked out to where his truck had been parked. We knew the route he would've taken home. After a block or so in the direction Strickland had gone, Pop would have turned left onto Brennan Street. Unless he was following the preacher.

We all stared the way Strickland had gone.

"I want to go to the spot where he was killed," Pop said. "I want to walk through it."

Drew locked up, and we loaded into the cab of the pickup and drove the two miles down the road. Drew pulled off where the church members had installed a marker with a plaque on it about the man they called "Brother Strickland."

Drew walked to the tree that still bore the scars of Strickland's crash into it. "I came by here after they arrested you, just to see what had happened. There were two sets of skid marks on the road. It looked like he had been run off."

"Did they make casts of the tire tracks?" I asked. "Compare them to yours?"

"If they did, they didn't use them in court."

"Why wouldn't they?"

"Maybe they made the casts," Pop said, "and it didn't fit the narrative that I did it. Just muddied the waters." He looked out at the street. "Whoever it was came up and threw the door open and shot him point blank with a .44 Magnum. I've never owned a .44. All I have is hunting rifles. That's what I had in my truck that night. Hanging on my back window where I always kept it. You boys know that."

I glanced at Drew. "How big were the wheel tracks?"

"They were big, like a truck. It made sense to me that it was Pop."

We stood on the dirt as Pop walked to the tree and looked at the ground as if trying to picture what had happened here and why. "Your mama has the pictures and all the files from my attorney's discovery. That's part of the reason we got the pardon. She sent the governor a ton of stuff. Evidence that pointed out everything they failed to follow through on. There were other people in this town who didn't like Strickland, you know. It wasn't just me. I think somebody that night saw an opportunity to kill him and figured it would get put on me. Two birds with one stone."

"That would mean that the real killer was in the bar," Drew said.

I wanted to tell my brother that he was tumbling down the rabbit hole. Pop did it. It was obvious. But I didn't want to fight.

We got back into the truck and were quiet

as Drew drove us back to my parents' house. As we pulled in, Pop said, "I know you boys don't believe me. You don't have any reason to. But I want you to humor me. If not for my sake, do it for your own sake, and for your mama's. She's worked so hard on all this. She believes in my innocence. I want you to as well. Come in, and I'm going to give you the box of files. It's a lot of stuff, but look through it and see if you can get to the place where you see me as innocent."

The last thing I wanted to do while I was in Carlisle was to dig through those old files, but we both muttered that we would. We followed him inside, and he had the box all ready. He handed it to Drew. "I'll be over there some, just looking through things again. I just don't want your mama digging back through it again. She's earned a break from all that. But there's a killer out there who I took the punishment for. He owes me."

"What if you can never prove it?" I asked.

"Then I'll have to live with it," he said. "But I at least have to try."

BRENNA

When I got off work, I headed to the other side of Carlisle to pick up my children. By the time we'd endured Rayne's fawning all over them, kissing and hugging them good-bye like she had given birth to them, they were starving.

I offered them the rare treat of dinner at McDonald's.

Instead of sitting across from me in the booth, both children begged to sit beside me, so we all snuggled up on one side of the table, munching on chicken nuggets and french fries and getting caught up.

"The dinner last night was boring," Sophia said as she dipped a nugget into her sauce. "They had this green stuff we had to eat, and I thought I was gonna throw up, but Rayne made us eat every bite."

"I gagged," Noah said matter-of-factly, "and Grandpa said I did it on purpose."

"He took him in the bathroom and spanked him," Sophia said, "then brought him back to the table and made him eat it."

Noah looked up at me with a smile. "That time when I gagged, I covered my mouth so he wouldn't see."

I felt the blood rushing to my face, but I didn't want Noah to see it. How dare that man spank my son? How dare he lay one finger on him?

I had to change the subject. "What kind of dinner was it?"

"He said it was a fun raiser," Sophia said.

"A fund-raiser?"

"Uh-huh."

The mayoral election was still more than a year away. How were my children going to stand it?

"After it was over, we wanted to come home, but Daddy wouldn't bring us. He said we should get used to sleeping in our rooms at his house."

"I cried," Noah said. "I wanted you."

I squeezed him against me. "You could've called me," I said. "I could've told you a bedtime story on Facetime."

"Daddy wouldn't let him. He said Rayne could read him a story, but Noah said never mind."

It made me sad to think of Noah having to show such adult restraint and going to sleep homesick. I didn't tell them how many times I had tried to call them, but Jack never picked up.

"Then I wanted to sleep with Sophia," Noah said, his face taking on the grief he'd felt last night, "only they wouldn't let me. Daddy said only babies sleep with their sisters."

"He could've slept with me, Mommy," Sophia said. "I wanted him to. I could hear him in there crying for a long time."

99

It was almost more than I could take. I pulled Noah onto my lap, blinking back tears, and struggled to find something positive to say. "Well, tonight you can sleep in your own bed. And when we get home, we'll climb into my bed and read stories until bedtime. How will that be?"

"Good," Noah said.

"Mommy, do we have to go back to Daddy's next weekend?"

"Yes, honey. He gets you on weekends."

"But that's not fair. We never get to be with you. And when we're there, all he does is go play golf or have meetings with Grandpa and leave us with Rayne."

"Yeah, and she usually leaves us with babysitters while she shops."

"We'd rather be with you."

My heart sank further. "Honey, I'd give anything in the world if I could have you all the time. You know that."

"Do you think that judge might fix it?"

I couldn't tell my daughter that the judge in question was a close friend of Jack's and her grandfather's — as all the judges in the county were — and that I feared what might happen in court. Judge Radison had known my family most of my life too, but we had nothing to offer him. "All we can do is hope and pray."

"I have been praying, Mommy," Sophia said. "I pray about it all the time. Do you think God hears me?"

"I know he does. Children's prayers are extra special. In the Bible it says that the angels who watch over children are always before him. That means he pays extra attention to them."

"Well, what do you know?"

Startled at the deep voice, I turned to see Nate standing at the fountain drink machine behind us.

He came around our booth. "This must be Sophia and Noah," he said, bending down to Noah and extending his hand to shake. "I'm Nate. I used to go to school with your mom."

I realized Noah had sauce on his hand as he shook, but Nate pretended not to notice.

He moved to Sophia. "Sophia, your mother told me you were pretty, but she didn't say how pretty. You're lucky, you know. You look just like her."

Sophia smiled. "Everybody says that."

"Everybody's right. Your mama always was the prettiest girl in Carlisle, but now it looks like there are two of you."

I smiled in spite of my effort not to. I looked up at Nate, wondering if I should ask him to sit down, but then I thought better of it. "I can't believe you'd eat here when you could have your mom's cooking."

"We've been out and about today." He nodded toward his father and brother in line at the counter.

My smile crashed as I recognized Roy. My father's killer stood just feet away. Suddenly I wanted to leave.

Nate stood there a moment longer, his eyes lingering on me. "Well . . . I guess I'll go order."

"Okay. Good to see you."

Nate shook Noah's hand again and winked at Sophia, then ambled up to the front.

And as I watched him go, I told myself again to put him out of my mind. Nate wasn't what I needed right now.

NATE

Pop waited until we sat down before he said, "That woman looked familiar."

I thought of lying, but Drew knew who it was. "Brenna Hertzog."

He dropped his Big Mac and gaped at me. "What?"

"I was just saying hello, Pop. No big romance."

Pop's face began to redden, the way it always had just before he launched headfirst into a brawl. "Do I have to remind you why I just spent almost a decade and a half in prison?"

I wished I'd never left Drew's house today. "That wasn't her fault. There was an actual murder. Someone shot her father. She was a victim."

"Do you still have a thing for her?"

I gave up trying to eat and set my food down. "I've been gone from here almost as long as you have. I barely know anybody here anymore. What kind of *thing* could I have?"

As Brenna and her children threw their bags away and went out the door, Pop eyed her. "She married?"

I really didn't want to talk about her to him.

"Divorced from Jack Hertzog," Drew said.

Pop frowned. "Oh, no wonder you perked up when you heard the name Hertzog, when I was telling who was at the bar that night."

Drew touched my arm to silence me. "It doesn't matter, guys."

But my eyes were riveted on my dad's. "Pop, if you think any of what happened was her fault, I've got to set this straight right now. Brenna and I shouldn't have sneaked out, but nothing happened. She probably wishes she'd never met me."

"She wishes? You don't know how many nights I lay in that cell wishing you and Brenna Strickland had never laid eyes on each other."

I glared at my father.

"If you start seeing her again, it'll be over my dead body."

I felt the blood rush to my face, and I thought about telling him I was a grown man and I didn't need his permission. But why bother? I picked up my burger and took a slow, deliberate bite, looking past him.

Pop watched me chew. "Did you hear me, son?"

I finally dragged my gaze back to him. "I heard you," I said. "But I haven't taken orders from anybody in a long time. And I'm not about to start now."

My father locked eyes with me, as though I was his peer and he wanted me to know he wouldn't hesitate to come across the table. My look back at him said that I didn't want to hurt him, but he had to know that if he came at me, I'd have no choice.

Drew broke the tension. "Hey, did anybody hear that one about the cowboy, the cop, and the coop-scooper?"

Pop finally looked away. "What in blazes is a coop-scooper?"

"You know. A guy who scoops coops. Any-way . . ."

As Drew went on with the joke, Pop began to eat again.

But I wasn't hungry anymore.

CHAPTER 10

NATE

A few days had gone by since I'd seen Brenna, though I'd spoken to her a few times on the phone. The first time she picked up I could hear the reluctance in her voice to get into deep conversation. Maybe she didn't want to take a moment away from her kids at night, and she worked every day at Georgi's boutique.

But Saturday I saw her and her kids out in their front yard. Noah was riding his bike with training wheels around the driveway, and Sophia was drawing with chalk on the front sidewalk. Brenna sat cross-legged on the grass, her laptop in her lap.

Instead of going in, I crossed the street. "What's up, guys?" I said.

Was it my imagination, or was that a genuine glad-to-see-me smile in her eyes? "Hey, Nate," she said. "Guys, remember Mr. Nate, from McDonald's?"

"I'm drawing a skop-hotch," Sophia said. "You jump backward."

I stopped and studied the hopscotch squares. "Did you invent this or is it a real thing?"

"I invented it. Try it."

Brenna got to her feet, laughing, as I lined up in front of the pink boxes and tried to figure out how to hopscotch backward. "One foot?"

"Except on the double ones."

"But if I can't see . . ."

"That's the trick!"

Noah stopped to watch. I bent one leg and tried to jump back, once, then twice, then again . . .

"No, that one's double! I got you!"

I toppled over and caught myself before I hit the ground. The kids and Brenna cheered as I got my footing. "No fair. I'm injured and not at my best."

"What's the matter, Beckett?" Brenna taunted. "You gonna let a little game of hopscotch do you in?"

"I'll make another one!" Sophia said. "This one will be different and you can't look. Mommy, it'll be your turn next."

"Better practice balancing, Mommy," I said as I crossed the yard.

She laughed, then said, "Seriously, you

don't have to do it again."

"Are you kidding? I have to master this."

Her laughter reminded me of when she was sixteen, before bereavement and divorce sapped laughter from her life. When Sophia was ready, they walked me backward to the squares, and I had to guess where the doubles were as I hopped backward. It was a disaster, but Sophia was thrilled that she'd gotten me again.

When Brenna tried it and fell, I caught her. "It's not easy, is it?"

"No, it isn't."

"I want to do it!" Noah cried, jumping off his bike. "My turn!"

We watched him hop backward, changing feet like a champion. "Both feet!" I yelled when he got to the doubles.

"No fair!" Sophia cried.

When he tried the double feet and went back to the left foot, he toppled over and I scooped him up. "Careful with your burns!" Brenna yelled.

"I'm okay," I said. "But I'm a little clumsy. I might drop him. Uh-oh!" He squealed as I pretended to drop him, then didn't at the last second.

"What burns? Can I see your burns?" Noah asked.

I put him down and showed him my

bandages. Brenna told him how I'd gotten them.

When the kid next door came over to play, they ran around to the backyard. I walked with Brenna around the house, but hung back at the gate. "I didn't mean to interrupt your time with them. I just saw you out and wanted to say hi."

Her smile seemed genuine. "You don't have to leave. I'm glad you came. You're good with them. That surprises me."

I grinned. "Why?"

"Because I've never seen you with kids. You're not even an uncle."

"I have friends with kids."

"Well, they really like you. You're a hit." She looked longingly at them as they pretended the garden hose was a fire-hose and hosed off the slide. "They love our new yard. I bought the house because it has this fort swing set. But they don't get to use it that much since they're always gone on weekends."

"Why are they home today?"

"Because Jack had an event last night and some kind of fund-raising brunch, so he's picking them up in a little while."

Her eyes glistened with a sheen of tears as she looked across the yard at them.

"Okay, well, that seals it then. I'm gonna

leave you to enjoy the rest of your time with them. Do you want to hang out tonight?"

She stared at me, as if running through all the reasons not to in her mind. "You can come by if you want."

I didn't know if she really meant it or if she was just being polite. But I wanted to see her, so I accepted. "Sounds good. I'll see you about four?"

"Yeah, okay."

I headed back across the street and looked back before going into Drew's house. She was leaning against the gate watching me. I smiled as I headed inside.

By four o'clock, I had almost convinced myself that this was a bad idea. Why did I want to keep pursuing Brenna when there was no clear indication she was interested? I'd had other relationships in the past ten years, but not with anyone who still occupied my thoughts like she did. She hadn't told me to stay home, and she had answered some of my calls. Maybe it wasn't futile.

Besides, I really wanted to spend some time with her.

I crossed the street again and knocked softly on Brenna's front door. She opened it, smiling. "Hey."

"Hey. Have you been okay this afternoon?" I asked.

"Yeah, I'm okay."

"Was he civil, or did he torture you?"

"Kind of a combination. Civil torture."

"I heard them when they drove up. Glanced out the window. She may be young, but she has nothing on you. The man is out of his mind."

"Thank you, Nate."

I could see that she didn't need me to insult the other woman. She wanted to change the subject. "So, you had a laptop outside today. Were you writing?"

"A little. It feels good."

"What are you working on?"

"I don't know. Maybe a short story. Or a novel. I have this character . . . but she's probably too much of me."

"Too much?"

"Yeah, she's kind of a mess. But I'll figure it out. It's just good to be doing it again. I'm working with my sister, Georgi, in her store, and that keeps me pretty busy most of the week, but the writing is a good escape when the kids aren't here."

"You were really good back in the day."

"You don't remember."

"I do. You wrote that story about the lake, how you used to swing on a tire your dad strung up in that big oak tree, and how you'd jump in . . ."

"You do remember."

"Sure I do. It was really good. And a few years ago, I read that story you had published in that *Agatha Christie* magazine."

"What? Okay, I know you're not a subscriber to *Agatha Christie.*"

"No, but I heard you'd had it published. I found a copy."

She seemed genuinely moved by that. "That was before I was married, but I was dating Jack then. He didn't even read it."

"It was good. I thought you were going to do it as a career. You could, you know."

"Actually, I couldn't. You can't have a career as a writer if you never write anything."

She showed me that she was marinating steaks for us to cook on the grill, so we went out back and started the charcoal. The smoke mixed with the scent of the crisp Colorado air, reminding me of the fires raging just an hour and a half north of here. I wondered if my team was still in the thick of it, or if they'd finally gotten a break. The news said that the fires were 50 percent contained. At least they were moving in the right direction.

We were outside waiting to put the steaks on the grill when I heard her front door slam. "Brenna! You home?"

"Uh-oh," Brenna said. "My sister. Wait here."

As Brenna stepped into the house, I looked in past her. Georgi looked different than she had in high school. She was two years older than Brenna. Back in high school she was a T-shirt and jeans girl, but now she dressed the part of the boutique owner. Her long hair was platinum blonde over brunette tips, and she had on way more eye makeup than she'd worn before.

"I wanted to check on you," she was saying as she crossed the house. "Since the kids were gone and you were . . ." Her voice trailed off as she saw me standing at the back door. "Are you kidding me?"

"Georgi, come on," Brenna cut in.

"No. Seriously? He's here?"

I cleared my throat. "Hi, Georgi. Nice to see you too."

Brenna stood between us. "Nate, why don't you put the steaks on? I want to have a word with Georgi."

"A word? You want a word with me?" Georgi asked.

I stepped out back and closed the door behind me. I drew in a deep breath. Of course she was angry. My father had been convicted of killing her father. How was she supposed to act toward me?

"How could you be with him?" I heard her say through the open window.

"His brother lives across the street. He's visiting. It's no big deal, Georgi."

"No big deal? Our father is dead!"

"Nate didn't kill him."

"But his father did! It's your relationship with him that led to that, Brenna. What are you thinking? If you hadn't sneaked around with him, Dad would be alive today."

"Oh, don't you blame me for that!" Brenna said. "You have to take some responsibility for that!"

"What do you mean?"

"I mean that your defiance of Mom and Dad paved that path of distrust before I ever even dated. By the time I was getting out of the house, they were so strict I couldn't breathe. Not because of me, Georgi, but because of you and Jacob Ferrell."

"Jacob Ferrell didn't get Dad killed. Nate did."

"Dad overreacted to everything I did after he caught Jacob sneaking through your window multiple times, Georgi! He even had him arrested for breaking and entering. If that hadn't happened, maybe Dad would have reacted in a normal way and not stormed into a bar looking for a fight!"

I stepped toward the door, my hand on the knob. Should I intervene?

"How dare you!" Georgi cried. "You're drinking again, aren't you? You would never say that to me if you weren't. I hired you so you could afford to buy this house. I gave you an income. I've been there for you through this whole thing."

Brenna dropped her voice, and she sounded like she was crying. "Then let me have dinner with someone who used to care about me, Georgi. Don't go nuts on me. And don't accuse me of drinking just because I'm defending myself."

I dropped my hand and backed away from the door. I didn't want to hear any more. I put the steaks on, hoping the sound of the sizzling would block out the voices. I wadded up the tinfoil that had been in the pan and took it to the garbage can I'd seen on the side of the house. I opened the can and dropped the tinfoil into it, but I couldn't miss the empty bottles in a paper sack at the bottom. Had she drunk all of that . . . alone?

I closed the garbage can and went back to the grill, wishing I hadn't seen that, and that I hadn't heard the conversation.

I heard the front door slam, and Brenna came back out wiping her eyes. "I'm so sorry for that. She's been great to me, but she's a little controlling."

"Look, if this is going to be a problem for you, I don't want to be here. I don't want to complicate your life any more than it already is."

"You're not complicating it. And I can't let other people call the shots on my life anymore."

"There's just a lot of water under the bridge. I get it. Just the thought of me brings up a lot of bad memories."

"I have bad memories and plenty of guilt about what happened. But seeing you this week has reminded me of how you used to make me feel. There were good memories too. Let's try to dwell on those."

"Okay," I said. My gaze locked with hers, and for an electric moment, I wanted to kiss her. I finally turned back to the steaks. "Georgi looks good. What's up with her? Married? Kids?"

"No, neither. She's married to her store. Loves it. She doesn't really even want kids."

"My mother shops there for gifts and stuff. She said it's nice."

"Yeah, we do a lot of business for wedding and shower gifts."

"Oh, speaking of a gift, I have a surprise for you."

"A surprise? What?"

I pulled a thumb drive out of my pocket and handed it to her with a grin.

She took it, inclining her head. "Are these national security secrets?"

I laughed. "They don't give those to smokejumpers. Where's your laptop?"

She went in and got it, and set it on her picnic table. "If you're giving me a virus, I know a guy who can break your kneecaps."

"Sounds painful. And weird." I took the flash drive from her and inserted it into the port. "Yesterday I was thinking about your writing. I had time on my hands, so I got on the internet and looked up advice about getting started, and it said you should go to a writers' conference."

"Yeah, I tried doing that when I was married, but it never worked out."

"Well, I looked up the ones close to here, and there's one in Fort Collins every May, but that's seven months away. But they had downloads of all their sessions from last May. I bought them and downloaded them to this."

She gasped and bent over to pull up the contents of the thumb drive. "Are you serious? All of them? That's expensive, Nate."

"I consider it an investment. I like to read."

Was it my imagination, or were her eyes growing teary?

"I believe in your talent," I said. "You just need a jumpstart."

She scrolled through the workshops. "Look at this. Plotting, point of view, character development, research . . . I can't believe you thought to do this."

"I figured you could listen to the ones that interest you and ignore the ones that don't. In May, maybe you can go to the conference."

Yes, those were tears. She seemed to struggle to keep them back. "Nobody's ever taken my writing that seriously."

"They would if they read your work."

She got a Kleenex out of her pocket and dabbed at her eyes. The vulnerable expression on her face broke my heart. She wasn't used to kind gestures. I wanted to change that.

CHAPTER 11

NATE

I didn't kiss Brenna good night, but we hugged at her door before I walked back across the street. We had hung out like old friends, talking and getting to know each other again, but I was ever aware that she was drinking a lot. I drank soda and kept my head clear, knowing that if we both waded into that foggy place, we might not turn back. I didn't want to give Brenna another thing to regret.

Drew was still at the bar when I got back to his house, so I turned on the news and waited for coverage of the fires. As I waited, I peeled off my bandages and checked out my burns, hoping they were healing faster than the doctors had warned me they would. I wanted to get back up there with my men. They couldn't afford to be a man down right now.

I applied the medication I needed, then

wrapped my leg with fresh bandages. My mind drifted back to the conversation Brenna had with Georgi tonight. I picked up my laptop, set it in my lap, and leaned my head back on Drew's recliner. I hadn't thought of Jacob Ferrell in years, but now I remembered Georgi's relationship with him. Georgi had been the wild child, the preacher's kid people gossiped about. Her boyfriend Jacob had been even wilder. He was probably the one who influenced her the most. No wonder her dad was so strict with Brenna.

I pulled up my browser and did a quick search for Jacob Ferrell from Carlisle, Colorado. I was stunned to see a mug shot and a prison record. I clicked on it and studied the photo that came up. This was taken about five years after I left Carlisle. The guy looked bad, with red circles under his bloodshot eyes, an unkempt beard born of neglect. His stringy hair looked like it hadn't been washed in weeks, and it hung into his eyes.

He looked like the kind of guy you would see on the street and walk the other way, for fear he would knife you. His arrest was for assault and battery. He had served a year and a half. I went back to the list of links in my browser and clicked on another one. It was a newspaper article that covered the barroom brawl, again at Flannigan's, that had gotten him arrested.

So he was a regular at Flannigan's? I went to my dad's box of files and found the list of those who'd been at the bar the night of Pop's fight with the preacher. Yes, Jacob Farrell was at the bar that night.

I sat on the edge of the recliner, thinking. I had thought there wasn't anyone in town who had anything serious against the preacher, but maybe I was wrong. Georgi's boyfriend probably had something against him. Hadn't Brenna said that he'd had Jacob arrested before for breaking and entering? I went back to my computer and searched through more records until I found the edition of the *Carlisle Chronicles* with the police blotter from that week. The police had reported an incident at Brenna's house, just months before Strickland was killed.

I looked through more of the links and tried to figure out when Jacob had been released for that charge. The charges were dropped a few days later, and Jacob was let go. But he was probably livid. After that, it was years before he was convicted of another crime.

I flipped through more of the files and found the one that described the police interviews with different witnesses who were at the bar that night. Jacob had been interviewed.

I read through his interview. Jacob claimed he had followed Pop and Brenna's dad out the door just for amusement and stood watching as the two men screamed at each other, then separated in the parking lot. He swore that my father had pulled out after the preacher and followed in the direction Strickland had gone.

I sat back and thought about that for a moment. That was the testimony that sealed Pop's fate.

What if Jacob lied? What if *he* had really been the one to follow the preacher? What if he had been the one to run him off the road and shoot him in the head? I wondered if he had a .44 Magnum that matched the gun that killed Brenna's father.

I found the transcript of the trial that my mother had gotten, and I scanned it until I found where Jacob had testified, something I'd completely forgotten about.

Jacob claimed he had gone home after that, and his roommate corroborated his story. His roommate. Who would that have been? I flipped through the pages until I found the name. Johnny Humphrey. He was a couple years older than me, in Drew's class. I wondered if he would stick by his story today, in spite of all that Jacob had proven about his character since then.

Maybe I would go and talk to him.

For the first time since Strickland's death, I considered the possibility that my dad could be telling the truth. He really could be innocent. Maybe I should give him the benefit of the doubt and dig into this just a little bit.

Sunday afternoon I googled Johnny Humphrey and got his address. I found his house in the neighborhood where my parents lived. I drove by and saw him out in his driveway, working on an old Mustang with the hood up. Two children played in the yard.

I circled the block, then came back more purposefully. I pulled along the curb in front of his house and jumped out. "Johnny Humphrey? I was driving by and I saw you. How's it going, man?"

Johnny peered at me over the hood, and when he recognized me, he started laughing and came to slap my hand. "How are you, Firebug?"

I winced at the nickname. Nobody had called me that in school. I wondered if someone had named me that since the church burned down, or if it was just because of my occupation. I told him I was back in town since Pop had just gotten out of prison, and I watched him carefully for a reaction at my dad's name. But there wasn't anything discernible.

"What you got here?" I asked, looking into the engine of the antique sports car.

"Sweet, right? I bought it a few years ago and I'm slowly rebuilding the engine."

I noticed something right away and reached to adjust it. "This isn't quite where it's supposed to be. I work on the fire dozer when we're not fighting fires, so I've picked up a few things."

"Help me out?" Johnny asked.

"Sure." I bent over the engine and made the adjustments, then he high-fived me and handed me a rag to wipe the oil off of my hand.

"So that pardon, huh? That blew my mind. Blew everybody's mind."

"Yeah, ours too. My mother had a lot to do with it. She's been working on getting him out ever since he went to jail. Hey, you were kind of close to his case back then, weren't you?"

He frowned and looked up at me. "No. Why would you say that?"

"Weren't you roommates with Jacob Ferrell?"

"Oh yeah, for a while. He was there, wasn't he?"

"I think so."

"Yeah. I remember he came home pretty jacked up, and he told me what happened."

"Jacked up how?"

"I don't know. You know Jacob. He liked to mix his moods."

I thought about him snorting cocaine while getting wasted on alcohol, and how that might have altered his brain enough to go get even when the fight moved outside.

"Yeah, come to think of it, his name was on the witness list at my pop's trial. What did he tell you that night?"

"He didn't say anything that night. But the next day he told me that he was on his way home and saw the police swarming all over the place on Mill Road, and it was the preacher. Somebody had shot him."

"So he came home *after* the shooting?"

"Yeah. Said he was at the bar when the fight happened. I don't remember a lot about it."

"But he wasn't home from around ten to eleven?"

He laughed. "Man, that was fourteen years ago. I don't remember what time he came home."

"But didn't the police ask you?"

"Me? No. Why would they ask me?"

"Just because they would have looked at everybody who was there."

"Dude. Everybody knew it was your dad."

I leaned back against the Mustang. "I figured that too. But what if it wasn't him? What if there was somebody else who had something against him? Took that opportunity to knock off the preacher. Perfect timing, when so many people witnessed their fight and my dad was stumbling drunk."

The kids got too close to the street, and Johnny yelled, "Joey, get back in the yard!" When the kids retreated, he turned back to me. "Are you suggesting that Jacob might have killed the preacher?"

I thought of trying to hedge, but he was on to me. "I'm just trying to work with my dad. He's had Drew and me running all over the place, looking at all the evidence again, studying alibis and witness testimony. I'm trying to give him the benefit of the doubt, you know?"

"Jacob did have stuff against Strickland. He hated the guy. He'd been dating Georgi, and her dad split them up. Had him arrested that time. But he wouldn't have killed him."

"What if he was high? I know he used cocaine, and there were rumors of crystal meth. Mix those with alcohol, and a person could do a lot of things they wouldn't normally do. Are you sure he got home later? Because I'm sure in his witness statement he swore that he went home after the fight, before the shooting, and that you could vouch for that."

He scratched his forehead with the back of his thumb. "I'd forgotten all about that. Yeah, they had me come in with him, and they asked me where he was during that time."

"You told them he came home around ten. Did you see him?"

"No, I'm pretty sure I didn't. I was sleeping when he came home. I had to get up super early the next day for work, so I was zonked out. I knew he came home at ten because he said he did."

"But if he said he drove by the scene after the shooting happened, that would have been around eleven, right?"

He looked confused, then thought for a minute. "You know, you better ask him. My memory is a little foggy. The last thing I want to be is Jacob Ferrell's defender. That guy has problems."

It seemed like Johnny was telling the

truth. His foggy memory came across as genuine. When I finally left him there with his Mustang, I thought back over Ferrell's timeline. The gist was that he'd been out until after the shooting.

Georgi's ex-boyfriend could have been the one who killed her dad.

CHAPTER 12

BRENNA

Labor Day weekend was when most of the country had a day off from work, but I dreaded that whole weekend. My children would have to stay at Jack's for an extra day. Sunday I had forced myself to go to church and look like everyone else, but the afternoon was long, and the night was longer.

I hadn't heard from Nate, though his car was home part of the day. But maybe after he'd seen how much I was drinking Saturday night, he decided I was poison. Or maybe he was giving me time to listen to the workshops on the flash drive. So I did. I listened to two hours' worth, taking notes as it played.

I could do this writing thing, I thought with a surge of hope. There was a learning curve, but the gift I'd had years ago was swelling inside me, reminding me that it wanted to be used.

I was being reminded of a lot of things.

When the two workshops were over, I tried to employ what I'd learned. I started to type.

You can't go back. That's what they always say. But maybe it isn't true. Maybe there are times when you have to go back, to make sense of what happened. To pick up the pieces you dropped along the way.

I wrote about a character who looked like Nate and a woman who looked better than me, and before I knew it, I had four pages written. It gave me a sense of peace and accomplishment. But soon that feeling faded, and loneliness set in. I wanted one drink, and maybe then I could write more. Hadn't drinking helped Faulkner, Hemingway, Kerouac?

What if Nate called? I wanted to be sober if he saw me again. But what difference did it make? I no more wanted to get into another romance now than I wanted to cut off my hand. All I really wanted were my children. If I just had them, nothing else in the world would matter.

Getting up, I went to the pantry and reached to the top shelf for the bottle of bourbon I had hidden there. It was almost

130

empty, just a quarter inch left. I poured it into the Coke I was drinking, mixed it with my finger, then swallowed it.

It did little to take away the edge of despair, so I dug through the pantry, searching for another bottle. I hoped I'd overlooked one that would miraculously appear out of nowhere. But there was none.

Grabbing my purse, I headed to my car.

The liquor store was busy this time of evening, as was the drugstore next door, and I scanned the parking lot for a car I recognized. Would people judge me if they saw the former preacher's daughter buying liquor? Would they gossip about me even more than they already did?

For a moment I sat in the car, not moving and wishing I'd made a trip to Golden yesterday, where no one knew me. But I'd told myself that I could make it, that I didn't have to drink to get through the hours until my children were home.

Now I hated myself for not being able to do it.

The front door of the drugstore opened, and Cass, my best friend, came out holding the hands of both of her girls. She saw me in my car and rushed over.

Feeling sick, I rolled my window down. "Hi," I said, trying to muster as much enthusiasm as I could. "How are you guys?"

"Great." She leaned in and hugged me. "What are you doing?"

"Just need to get some things at the drugstore."

"Are the kids with him?"

"Like always," I said.

"Well then, you're free tonight?"

For a moment I didn't want to admit it. "I actually have lots of options. You know, like cleaning my baseboards. Rearranging my books in alphabetical order. Hanging my dresses according to length. That sort of thing."

"You're not writing?"

"I did. It was good. But then I started thinking again."

"So come home with us. David is helping his brother move furniture, so the girls and I just rented some Redbox movies."

I tried to smile. "No, it's your girl night."

"Come on, Brenna. It's *Frozen.* I've seen it fifteen times. I'd love having an adult to hang with. We can catch up. I want to hear about Nate."

I grinned. Maybe it would make me feel better to talk to her. I glanced toward the liquor store. "Yeah, I guess I can come for a little while."

"Do you want us to wait while you go in?"

"No, you go on. I'll head that way after I get what I came for."

Cass wasn't much of a drinker, so I was surprised when she pulled out a bottle of wine and poured me a glass as Finn and Anna trekked up the snowy mountain to find Elsa.

I drank more than I intended to — more than I realized.

When she put the kids to bed, we took over the living room and curled up on each end of the couch with throw blankets over us.

"I did everything for Jack," I said. "I kept his socks lined up in perfect rows according to color in his drawers. I polished his shoes. I ironed his shirts. I made him huge breakfasts every morning and brought him coffee in bed."

"No wonder you couldn't write."

"He thought it was like being on social media or something. That it was something I should feel guilty about. A waste of time. But when my marriage was lacking, I always felt the kids made up for it."

"But now you have another chance," Cass said. "Now you can start over and find someone who *does* give back. Someone who appreciates you."

"But I'm divorced. I never wanted that. Now I don't know how God even feels about me remarrying."

"Jack broke your covenant. He walked out. I researched this when we studied it in my Bible study, and according to Jesus, adultery is a biblical reason for divorce. He walked out on you, and he's married now. So you're free to remarry."

"I don't know if I can ever let myself be that vulnerable again." I picked up my glass and realized I'd already emptied it. I hoped she'd offer me another one, but I doubted she had more. "If I lose my kids, nothing else will ever matter. Nothing."

"You won't lose them," Cass said. "Come on, Brenna. You're the best mother I've ever seen. No judge is going to take them from you."

"Jack's father . . . William Hertzog made my life miserable when we were married. He was always there ordering Jack around, and Jack ran around like a little boy trying to win his approval. The kids tell me such stories every time they come back . . ."

I had talked myself right over the cliff, and tears rolled down my face. Cass listened intently and poured me more wine.

I'd had too much to drink, I told myself, and now I was losing control. But if I could just have a little more, maybe the pain would clear. Maybe the misery would be numbed.

"You know," Cass said, "I think Nate being back in town might be a God thing."

"Still, there's a lot of bad history there. My father and his father   and the church. My sister saw us together the other night, and she had a fit."

"Nate didn't do anything wrong."

"He may as well have, as far as she and my mom are concerned. Plus, half the town thinks he burned the church down."

"He wasn't like that. I never thought he did it."

"But he disappeared right after that. Left town."

"I think he'd probably had enough."

"Yeah." My mood sank, and I realized I was getting too sleepy to drive. "I better get home. Maybe I need an Uber."

"Stay here tonight," she said. "You shouldn't be driving, and I don't think you should be alone."

"I'm fine, really. I can make it." I wanted to go home in case Nate came over, or call him and ask him to. But when I stood up, I almost fell over. Cass caught me and sat me back down.

"You're staying here. I won't take no for

an answer."

"I don't know what's wrong with me."

"You had too much to drink."

"I didn't mean to."

"Hey, I was the one pouring. Come on, just stay. You'll love my guest room."

"Well, okay. If you're sure it's no bother."

Cass helped me to the guest room, and as I collapsed on the bed, she covered me with the quilt and sat down beside me. "Brenna, I know this is one of the most dismal times of your life, but believe me, it'll pass. It really will."

"I've had dismal times before," I said, closing my eyes. "I'm not sure they ever did pass."

"I wish there was something I could do to make you feel better."

"I wish it too."

Cass kissed me on the cheek, then tucked me in like I was a child.

And I was asleep before the light even went off.

Chapter 13

NATE

Monday morning, I found my father sitting in Drew's kitchen, paperwork from the boxes spread out across the table. He had started a pot of coffee.

"I didn't know you were here, Pop."

"Drew let me in before he went to bed. I wanted to look through this stuff." He sighed and sipped on his coffee. "I get up early these days. Have trouble sleeping on that soft mattress. Never thought I'd say that. I thought it would be like lying on a cloud after sleeping on a six-inch-thick piece of foam. But it takes some getting used to."

I poured my coffee, stirred in some sugar. "Yeah, I've been looking through those. Refreshing my memory."

My pop looked up at me with soft gratitude in his eyes. I pulled out a chair and sat down.

"I could tell somebody was looking," Pop

said. His eyes glistened a bit. "It made me feel good, to know you're taking it seriously. I know you don't completely believe me yet, but maybe you could at least consider that I'm telling the truth."

"I have an open mind. So what are you looking at?"

"You had that file about the interviews sitting on the top. I thought I'd start there. I was reading back through my own interview. Man, I was still half drunk when they interviewed me that first night. They told me they were arresting me for murder. If I'd been in my right mind, I would have called a lawyer. But when you drink you think you're invincible, like you can handle anything. You never even consider that somebody might be setting you up."

"You think they set you up?"

"Not the cops. But whoever killed him did. I was an easy target — the town drunk."

"I don't know if you were the town drunk, Pop. You drank a lot, yes. But so did others. Some of them are still at it."

Pop rubbed his hand hard against his jaw. "I was just remembering when they came to our house that night. Banged on the door, screaming, 'Police!' Your mama let them in and they bolted through the house, rattling the walls, woke me out of a dead

138

sleep. I didn't know what was happening. They told me I was under arrest for the murder of Richard Strickland. I thought they got the story wrong. It was just a fight. We didn't really even come to blows. Just a little shoving. I'd just seen him an hour earlier. When it hit me that he was really dead, I figured he had a car wreck on the way home."

I tried to imagine what a shock that had been for my mother. She'd been hysterical when she called me.

"It hurts, you know? I mean, I know I drank too much. I was an alcoholic. I'll give them that. But they knew me. They knew I wasn't capable of killing somebody, especially the preacher. You mean to tell me that of every single person in that bar, nobody saw that I took a left on Brennan?"

"Yeah, you've got a point there," I said.

"I just wanted Strickland to leave. I didn't want him dead."

"Well, somebody did."

He looked at me hopefully. "You believe me then?"

I knew it would mean a lot to him if I said yes, but I wasn't ready to say that yet. "Pop, I promised you that I would look into it and I'd listen and consider it. That's what I'm doing."

"All I'm asking, son, is that you give me more consideration than the rest of this town did."

When I knocked on Brenna's door Monday night, I heard running footsteps inside and a child's voice yelling, "I'll get it!" and then another child yelling back, "No, you can't! What if it's a robber? We have to ask who it is!"

I grinned and looked down at my feet, waiting. "Who is it?" both children yelled through the door at the same time.

"Nate Beckett," I said.

Noah yelled, "Mom! It's that fireman guy from across the street!" I stepped back from the door, offering full view through the peephole, and finally the door swung open.

"Nate!" Brenna looked so bright-eyed and pretty. I liked seeing happiness in her eyes, even though I knew it had nothing to do with me.

"I know. I should really call first."

"Don't be silly. Come in."

Was it my imagination or was she really glad to see me?

I smiled down at the little boy hanging on to his mother's leg and the little girl standing in front of Brenna, her hair a corkscrew mop falling into her eyes.

"He could eat with us," Sophia suggested. Then, looking up at me, she said, "Mom's the best cook ever. Isn't she, Noah?"

She nudged her little brother, but he only raised his shirtsleeve and said, "See my tattoo?"

It was a stick-on picture of a Power Ranger, and I stooped down and examined it. "Wow. That's a sharp-looking tat, all right."

"You want one?"

I shrugged. "Sure. You got a little mobile tattoo shop in your room?"

"No, I have it in my pocket." Noah dug into the pocket of his jeans and pulled out a rock, a penny that looked as if it'd been run over, a wadded-up and dying flower, and a tattoo sticker. "Where do you want it?"

I looked down at my hands, then rolled up my sleeve. Exposing my forearm, I said, "How about here?"

"Okay," Noah said and carefully applied the sticker. "Are you still a fireman?"

"Yep. Sure am."

"Can I wear your hat?" Noah asked, his eyes growing wide.

"Uh . . . I don't have it with me."

"I have one," Noah said and quickly disappeared into the house.

"He's going to get it," Sophia said, rolling

141

her eyes.

I got back up and glanced at Brenna.

"So do you want to eat with us?" she asked.

I couldn't hide my delight, but tried to. "Well, I don't know," I said facetiously. "What are you having?"

"Spaghetti," she said. "Sophia made the garlic bread, and Noah tore the lettuce for the salad."

Noah came running back out of his room with a little plastic fire hat on his head. "See? I told you."

"You sure do have one," I said. "Only mine doesn't look like that. Mine's more like a helmet."

"Then you're not a real firefighter," Noah said.

"Noah!"

Laughing, I stopped Brenna from correcting him. "Nothing I like more than a challenge," I said. "I'll have to prove myself while we eat spaghetti."

BRENNA

I watched through the kitchen window as Nate played kickball outside with Noah. Sophia sat heckling them on her swing.

Nate's gentleness came back to me, and my cheeks reddened as I thought of how

142

comfortable I had been with him the other night.

Trying to rally from my thoughts, I took the last two plates to the table. What was wrong with me? I couldn't afford to get caught up with Nate Beckett again. I had too many complications in my life already. It was only when I was alone on weekends that I felt so vulnerable.

I heard laughter outside the window and smiled at the sound. That was what kept me sane. The laughter of my children. As long as they were here, I could be happy. As long as I had them, I could function, without crutches or grief or regrets.

They came running back into the house, and I shouted for them to wash their hands, including Nate in my order. His grin as he saluted and headed for the bathroom reminded me of that teenage rogue he'd been at the homecoming dance. That grin had knocked my socks off then too. But I was older now. And I wasn't supposed to be bowled over by men like that anymore.

But I was, just as I had been then.

We laughed a lot as we ate with the children, and when the dishes were cleared and loaded into the dishwasher, Nate thanked me. "I know you have a lot to do, so I'll go on home now."

I hesitated, part of me wanting him to stay and the other part hungering for my and the children's nightly routine of crawling into bed together and reading until bedtime. "I'm glad you came over," I said.

He stepped close to me and gazed down into my eyes. "How about this weekend? I can take you to a little place in Golden where no one knows us, and we can catch a movie and . . . maybe laugh some more."

I smiled. "All right. How about Friday night, since the kids will be with their dad?"

Looking up to the ceiling and mouthing, "Yes!" he dropped a kiss on my cheek and headed for the door.

CHAPTER 14

NATE

Tuesday morning I told Drew what I was thinking about Jacob Ferrell, and he got right on it, making phone calls to find out where Ferrell was now. "Got it," he said after the third or fourth phone call. "Ferrell is living in Golden."

"Let's go talk to him."

"Just like that?" Drew asked.

"Sure. You can learn a lot by surprising a person."

We drove the thirty minutes to Golden and found the apartment complex where Jacob lived. Trash spilled out of dog-torn garbage bags alongside the parking lot, and broken beer bottles littered the cracked pavement.

We got out, found the right building, and knocked on his first-floor apartment. He didn't answer, and we listened but didn't hear footsteps or a TV. "Probably at work,"

I said. "Did you find out where?"

"I was told he drives for one of those food delivery services. Like anybody would trust him to bring them restaurant food."

"If they knew. I doubt he put 'ex-con' on his résumé."

"You don't need a résumé to deliver food orders. Just a car and an app."

We got back into the truck and sat there for a while, waiting to see if he came home.

Drew glanced at my arm where Noah had placed my "tattoo."

"What's that on your arm?"

"Power Ranger, of course."

He laughed. "Want to elaborate?"

I chuckled. "I ran into a friend and her kids."

"Was it Brenna?"

"How'd you guess?"

"You're pretty predictable."

"No, I'm not."

"Pop is gonna have a coronary if he finds out you've been seeing her. Mama just might too."

I was quiet for a long moment, my eyes fixed on a squirrel running past on the ground. "I spent an awful lot of my life reacting to what other people did and said and thought, Drew, but I got over it. I'm not going back now."

"Just be careful, man. Things have a way of cutting deeper in Carlisle."

My brother was one of the few in the world who fully understood that. "I've given this a lot of thought. I've known a lot of women, come close to falling in love with a few."

"But?"

I sighed. "But I don't think a day's gone by in the past fourteen years that I haven't thought about Brenna Strickland. It's real ironic that I'd have to come back to Carlisle to find the missing piece of my life."

"Sounds serious."

"It may be," I said. "And I have to explore it."

"She's got a lot of problems, man."

"I know she does. She's been through a lot."

"So you're going to rescue her?"

"I might."

He chuckled. "My brother, the defender of damsels' psyches and souls."

"Hey, maybe it's *my* psyche I'm defending. Maybe *my* soul is the one on the line."

"It's your *neck* I'm worried about, when Pop finds out."

"He'll have to get used to it," I said.

"And Brenna? Is she used to it?"

"No," I said. "I have to convince her."

An old car with a bashed-in front fender pulled into the parking lot too fast and bumped over a pothole. It pulled in right next to us.

"Is that him?"

We watched as he got out. Yes, it was Jacob Ferrell, though he looked different. He was skinnier than he'd been in high school and had deep lines etched into his face. His hair was long and greasy and hanging into his face. He had a week's growth of beard, and he was missing a front tooth.

Drew got out and called to him. "Ferrell!"

Jacob turned around and saw Drew, then me as I got out. He gave us a tentative smile. "Drew? What are you doing here?"

"Came to talk to you."

His smile was full blown now, and he slid his keys into his skinny jeans pocket and came toward us. He fist bumped with Drew, then slapped hands with me. "Good to see you guys. I'd invite you in, but I haven't cleaned. Like ever."

"Did you know my dad got out of prison? Pardoned by the governor?"

"No, that's great," he said, and he looked genuinely surprised. "Pardoned, huh? Who would think? How long has it been?"

"Fourteen years. He still claims he didn't do it."

Jacob shook his head. "Yeah, I never thought he could have pulled that off that night. First of all, he was stumbling drunk."

"But you're the one who said you saw him driving that direction."

"Yeah, but I didn't mean he killed the guy. And I wasn't even sure. Things happened so fast, and honestly, I'd been drinking a lot too."

"I talked to Johnny Humphrey yesterday," I said. "He was telling me you came home after the shooting. Not before."

"Yeah, so?"

"So did you go back into the bar after they drove off?"

Jacob leaned back on Drew's truck. "Oh, I see where you're going with this. You trying to pin this on me? Since I have a record and all?"

"We're not trying to pin it on anybody," Drew said. "We're just trying to give our dad the benefit of the doubt."

"Well, I'm all for that. But I went back in, man."

"Did others see you?"

"Of course they did. Everybody there saw me."

I doubted anyone would remember, but I figured there must be some way to confirm that.

"Look, I know I don't have a lily-clean life, and I've gotten into fights. But I never shot a preacher. If I had, I wouldn't have gone anywhere near the cops. But I let them interview me two or three times."

When we left, I looked over at Drew. "What do you think?"

"I think he may be telling the truth. I know that guy. He used to have tells."

"Tells? Like what?"

"Like he would sniff before he lied. And he'd look off to his right. Dead giveaway. I know that because Coach Landruff called him on it in front of the whole class. Told us what he'd noticed. He didn't buy that the dog ate his homework or whatever."

"I didn't notice any tells. I think he is telling the truth. But we can check up on his story. Somebody would remember seeing him."

"I'll ask around at the bar tonight."

The next morning, Pop was at Drew's again before I got up. I found him in the dining room going over those files again. "I had a dream last night," he said in greeting when I came in.

"Oh, really? What about?"

"You and that girl."

I braced myself. "I thought you said this

was a dream."

"It was. And it was pretty unbelievable. In fact, it was downright silly."

But I could tell my father didn't really think it was silly. I felt the defensive barriers rising inside me with surprising speed. "All right, Pop. Hit me with your best shot. What girl?"

"Brenna Strickland."

"Hertzog." I took a sustaining sip of coffee. I looked at my father and saw that wrath was beginning to take hold of his face.

"Have you been seeing her?"

I decided it was best to get this over with. "Yes, I have."

Pop slowly set his cup down and sat straighter in his chair. "Is that what you've been doing with your time?"

"Some of it."

My father's face reddened as we stared each other down, like enemies finally face-to-face. "Are you out of your mind?"

"Pop, she's never done anything to you."

"She and her family sent me to prison for fourteen years!"

"I'm not going over this again."

"Of course not, because it didn't cost you anything."

"It cost me *everything!*" I bit out. "I still had to live in this town. I had to go to school with people who whispered about me, but they didn't whisper to my face, Pop, because they feared me."

"They *should* have feared you! They should have feared for their daughters and their churches!"

I flinched at my father's implied accusation. "You know I didn't set that fire!"

"Then why did you run? Everybody in town thought you did it, and they're gonna keep thinking that until you prove differently. That disappointed me, son."

I sat motionless, then spoke with slow deliberation. "I *can't* prove anything after all this time. All I can do is let them think what they want." I got up and headed back to my room. "I can let *you* think what you want too."

I got dressed and grabbed my keys, then headed out to my truck.

The new church couldn't have been more dissimilar from the church that had burned down so long ago. It was bigger and more modern, and over the years the congregation had added on a wing here and an addition there, always trying to accommodate the growing membership. But Angus, the gardener, was still working there.

I'd seen him a couple of times earlier in

the week as I'd driven through town. It had occurred to me that morning that Angus might remember key details about the church fire. Despite what I'd said to my dad about not being able to prove my innocence, I really wanted to.

I sat in my truck, looking at the groomed grounds, the perfectly pruned shrubs, the little flowerbeds circling the trees. The sidewalk was wet, and there were fresh grass clippings that hadn't blown away yet. Angus was probably around here somewhere.

Leaving my car parked on the street, I got out and strolled up the sidewalk. There hadn't been a sidewalk before — only grass that butted up to the gravel parking lot. And the building had been less than a third this big.

I heard a man whistling and went around the building. Movement between two shrubs caught my eye, and I left the sidewalk and wandered over to him.

Angus hadn't changed much, but there were deeper wrinkles in his face, and his hair was grayer. I doubted he'd grown much mentally. Angus had Down syndrome, and while he worked harder than anyone I've ever known, intellectually he was like a six-year-old.

"Angus?" I asked, and he jumped.

"I was just prunin' this bush," he said as if he saw me every day.

"I know. I'm sorry to interrupt you."

"It really does need prunin', sure does. Look at these dead limbs. Wanna see my pile of dead limbs?"

I shook my head. "No, you go ahead with what you're doing. Do you remember who I am?"

Angus got up and dusted off his pant legs. "Yes sir, I sure do. You're that preacher fella from that other church."

I smiled. "No, I'm not a preacher."

He looked crestfallen.

"I'm Nate Beckett," I said. "You remember? I lived here when I was a boy. Used to run around here with my brother, Drew."

"Yep," Angus said, nodding and laughing. "April ninth."

"April ninth? That's my birthday. How did you know that?"

"Yes sir, that preacher from the other church."

"No, I'm not a preacher, Angus. I'm a firefighter."

"Don't play with fire, no sir."

Sighing, I patted him on the shoulder. "That's right, man."

"I got a pile of dead limbs. Over here. I'll show you."

I glanced at the front door of the church, hoping no one inside saw me and got concerned. "All right, Angus. Show me."

With his gloved hands, Angus picked up some of the clippings he'd just cut and carried them around to the side of the church, where he dropped them in the big pile he was so proud of.

I congratulated him and wished I could take half as much pleasure in such things.

"How long have you been working for the church?"

Angus looked down at his hands and began to count on his fingers. "About two years, three months now."

I knew Angus had been here at least twenty years.

"Do you remember when the fire burned down the old church?"

Was it my imagination, or were his ears turning red? "I was prunin' bushes," Angus said, his voice lower now. "Just prunin' them bushes. They sure did need it."

"I'll bet they did. But do you remember the fire? The one that burned down the church?"

"This new church is solid, yes sir," Angus said. "It won't burn up like the other one."

"You don't remember, do you?"

"No sirree, don't play with fire," Angus

155

said. "Those bushes sure needed pruning."

I patted his shoulder again. "You get back to it. I didn't mean to stop your work."

I drove around until Pop's car was gone, then I went back to Drew's. My hand was hurting and itching, as was my leg, so I went to the bedroom and peeled off the bandages. Throwing them away, I got out the ointment and unwound some gauze to redress the wounds. I winced when I touched them. They didn't look good.

But if there was an upside to having these injuries, it was that they'd reconnected me with Brenna.

Drew knocked and called, "Nate?"

"Yeah, come in."

He opened the door. "You okay?"

"I'm fine."

He saw me trying to wrap my wounds and came to the bed. "Cool. Those are wicked."

"I'm pretty proud of them."

"Need help?"

"Now that you're here."

He took the gauze. "Seriously, man. I didn't picture them this bad."

"It's not so bad," I said. "It's probably a worse-before-it-gets-better kind of thing."

He wrapped them better than I could. "Hey, listen, Mama called, said you had an important message this morning from the

White House. They tried to call your cell, but you didn't answer."

"What white house?"

"Uh . . . the one in Washington, dude. You're not in some kind of trouble, are you?"

"No. I can't imagine . . ." I picked up my phone and checked the voice mail, and realized I'd put it on silent when I was at Brenna's and forgot to change it back. I didn't recognize the number.

"Well, you'd better call them back. It might be a matter of national security. The entire free world could be hanging in the balance while they wait for you to return their call."

"Yeah, okay."

He finished wrapping my leg and side, then said, "You are going to tell me what it's about when you get off the phone, aren't you?"

"If it's not about nuclear war."

He grinned and left the room. I hit Call Back, and a woman answered. "Sean Guthrie's office."

I gave her my name and said I was returning a call, and after a moment, a man came on the phone.

"Mr. Beckett, thank you for returning my call. I was beginning to think I'd never catch up with you. I tried calling you at your apartment, and then I spoke to your superior, and he told me you'd gone to Carlisle to recover from injuries."

I nodded. "Yes. Sorry to send you on a wild-goose chase."

"Well, those injuries have a little something to do with why I'm calling you."

"Oh yeah?"

"Yes. Mr. Beckett, I'm sure you're aware that the family you rescued in the fire a couple of weeks ago was Senator John Livingston's."

"Yes, I found that out after the fact. There was a lot of publicity about it."

"There certainly was. And the senator has brought the matter to the attention of the president. The president was so deeply moved by your heroism that he'd like to honor you at a dinner he's giving for the men and women he considers to be some of the country's greatest heroes."

"The president?" I asked, coming to my feet. "Of the United States?"

"Yes, that one."

"Well, I didn't do anything for that senator I wouldn't have done for anybody. My teammates were the real heroes. They're the ones who noticed that people were in the house."

"But the president was particularly struck by your self-sacrificing determination to charge in and save that family at great risk to yourself. We've interviewed your teammates, and they seem to agree. Your burns only testify to that heroism."

I looked down at my bandaged hand. "What would this involve?" I asked finally.

"We'd fly you to Washington, and you and a guest would be among the guests of honor at a dinner at the White House, with the president in attendance. The next day, the awards ceremony will take place in the Rose Garden."

I took in a slow, ragged breath. "I'd be honored, sir."

"Good. Now, I'm sure you have friends and family you'd like to attend the awards ceremony. I'll have my secretary get in touch with you to take care of the number of people you need reserved seating for, and you'll be receiving an official invitation in the mail shortly."

After I hung up, I sat paralyzed. The White House was honoring me with an award for heroism, yet I couldn't prove to people in my own hometown that I was anything better than a petty arsonist.

I had to tell my mother. She would love this. I grabbed my keys and headed to my parents' house.

One part of me wanted to run up those front steps and shout, "Pop! Pop!" as I had as a child when I won the science fair competition at school. I'd been so desperate to see my father's smile, feel his pat on the back, hear him tell me he was proud of me. But that never happened. Pop had been drunk and asleep on the couch, and though my mother had been proud enough for both of them, it hadn't been the same. I never made more than a C on science fair projects after that.

Regardless, I had to tell them. I got out of my car and ambled up the steps to the front porch. I hesitated to go right in, so I knocked on the door.

My mother answered it instantly. "Nate, you don't have to knock!"

I let my mother pull me in and followed her into the living room. As modest as the home was, the afternoon sun pouring through the side windows of the house always painted the room with luxurious brightness. "Where's Pop?"

Mama had been folding clothes, and she moved the neat stacks of towels from the couch for me to sit down. "He's out cutting firewood. Now, you didn't come over here to start another fight, did you?"

"No. If he told you about yesterday, I'm sorry I lost my temper."

"Well, I am too, but it couldn't have surprised you. You knew how your father would feel about your seeing Brenna Strickland again. You should be a little more considerate of his feelings."

I strolled to the window and saw Pop swinging the ax and splitting the wood. "Why do you always defend him?"

"The man has spent the past fourteen years separated from the wife who loves him and the home that comforted him and the sons who followed him everywhere he went. He has a lot of adjustments to make, and a lot of anger just simmering in there. He's spent all those years living with his regrets and wishing he'd done things differently. I just want him to have some peace now."

"Has he changed at all, Mama?"

"Yes," she said without hesitation. "He's changed a lot. He doesn't drink anymore."

"I'm glad. It's time he started treating you right."

"Give him time, Nate, and he'll treat you right too. Changes like we need don't happen overnight."

I glanced out the window again and saw Pop wipe his face on a towel he'd hung on a tree limb, then he headed back inside.

"I actually came to tell you both some good news," I said.

"I love good news," she called from the bathroom.

The side door opened and Pop came in. He shot a glance at me. "Didn't know you were here."

"Just got here. That's a lot of firewood you've got out there."

"Yeah," Pop said. "We'll be set for winter."

Mama came back in. "Could you guys sit down for a minute?" I said.

Mama went to the couch. Pop settled into his favorite chair. "If this is about what we discussed yesterday . . ."

I almost grinned at my father's persistence. "No, this is something else. Mama, you remember when that man called from the White House today?"

"Yes! You called him back, didn't you? Was it a prank call or one of those telemarketers?"

I sat down across from them, propping my elbows on my knees. "Yes, I called him, and no, it wasn't a prank."

"It was the real White House?" she asked.

"The one and only. The fact is, the president wants to give me an award. He wants me to come to the White House for a special dinner and then an awards ceremony in the

Rose Garden. Not just me, of course. There are some others getting awards too."

"Award for what?" Pop asked, sitting straighter and fixing his eyes on me with more interest.

"Well . . ." The word *heroism* seemed overblown, so I sought another way to say it. "You see, that fire I fought last week . . . well, I was burned trying to get a family out. Any of my teammates would've done it. I mean, it's our job. But it was the family of a senator, and I guess he recommended me for a presidential award."

"You're really getting recognized by the president of the United States?" Pop asked, the hint of a smile narrowing his eyes.

I smiled. "Yeah. Pretty wild, huh?"

"For saving a family?" he asked. "You're the one who saved that senator's family?"

"Well, me and my team."

"But the news said only one man got the family out," my mother said. "Was that really you?"

"Guess so."

"Why didn't you tell us? You weren't even going to mention it?"

I shrugged. "There was a lot going on."

"But it's a big deal! I'm so proud of you!" She popped up and threw her arms around my neck.

Pop began to laugh, and I watched him apprehensively, not sure where this was going.

"The man said I could have reserved seats at the awards ceremony in the Rose Garden. Do you both want to come? I'll ask Drew too, but I haven't told him yet."

Mama gasped with excitement and turned to Pop. "You hear that, Roy? We're going to Washington!"

Pop's eyes lost their glint as he thought that over. "You sure you want us there, son?"

I met his doubtful eyes. "Of course."

"There's going to be a lot of publicity," he said. "I don't know what that's going to look like, or if I even want to be part of it."

I frowned. "Why would you say that?"

He rubbed his face. "I just . . . I don't know if I can go. Your mama doesn't like to fly much —"

"I'll do it for this," Mama cut in.

"Well, *I* don't like to fly," he said quickly.

Pop was trying to get out of it, and that fact knocked me breathless. My gaze moved to my mother, her own crushing disappointment apparent on her face. "Mama, you can come alone if Pop won't come."

Mama turned pleading eyes to Pop, but I knew she wouldn't cross him in front of me. It was one of the rules etched in the very foundation of our family. "We'll talk about it, Nate."

"Well, I have to go," I said finally, my voice quieter. "I want to see if I can track down Drew and tell him."

Mama walked me to the door, but Pop kept his eyes fixed on the floor.

"We're so proud of you, angel," she said. "You're a real hero. All the world's going to know it."

"Yeah, well, I'd like to keep it to myself until then if it's okay with you, Mama. I'd hate for word to get out, then have something happen and it all fall through."

"What could happen?"

I gave a joyless laugh. "I just don't like to count my eggs before they've hatched."

Pop looked rattled as he got to his feet and headed for the back door. "I'll see you later." And then he went back outside to chop more wood.

After I left my parents' house, I drove around for a while, thinking. My father's reaction had thrown me into a state of melancholy, and that surprised me. My first thought after I talked to the White House had been that my dad would be proud. And I had seen some pride, hadn't I? For a moment there, when Pop was listening, hadn't I seen a flicker of something?

But it wasn't enough. When it came right down to it, he wasn't all that impressed.

"You're a grown man, Nate," I said aloud to myself. "Get over it." I found myself driving past a mall with a ten-screen cinema and decided to catch a movie to pass the time. Then I could go back to Drew's and call Brenna after she'd had time to get her kids into bed. Maybe she could lift my spirits.

The burns on my hand and leg began to ache as I sat in the theater watching a movie I had trouble following, but I stayed nonetheless. For all my accomplishments and all my growth, I still had no place I had to be, no one waiting for me, and no one to celebrate with. Not really.

Man, I really felt sorry for myself.

I was no better off than I'd been at eighteen, branded an arsonist and fleeing town. Just because they'd stamped me with the label *hero* didn't mean I was one.

CHAPTER 15

BRENNA

I stood in the doorway of Sophia's darkened bedroom, where both children slept peacefully. Lately little Noah always crawled into bed with his sister, as though that was the one consistency he could count on. It didn't take more than a moment for either of them to fall asleep these days because they were usually so tired from the weekends with their dad. Their bedtime wasn't regular there, and their schedule was brutal.

Quietly I tiptoed to their closet and pulled out the things they would need to take to their father's this weekend. He would pick them up at day care after school tomorrow, since it was Friday, and my weekend darkness would start all over again.

I heard the doorbell ring, and glancing back at my children to make sure they hadn't been disturbed, I hurried to the front door.

167

When I peered through the peephole and saw Nate standing under the porch light, a gentle smile came to my face. I opened the door. "Hi, Nate."

He looked expectant, almost apologetic. "Hi, Brenna. I know it's kind of late, but I wanted to give you time to get the children into bed."

"They're both sound asleep." I stood looking at him for a moment, wishing my heart didn't pound so wildly whenever he was around. It was adolescent and it was dangerous. "Come in."

I saw the relief on his face, and as he stepped into the living room, I noted the way he held his hand at his side, as if it was bothering him. "How are your burns?"

He reached the sofa and turned back to me. "Okay."

"Are they really?"

He shrugged and sat down slowly. "Yeah. They're okay."

But there was no conviction in his voice, and I knew his injuries must be bothering him a lot.

I thought of sitting in a chair safely across the room, but something about his manner, his quiet mood, the melancholy in his eyes, compelled me to sit closer, on the other end of the couch, my feet pulled under me.

"I should've called first," he said, his soft eyes assessing me. "But I was afraid you'd tell me not to come."

I smiled. "Maybe not."

He stared down at the floor, and I could see the struggle on his face.

"Is everything all right, Nate?"

He sighed. "Yeah. I've just gone from getting the biggest pat on the back of my life, to getting dumped on by my father . . ."

I was quiet, listening, taking in every nuance of his expression.

"So what was the pat on the back?"

He shrugged. "An award I'm getting. It was a nice surprise."

I smiled. "For what?"

When he didn't answer, I asked again. "Nate, for what?"

"For doing my job," he said. "Seriously, that's really all it is." He told me what it was about.

I reached over and touched his wrist, and he met my eyes. "Nate, is that when you got these burns?"

"Yes. But my team was at risk too. They took the same chances."

"Are they giving all of you an award?"

"No, just me. But I was in charge of that particular team, so I get all the credit. It's not fair, really. But that's the way it is." He smiled. "Anyway, I figured if I told you that, you'd at least feel kind of obligated to keep our date tomorrow night. Remember, we were going to Golden?"

"Our Golden date. I remember."

"I mean, you wouldn't refuse to celebrate with me, would you?"

I laughed then. "I wouldn't miss it."

He chuckled. "Well, you know how it is. I didn't want to take any chances. Your kids are going to their father's, aren't they?"

My smile faded instantly, and I glanced toward their bedroom. "Yeah. They are."

He seemed to note my mood change and shifted to face me. Taking my hand, as if it was the most natural gesture in the world, he leaned toward me. "You're already getting depressed again, aren't you?"

I hated being so transparent.

"You know, it's been good seeing you this couple of times with your kids. You seem so much happier. At peace."

"And when they're gone, I'm a basket case."

"When they're gone, you're not yourself."

I looked down at his bandaged hand, his unbound fingertips stroking mine. There was something about his presence that provided a security I hadn't felt in months — maybe years — and I longed for it to be more than that.

But my mother would kill me if she knew, and I wasn't sure my own heart was strong enough for another heartache.

"I really haven't been myself in a long time."

"Well, that'll be over soon, won't it? Court's in a couple of weeks, right? Maybe then you won't have this threat hanging over you."

I withdrew my hand and pulled my knees up to my chest, hugging them. "The truth is, I'm scared to death."

"Why?"

"Because he's got the money, Nate. He's got the connections. He has the power. His father has every judge in the area in his pocket. They owe him. William Hertzog is very 'generous' with people he might be able to use later. And Jack has a wife who doesn't work, who claims she'll devote every waking moment to raising my children. I have nothing."

"Of course you do. You're their mother. They love you. They depend on you."

"I've only had a job for a year or so. I don't make very much money, and they have to go to day care after school. Besides, even my lawyer's intimidated by Jack's father. William's one of the most powerful men in Colorado." My eyes filled with tears, and I pressed my tear glands, trying to hold them back. "I'm sorry. I didn't mean to be one more person to dump on you today."

He didn't say anything, but when he slid his arms around me, I felt all my strength ebb away.

Tears burned my eyes, and I wrapped my arms around his neck and buried my face against the collar of his shirt. "I'm scared, Nate. Not just for me. For them too. They want to be with me. I've been there for them since the day they were born. That woman Jack married cared so little about them that she lured their father away and intentionally broke up his family. And now she claims she's a better mother for them than I am?"

"No judge is going to buy that, Brenna."

"Judges can be persuaded," I said. "It depends on who's selling."

"Is your attorney a good one?"

"I think so," I said. "But there's no guarantee. What if Jack wins?"

"He won't, Brenna." Nate lifted my chin and made me look up at him. "Listen to me. I'm gonna be here, okay? I'll help you. You don't have to go through this alone."

The gentle words melted me and made me cry harder. It had been so long since I'd been able to lean on someone else. Years.

Maybe even since Nate had dropped out of my life.

"I don't want to lean on you," I whispered. "I want to be strong, like your mother."

He sat straighter and looked down at me, confused. "My mother?"

I lifted my face. "She's the strongest woman I've ever seen. Your mother always did more for other people than she did for herself. She never let her pain or her loneliness stop her from doing what had to be done. She lost her husband and her reputation, but she kept going with her head held high. I wish I could be like her."

Nate sighed. "That's funny. I've always thought of my mother as weak. The way she let Pop walk all over her. The way she served him even when he was in prison."

"It wasn't weakness, Nate. Your mother keeps her commitments." I drew a deep, cleansing breath and tried to pull myself together. "I've watched her over the years, and when Jack was treating me terribly, cheating and lying, I'd remember her. I'd remember how she kept that family together for you kids, and how she tried her best to give you stability and love. I don't even know how she held up after your father went to prison. But she did, Nate. She always did, without any self-pity or any expectations that someone was going to come bail her out. I wish I had that kind of faith."

His face twisted as he watched me descend into someplace deep inside myself, someplace he couldn't go. "You don't think you have strong faith? You used to have so much."

"Yeah, but that was before anything bad had happened to me. The difference between your mother and me is that your mother's problems have built her faith. My crises have only shaken mine. I wish I could get it back."

I pulled away from him and hugged my knees again. I tried to smile. "I'll bet you're sorry you came over here tonight, aren't you? You with your great news, and me being a psycho."

He laughed softly. "I can't remember a time when I've ever been sorry to be with you."

"But I'm not the same person I used to be. You probably won't like me once you get to know me."

"Oh, you're still the same," he said. "You're just a little burned. But trust me. Burns heal."

I looked down at his hand then and lifted it gently. "Do they? Are you sure?"

"Positive," he said. "They're my specialty. I've recovered from lots of them."

"What do you recommend?"

"Well, for starters, a Golden date. Forgetting your problems for one night. Having some fun. That's the first step."

I sighed heavily. "My mother would kill me if she knew."

"I get it. My father would kill me too," he said. "That's why we won't flaunt it. Nobody really knows us in Golden."

I studied him for a long time, then touched his face. "Okay. Tomorrow night? Is seven all right?"

"It's terrific." He got up and looked down at me. "You should get some sleep. I'm going now."

I stood, the top of my head barely reaching his chin. "Thanks for making me feel better, Nate."

"Did I?"

"You always do somehow."

He looked down at me for a long moment, his gaze like a drug that pulled me into a spell. When he breached the distance between us, I leaned in. He kissed me then, a gentle, sweet kiss that demanded nothing but offered everything. It felt just as it had at sixteen, restrained but full of promise, respectful but full of hope. I didn't want it to end.

When he pulled back, he pressed his forehead against mine, and I saw the gentle smile sweeping across his lips. "I hope that was all right," he whispered.

I couldn't speak. I just nodded.

He opened the door, then looked back at me. I felt the blood rushing to my face, the self-conscious smile that emerged from deep inside me, the awareness that I didn't want to keep him at arm's length anymore.

As he walked back across the street, I closed the door gently. I couldn't wait for our night in Golden.

CHAPTER 16

NATE

My new firefighting jumpsuit came in the afternoon UPS delivery, and I pulled it out of the box, my chest tightening at the stiff feel of the textile. Mine was charred and damaged. The new one wasn't perfect, but I could make it work. If I could use my mother's sewing machine, I could make it just like I wanted it. That is, if she had strong enough needles in her supply cabinet. I'd have to order the right kind of thread.

I chuckled at what my father's reaction might be when he saw me sewing. Most people didn't realize that smokejumpers made a lot of their own gear, adding pockets where they were needed, improving where things lacked, and making it altogether easier to stay alive while fighting a wildfire. I'd probably be toast right now if I hadn't had a Kevlar outer layer.

It was possible I could have saved my old

suit, but after flames had held on for several seconds, I worried that the protection it offered might have been diminished. It was the most important part of my gear, even more important than food and water.

This one would need a few tweaks before it would be adequate.

I stepped into it, zipped it up, and looked at all my gear spread out on my bed. The items reeked of smoke, but I liked that smell.

The suit was heavy, and the coat I had to wear under my parachute would be even heavier. A panicked feeling rose up in me that I was getting out of shape from not running with all that every day. I needed to pack my gear — all one hundred pounds of it — and trek uphill, even if I only walked. If I ever lost the ability to do that, I was finished as a Hotshot.

I packed my let-down rope in one of the big outer pockets of my right lower leg, then the pack-out bag in the same pocket on the other leg.

I stepped out of the suit and opened the pack with my undergarments — fire pants and shirt that I'd paid for out of my own pocket. Though the government issued those, I'd opted to pay for my own so I could buy them from a company that manufactured the latest in fire-resistant apparel that would still be cool enough and would wick my sweat. I liked them, so I pulled them on.

I set aside my helmet and mouth and face guards, which I would wear when I ran. I loaded my hammock, rolled up in a flat pack, inside another side pocket of my jumpsuit, then slipped my knife in the pocket on my right hip. One of my teammates had already inspected my chute, so I folded it and put it inside my deployment bag. I'd inspect it again when I went back to work. I put that bag in the pocket designed for it, then loaded the rest of the gear. Yep, with the coat, which hadn't been delivered yet, the weight of this jumpsuit would be the same as my old one.

I winced at the pain as the items on my right side rubbed against my burns, but I would push through. I went out to my truck and drove up to Simon Plateau Park, where people left their cars for the hike up to Nugget Peak. I parked and put on my helmet and face guard, popped in my mouth guard, and walked as fast as I could to the steepest area I could find.

A few heads turned as I passed tourists and hikers, but I didn't care. I had to do this.

I tried to run at first, but the pain was too great, so I told myself that walking was better than nothing. After I'd been walking uphill for a while, I picked up my pace, following the beaten trail left by other hikers. I wouldn't have that in the field, but for now, I'd use it.

I tried to refocus my mind. Brenna. I would think about her.

As I jogged, sweating already where my skin had functioning pores, I prayed for Brenna, that I wouldn't bring more turmoil into her life.

I thought about her having to leave the kids with Jack tonight. A feeling of overwhelming sadness and lifelong regret flitted through me. I loved my job, especially when there were people whose lives were spared because of us. But most of the time nature was the victim, and it didn't show much appreciation.

Smokejumping was tough-guy stuff, but not like having a family of my own, and children . . . Now, that took courage. That was what made life worth living.

I prayed Brenna wouldn't lose her kids. She deserved so much better. As I trudged upward, I asked God to change Jack's heart so he would put his children's needs first. They clearly needed their mom. They needed both of their parents. Every kid did.

When my burns told me I shouldn't go any farther, I slowed to a walk and went to a lookout. I sat on a bench halfway up Nugget Peak and stared out over the landscape, where gold miners used to pan their gold. The landscape this time of year was still lush and beautiful, but it needed to be pruned and cleared. Someone should have created firebreaks to prevent wildfires from having the chance to spread. The drought had gone on too long, and the vegetation was still brittle.

I looked down the mountain to see how far I'd walked. Maybe two miles? I didn't like this. I should be able to do much more, injuries or not. I prayed that when my bandages came off, I could do what I used to do.

I started back down, letting gravity help me. When I reached the bottom, I pulled off my helmet and wiped my sweat-drenched face as I cut across the parking lot. I noticed a guy snapping my picture as I slogged to my car. Tourists would photograph anything.

I sat for a moment behind the wheel, letting the pain of my burns calm down now that the weight was off my legs.

The sky went from dusk to dark as I drove

home, and I pulled into the driveway the same time Drew did. "You go to the grocery store in that getup?" he asked as he got out of his truck.

"No, I was trying to stay in shape," I said. "Heavy gear. Got to carry it. Went up Nugget's Peak."

"That stuff must be hot."

"You have no idea." I unzipped my suit as I went into the house and was almost out of it by the time I got to my room. Drew followed behind me.

"I heard about your award, man," he said as I ditched my boots and peeled the jumpsuit off my legs.

"Pop doesn't want to come."

"Yes, he does," Drew said.

I chuckled. "You're wrong. He couldn't care less."

"The old man was so proud when he told me about it I thought his face would split in two. You'd think you'd just won a Nobel Prize."

"He wouldn't have come for that either."

"He's afraid," Drew said.

I turned to Drew in irritation. "Afraid of what?"

"Think about it," Drew said. "He goes with you to get a presidential award, and it comes out that your father was in prison for murder."

I closed my eyes. "That wouldn't happen. It's not like I'm being appointed to something. People aren't going to be that interested in my past."

"I agree. They'll be so busy congratulating you and talking about the family you saved that nothing negative will even come up. But try telling Pop that."

"Give me a break," I said. "Pop doesn't think about other people. He wouldn't think that far ahead, especially not about how something affected me."

"I do see changes."

"I'm not sure I do."

"Come on, man. He's as proud of you as a guy can be of his son, and I know there's nothing he'd rather do than be there. But he doesn't want to ruin your moment."

"What about Mama's moment? Doesn't he realize she might like to be there?"

"Probably not," Drew said. "Right now, he's only thinking about you. But if Mama wants to go, she'll be there. She can go with me. Pop's not going to stop her."

"I don't know about that."

"It's been a long time since you've seen much of Mama," Drew said, "but she's no doormat. She's devoted to him, but she's not going to lie down and let him walk on her."

"She did for years."

"Fourteen years of independence has taught her a lot. Don't underestimate her."

I peeled off my socks. "So what, exactly, do you suggest I do? He hasn't told me the real reason he won't go. He acts like he just isn't interested."

"Tell him *I* told you, if you have to. But somebody's got to bring it out in the open. Talk to the man. Maybe he'll surprise you and listen. Do it for Mama."

"I'll think about it," I said.

CHAPTER 17

BRENNA

The call from Noah's school on Friday afternoon shook me. He'd had an asthma attack, his teacher told me, but he'd used his inhaler and was feeling better. I still rushed to the school. His attacks were terrifying and upsetting, and I wanted to hold him. He'd been upset when we said goodbye this morning because he didn't want to go to his dad's for the weekend. Stress often caused these episodes.

I headed into the kindergarten wing and found Noah sitting in a chair in the nurse's room. "Honey, are you all right?"

He coughed, a croupy, wet cough that he hadn't had that morning. "I couldn't breathe."

I felt his forehead. He was warm. "Did you take his temperature?" I asked the nurse.

"It was 99.8. We've had a lot of kids getting sick this week, but for him it's a trigger."

"Okay, big boy. We're going home."

"Home home? It's Friday. Can I stay with you tonight?"

I glanced at the nurse, embarrassed that she'd heard that. "We'll talk to Daddy."

I knew how that would go. I'd tried keeping them home once before when they both had a virus, and Jack had almost agreed. But then he'd called back and threatened to call his lawyer if I didn't bring them anyway. I knew Jack's father had changed his mind. It was his way. I was the enemy, and Jack couldn't give me an inch or he'd lose his ground.

When we got to the car, Noah asked me again. "Please, Mommy! Don't make me go."

"Honey, it's not up to me. Daddy just loves being with you."

"But what if I need a breathing treatment? I want *you* to give it to me."

I wanted that too, but I knew what Jack would say.

By the time we got home, Noah was wheezing again. What he really needed was his medication in the form of the fine saline mist his breathing machine put out.

Carefully I mixed the solution and put it

in the cup that was attached to the little mask that would fit over his nose and mouth. I stretched the mask's elastic over his head to hold it in place. The nebulizer came on with a hum, and the mist that would open his bronchial tubes began to fill up the mask. I got his favorite book out from a shelf under the table and handed it to him as he inhaled the mist. "Look at this for a minute while I call Daddy."

I breathed a silent prayer for strength before dialing Jack's number. After going through a receptionist, a secretary, and then his personal executive secretary, I finally got him on the phone.

"What is it, Brenna? I'm busy."

I closed my eyes. "Jack, I had to get Noah from school. He's had an asthma attack and he has a fever. He's wheezing and croupy. It always gets worse at night. Let me keep them home tonight so I can take care of him."

"Absolutely not. Rayne can take care of him if he's sick."

I lowered my voice so Noah couldn't hear. "He wants me. I'm his mother."

"Well, I'm his father. I'm perfectly capable . . ."

I glanced at Noah and hoped the hum of the machine was keeping him from hearing me. "Jack, have you ever given him a breathing treatment in his life?"

"Well, no, but you can send that little inhaler thing. He knows how to do those himself."

"He needs more than that this time! He's taking a breathing treatment right now, and he's probably going to need one every four hours. Even during the night."

"Then Rayne can do it."

"I don't trust her, Jack! She hasn't been taught how!" My hands were beginning to shake, and I rubbed my temple. "When I learned how to do it, a respiratory therapist came and taught me. Rayne has to know how to clean the thing so that it's sterile for the next treatment. One drop of water can grow bacteria, and that can go into his lungs and cause pneumonia. This is not a game or a competition, Jack. It's our child!"

"Rayne is very intelligent. You can show her how to do it."

"I don't want to show her anything!" I tried to calm my voice, then said, "Look. Can't you just take a weekend off from the kids? You and Rayne could get away or have a night alone."

He hesitated, but quickly rallied. "He should be at home with me."

"This is his home too," I bit out.

"He's coming with me, Brenna. Have him at my house at five thirty. And just send the inhaler. He'll be all right with that."

"I'll bring the breathing machine, but you have to use it right."

"I'm not stupid. I can figure it out. My father's coming over tonight and expects to see them."

"Jack, why can't you listen? Noah is more important than your father!"

"Have him at my house at five thirty, Brenna."

Jack hung up, and I sat with the receiver in my hand, listening to the hateful sound of the dial tone. Gritting my teeth, I clicked the phone off.

I went to the pantry and found the bottle of wine on the top shelf. I didn't grab it, but the thought that I could have it after I took the kids helped me somewhat. When I got back to Noah, he looked up from the book.

"What did Daddy say?" he asked as a small cloud of mist circulated inside his mask.

I took a deep breath and tried not to appear so angry. "He says you have to come tonight. But he's going to take good care of you. I'll take the machine so they can give you treatments."

"But I don't want to go!" Noah said, starting to cry. "I want to be with you! What if I can't breathe?"

I pulled him onto my lap and closed my eyes against my own tears. "You'll be fine. Your daddy loves you as much as I do. He likes to take care of you too."

Jack was waiting when I delivered the children, and in the massive marble-floored foyer, his father stood with his thick eyebrows knit together and a look of condemnation on his face. "You're late," Jack said.

"Noah needed another treatment before we left. I had to finish it."

The children were hovering around my legs, neither making a move to go in, when Rayne appeared at the door between Jack and his father. She tried coaxing. "Hi, sweetie," she said to Noah.

Noah didn't answer.

"Come on in, Sophia," Jack ordered.

Sophia looked up at him with sad eyes. "Daddy, can't we stay with Mommy until Noah's better?" I held my breath and hoped Sophia's sweet voice would have some impact.

But William Hertzog made it clear it had none. "For heaven's sake, Jack, don't let these kids call the shots. Be a man. You're their father."

"But, Daddy —" Sophia tried again.

"That's enough, Sophia," Jack said, sterner now. "Tell your mother goodbye."

Fighting my tears, I leaned down to kiss her. "Bye, honey. See you Sunday."

Sophia disappeared into the house, and Rayne followed her.

"Rayne."

It was the first time I could remember speaking directly to the woman who'd set out to destroy my marriage, but it had to be done.

Rayne looked back at me. "What?"

"I want to show you how to do these breathing treatments. Noah's going to need them tonight."

"Aw, he's breathing fine," his grandfather grumbled.

Like a puppet, Jack agreed. "Brenna, you're overreacting. He's breathing fine. He won't need them."

I felt Noah squeezing my hand, and I tried to keep my voice even. "Fine. If he doesn't need them, he doesn't need them. But let me show you what to do just in case he does."

When they didn't invite me in, I opened the bag and pulled the small machine out right there. "This tube hooks onto it right here, see? And then the cup and the mask . . . You put in a dropper of this medicine, right to the point-two mark. See? No more. It's really important you put exactly that amount, and then add four squirts of the saline in this bottle —" I dug into the bag for it. "Right here. Four squirts."

They all stared blankly, stubbornly, at me, and finally I let out an exasperated breath. "Jack, I'll text you the instructions. Please read them before he needs it. This is really important."

"Take that thing home, Brenna," William said. "Noah is fine."

Noah looked up at me with pleading eyes, and I stooped and drew him into a hug. He clung to me longer than he needed to, and already I could hear a faint whistle in his breathing. "You call me if you need me, okay? Or get Sophia to."

"There's not going to be any calling," Jack said, pulling Noah away from me. "We can take care of whatever he needs. Can't we, Noah?"

Noah shrugged, but his wet, sad eyes were still fixed on me. "Bye, Mommy."

My heart broke at the disappointment in those words. Jack must have heard it too. Didn't he care?

I looked at Jack and saw that Noah was getting to him. He picked him up and kissed his pale cheek.

William shook his head. "He's only whining for your benefit, Brenna. Just go."

I ignored him and patted Noah's back. "You'll be okay, sweetie."

Jack handed Noah to Rayne, and she took the cue to usher the kids away. I heard Noah's crying grow louder, and with my own eyes full of tears, I glared at Jack.

"He doesn't feel well. He isn't acting. You could show a little more compassion."

"He said to go, Brenna," William said.

"I wasn't talking to you," I bit out. I turned back to Jack. "Your father isn't always going to be here pulling your strings for you, Jack. Someday you're going to have to get a spine."

"I'll have the kids home Sunday night," Jack said.

I started down the steps, but William stopped me. "Take this contraption with you," he said.

"No! You're going to need it!"

"Take it, or I'll throw it away."

Furious, I jerked up the bag with the nebulizer in it, thinking he'd have to learn the hard way and sick that it would be at my sweet little boy's expense. As I went

193

down the front steps, my mind raced. How could I force them to give him a treatment? Would my lawyer be able to get anything done tonight?

By the time I was back in my car, I was sobbing, but unwilling to let them see me like that, I drove off. I called my lawyer, and he tried to calm me down. "Have you ever known Jack to be abusive with the children?"

I tried to think. "No, not outright abuse. But some of the things he does are indirectly abusive."

"That's hard to prove. So would you say that he loves the children?"

"Yes, he loves them. He's their father."

"Then don't you think he'll call you if he needs the nebulizer? He's not going to ignore Noah's condition, is he?"

"What if he's not home? What if he's playing golf or something? I don't know what Rayne or a sitter might do."

"I just don't have grounds to get an emergency court order until something actually happens, Brenna. The judge won't look kindly on your simply anticipating that something is going to go wrong."

"He has a fever and asthma!"

"But we don't know yet if his father is going to take care of him."

I gave up, realizing he was right. Noah would be all right. Sophia would tell me if her brother was in trouble. She wouldn't let them ignore him.

But the nebulizer was with me!

It would be all right, I told myself. I'd leave a key where Jack could get it if he needed to get it while I was in Golden. I'd leave the nebulizer packed up by the front door so he could find it easily.

Nate would make me feel better. I wouldn't have to dwell on the injustice or the uncertainty all night.

But I couldn't stop crying, and I realized there was no way I'd be able to sit through a date, worrying about Noah and stewing over Jack and his father.

Then I saw the liquor store. I knew there was a bottle of wine in my pantry, but I doubted that would be enough tonight. It sure wouldn't numb me through the whole weekend.

Crossing two lanes of traffic and almost hitting a car, I pulled into the parking lot. Within minutes, I had several bottles and was on my way home.

No sooner had I gotten through the door of my house than I had the vodka bottle open and was drinking from it. Not waiting for the buzz to numb me, I poured some into a tall glass, filled it with ice cubes to chill it, and tried to relax.

But the numbness came too slowly, and the pain held on.

So I drank a little more.

NATE

I was prepared for Brenna's melancholy, but I had a plan. I was going to make her laugh tonight.

But that plan shattered when she answered the door, her eyes too bright and her smile exaggerated. She'd been drinking. "Wow," she said, giving me a bold once-over. "You look great." Standing on her toes, she set her hands on my chest, got close to my neck, and breathed in. "I love the way you smell. Breathtaking."

I felt her wobble and I caught her shoulders as I looked down at her with an expression that was both a smile and a frown. Something was wrong. I'd seen several sides of Brenna in the past few days, but this flirty side was new. It didn't ring true. "Are you all right?" I asked.

She laughed softly and stepped back, letting me in. "I'm great. What could be wrong?"

"I don't know. I just wasn't expecting a greeting like that."

She laughed again. "What did you think? That I'd spit on you and curse you?"

I watched her plop onto the living room couch and pat the place next to her.

"Well, it's not like it hasn't been done before," I teased.

"Not by women, I'll bet."

Cautious, I sat down next to her. "So . . . how was your day?"

"Terrific," she said, then quickly leaned forward and reached for the tall glass on the coffee table in front of her. She took the last drink in it, then whispered a curse under her breath. "It's empty. I'll get some more. You want some?"

"No, I don't want any." I followed her to the kitchen counter, where the wine bottle sat with only a fourth of its contents left. Had she drunk all that tonight? There was a bag of other bottles sitting next to the sink. She had stocked up.

"So, where are you taking me?" she asked.

I watched her from across the room. "There's a little French restaurant in Golden. It sounds like a nice place. I thought we'd try it, but . . . are you sure you're up to it?"

She looked at me, surprised. "Why wouldn't I be?"

I didn't want to accuse her of drinking

too much. I'd looked forward to this. I wasn't about to spoil it now. There was a reason she'd decided to tie one on before I got here. Maybe it was prompted by nerves because of this date, which would be understandable after all these years, but she'd never seemed that nervous before. Could it be something deeper? "Well, I just get the feeling something might be on your mind. Is it the kids?"

That overbright look faded from her face. "My sister told me not to talk about my children or my ex-husband on dates. Not that I've tried it. You know that you're the first date I've had since my divorce?"

She was evading. "Well, I'm happy to oblige." I walked over and sat down next to her. "Brenna, really, what's wrong?"

She clutched her glass tighter. "Why do you think something's wrong?"

"Because you aren't yourself. Something happened today, didn't it? Something with the kids."

Her eyes filled instantly, and she struggled to hold the tears back.

"You can tell me," I said, taking her hand. "I want to know. It's just me, Brenna. Not some guy who asked you out for your first date. I understood you when you were sixteen, didn't I? And I'll understand now."

Before I knew it, those tears were streaming down her cheeks, and she pulled her hand from mine and covered her face, not wanting me to see. Leaning forward, I set the glass on the table.

"Noah has asthma," she said. "I had to go get him from school today, and he's having trouble breathing. But Jack wouldn't let me keep him for the weekend, and he claimed I was overreacting to his illness. He wouldn't take the breathing machine that Noah needs. And neither of the kids wanted to go. They wanted so much to stay home with me, just for one weekend."

I slid my arms around her and held her, letting her cry against my shirt. "He's a fool, Brenna. He's going to have to learn the hard way."

"But he's learning on my baby," she whispered. "His father was there. William. That man ruined him and now he's trying to ruin my kids. Jack's trying to please him, but even after all these years he doesn't realize that's impossible. As long as I can remember, he's been trying to make his father respect him, but nothing he's ever done has been good enough. I honestly think this whole custody thing is to please his father. I know the mayoral campaign is."

"Jack's father is no excuse. It's his children

at stake — not his father's. If he were a decent man, he'd be thinking of the best interests of the children, not how he looks to his father."

"It's like they want to erase me from their lives completely and replace me with that younger, prettier woman who couldn't care less about my children or their feelings —"

"Wait a minute," I said, looking straight into her eyes. "Stop right there. She may be younger, but there's no way she's prettier. I saw her. Trust me, she's not."

Brenna was able to smile slightly through her tears. "The truth is, I never thought she was that pretty. Which really ought to make me feel worse. I mean, he left me for her. What does that say?"

"That he has bad eyesight and incredibly poor judgment. And one day he'll regret it. But you won't care. By then all the pain will be gone, and there'll be someone else loving you."

"Yeah?" she asked hopelessly. "Who?"

I only smiled. "My guess is that you'll be able to take your pick. And I'll have to be worked into your social schedule."

"Fat chance," she said, wiping her tears.

"Look, if you don't want to go out tonight, I could go get us a video and some takeout."

She thought that over for a moment. "No.

We may as well go out. If there's an emergency, I'll have my phone with me."

"All right, then. Are you ready?"

"I will be in a minute. Just let me go freshen up." I watched her hurry to the back of the house, and leaning forward, I picked up her glass.

There was no harm in her having a drink or two when she got off work, was there? And I had no evidence she'd finished off the entire bottle tonight. There was nothing to worry about. Brenna was all right.

She was back out in a flash, her face looking beautiful again, though her nose had a red tint to it and the rims of her eyes were still red.

"I'm glad my first date is with you, Nate," she said as we started out of the house. "In a lot of ways, it feels like coming home."

"I was thinking the same thing."

CHAPTER 18

NATE

I had hoped the food we ordered for dinner would help neutralize the effect of the wine on her, but Brenna only ordered more wine. As she drank, she got deep into the story of how her divorce had come about, and alternated between crying into her hands and laughing hysterically at the irony of it all.

"Who would've thought?" she asked, sloshing her drink, then wiping up the spill. "Back then, when we were kids. Who would've believed how our lives would turn out?"

I smiled. "Most people would've bet money on my being in prison by now."

"And they would've staked their lives on my being a happily married wife and mother." She looked up at me. "Nate, what if you and I had gotten married?"

I smiled. "What if we had?"

"I mean, really," she said seriously. "What if none of the nightmare had happened, and we'd kept seeing each other? Would we have gotten married eventually?"

"Maybe. I was crazy about you, you know."

"And I was crazy about you. I saw things in you nobody else could see."

"Maybe you still do," I said.

"We complemented each other well. What would it have been like?"

"Amazing," I whispered.

Her eyes filled with tears again. Her words were slightly slurred. "Would you have traded me in when I hit thirty?"

"Not on your life."

"Jack would have promised that too. But he sure snowed me, didn't he?"

I looked down at her empty glass, hoping she wouldn't order more. "But I thought we agreed that Jack is a moron."

She giggled. "Yeah. We did agree on that."

She glanced down at the empty glass again, then scanned the room for a waiter. "Could you get me another drink?" she asked.

I hesitated. I wanted to say no, but would she think I was judging her? But if she had more, I doubted she'd be able to walk out of here.

I pretended to look around for a waiter. But just as I did, a man a few tables away got up and came toward us.

"Brenna, is that you?"

Brenna jumped, knocking over her empty glass. Quickly righting it, she looked up at the man. "Stocker!" she said. "I didn't see you."

She got up then, and I wasn't sure why.

He studied her with a curious frown. "How are you?"

Brenna reached out for the chair back and tried to steady herself, but the chair almost fell backward. Stocker caught it, then grabbed her arm to steady her. "Sit back down, Brenna. You don't seem to be in any condition to be standing up."

She sat back down. Her hands were shaking.

I stood up and shook his hand. "I'm Nate Beckett. And you are?"

"Gene Stocker. I'm her husband's lawyer."

"Ex-husband," Brenna said.

She reached for something, knocked over her glass of water, and swept her sleeve through the sauce from her veal parmigiana.

Stocker only snickered and glanced at me. "Maybe you should get her home."

"She's fine," I said.

"Nice of you to care about me," she said

through gritted teeth as she blotted her sleeve with her napkin. "I don't care what they say about you. You're not a ruthless, bloodsucking slimeball, are you, Stocker? You're just a genuinely nice guy."

The man seemed amused by her indictment and, shaking his head, went back to his table. The woman sitting with him there had her phone up, and I suspected she was taping the encounter.

Brenna had tears in her eyes again. "Can we go?"

I sat down slowly, thinking through what had just happened. Jack's lawyer had seen her drunk, and he wasn't likely to let it pass. If he had it on video . . .

I waved at the waiter. "We need our check," I said.

In moments, I had paid the check, but I worried about walking out. What if Brenna couldn't walk straight? What if she fell? What if she drew more attention to herself while they videotaped?

But she was on her feet before I was. I caught up to her and put myself between her and Stocker's table. She stumbled between the tables, and I tried to steady her. The harder she tried to appear sober, the worse her balance. I put my arm around her waist and guided her out the door. I helped her to my truck, and she managed to climb inside. "I can't believe it," she mumbled.

"Can't believe what?" I asked gently.

"He thought I was drunk."

I just looked at her.

"I am drunk," she slurred. "I drank too much."

"It'll be okay," I said, though I wasn't sure it would be. I got in on my side. If I could have taken away the misery I saw on her face, I would have.

"Being drunk doesn't help any of this."

"No," I agreed.

"What is wrong with me?" She started to sob then, and I pulled her against me. But after a moment, I didn't feel her shaking anymore. I looked down at her and realized she was asleep.

Moving her head back to her headrest, I hooked her seat belt, then switched on the ignition.

Years ago, I'd been the one known to tie one on, and she was the one who would've shaken her head and wished she could stop me. I didn't like what alcohol was doing to Brenna, and if she could see it clearly, she wouldn't like it either.

She slept all the way home, and I prayed silently that I could figure out how to chip away the broken pieces of her life. I wanted to find Jack Hertzog and break his jaw for hurting her.

When I pulled into her driveway, I gripped her shoulder and gently shook her. "Brenna, we're home."

She didn't stir.

"Brenna?" I shook her again, and this time her eyes fluttered open.

"What?"

"Come on, sweetheart. We're home. Let me help you in."

I came around to her side, got her purse, and coaxed her out. She stumbled and staggered as I got her to the door, and then I quickly dug into her purse for her keys. I unlocked her door, then walked her in.

She tried to stop at the couch, but I made her keep going. "The bedroom," I said. "You're going to bed."

"Stay with me," she pleaded, clinging to me. "Don't leave me, Nate."

"I won't," I heard myself say, then quickly wondered at the wisdom of making such a promise. "Not until you're asleep," I added quickly.

I pulled back the comforter on her bed, and before I knew it, she'd climbed in and curled up in a ball. Her eyes closed again, and I sat beside her and stroked her hair back from her face.

"I'm sorry, Nate."

"For what?"

"For ruining our date."

"You didn't ruin our date. I had a wonder-ful time."

"Me too," she mumbled, and then she was sound asleep.

For a while I sat beside her, stroking her face, brushing her hair with my fingers.

"God help me, Brenna," I whispered, "if it's the last thing I do, I'm going to help you see what I see in you."

But she was too deep in her intoxicated sleep to hear me.

I let myself out just before midnight and moved my truck across the street to Drew's, wishing things had gone differently, and renewing my vow to make sure they did from now on.

CHAPTER 19

BRENNA

The doorbell penetrated my sleep, and I woke up groggy and looked around. My head pounded with the force of a sledgehammer, and my mouth tasted as if something had crawled into it and died.

The doorbell rang twice more, and then an urgent knock followed. I forced myself out of bed and looked for my robe. But then I realized I still had on my clothes from last night. I pulled the robe on anyway.

What if it was Nate? I glanced in the mirror and cringed. I reached for my brush and ran it through my hair, then squeezed out a glob of toothpaste on my finger and put it in my mouth as I hurried to the door.

When I opened the door, Jack burst in, looking agitated and tired. "Guess I woke you," he said.

I closed the door and followed him into the living room. "Where are the kids? Are they all right?"

"Of course they're all right," he said impatiently. "I just came to get that blasted machine."

"The nebulizer?" I asked, gaping at him. "Did Noah have a bad night?"

"Yes, he had a bad night," Jack flung back. "Everybody in the house had a bad night. Now where is it?"

"By the door." I went and got it and handed it to him. My hands were trembling and my head throbbed, but I tried to hide it. "Jack, if he's that sick, why won't you let him come home? I can take care of him, and then you and Rayne can get a good night's sleep tonight."

"Yeah, right," he said, jerking it out of my hand. "You'd be a big help with that hangover."

"What?"

"Stocker told me he saw you last night."

"What did he do? Call you from the restaurant?"

"He said you were falling all over some guy and staggering like a drunken sailor."

"Yeah, well, Gerald Stocker always has had a vivid imagination. He's even been known to lie outright."

"Look at you, Brenna. You look like death warmed over. And what's this?" He went to the kitchen and grabbed the empty vodka bottle off the counter, then saw the bag of other bottles I'd bought.

I jerked the bottle away from him and tossed it in the trash. "Could we get back to Noah? How bad is he right now?"

He shrugged. "Coughing and wheezing. And he threw up a couple of times. How do you use this thing, anyway?"

Summoning all my strength, I tried to explain it as carefully as I could. "First, you measure off the medicine. Write this down. Too much could kill him."

He got out his phone and thumb-typed it in.

"I emailed it to you yesterday. It's all there in case you forget. Remember, you have to clean it after each treatment."

When I'd gone over everything from administering the medication to cleaning the machine, I followed him to the door. "If he got worse, you'd take him to the emergency room, wouldn't you? You wouldn't just ignore it to spite me, would you?"

"Spite you?" Jack looked genuinely surprised. "Brenna, none of this is to spite you. I never give you a thought."

"Then why are you standing in my kitchen asking me how to take care of our son?"

"Because you took the medication with

you last night."

"Is that your story? Your father forced me to take it, and you stood there like a child and let him call the shots! Oh, and by the way, I also happen to have the womb that carried those children. I'm their mother, and I will be no matter what your big-shot father or your sleazy lawyer says when we get into court!"

The doorbell rang, and touching my splitting head, I threw open the door. Nate stood there with a mug of coffee. "I saw his car," he said. "Everything all right?"

I hated myself more than I ever had before. I wiped my tears, letting him in.

Nate's expression was hard as he stepped toward Jack. "What's going on?"

"He came to get Noah's breathing machine since he wouldn't take it last night."

"Is Noah all right?"

"No," I said.

"He's fine," Jack bit out. He looked at Nate. "Were you spending the night here? Did you go out to get coffee?"

Nate just stared at him, as if he didn't owe him an explanation, so I spoke up. "He's staying with his brother across the street," I said. "He didn't spend the night."

"You have what you need now?" Nate asked Jack.

212

Jack didn't like the question, so he gave me one last, tight look, then headed for the door.

"Jack," I called before he could get to his car.

Jack turned back, his chin set.

"Please if Noah gets too bad, take him to the hospital. Or bring him home and I will. People have died of asthma. It's not something to play with."

"I know what to do, Brenna."

"And . . . if you do take him to the hospital, you have to call me. I have the right to be notified. It says so in our divorce decree, and if you don't do it, I guarantee you it'll come up in court."

"Goodbye, Brenna."

"Jack," I said, stopping him again. "Can I call Noah later on today? Just to let him know I'm thinking about him? It might make him feel better."

"He won't be there," he said.

I grunted. "Where will he be?"

"Rayne has a Junior League meeting, and they're going to stay with her mother. I have an appointment."

"You mean a tee time? So keeping the kids isn't about your wanting to be with them at all, is it? Why can't you admit you just don't want them with me? Or more likely, your father doesn't want them with me."

Jack just got in his car and pulled out of the driveway.

I was trembling — and I reached for a bottle of whiskey out of the bag on the counter.

"Brenna, don't let him win!" Nate said.

Shaking my head as if there was no use in even trying, I poured the brown liquid into the coffee he'd brought and stirred it with my finger. "He already won."

I brought the drink to my lips, but he took the mug. "Brenna, you don't need that."

"You don't know what I need," I said.

"Yes, I do. You're in the middle of a war, and you're falling right into the hands of the enemy."

I wilted then, breathing in a sob, and dropped my hands. "I can't believe this is my life. It's like I'm watching some B movie with a bunch of bad actors and a lousy plot. Why are you even here? After seeing me like that last night?"

Nate smiled and set the mug down and pulled me against him. "Because you're the beautiful heroine of that B movie, and you'll pull through and see how blessed you are that that blind ingrate is out of your life. He's going to get his. Watch. What goes around comes around."

"To others maybe. To me, it just comes around and around, and around again."

"I want you to do something for me," he said. "I want you to visualize what you want your life to look like, say, three years from now, after you've come out of this tunnel."

"Is it really going to take three years?"

"Probably not. Make it one year if you want."

I sighed. "All right, let's see. I'd have my kids, without the constant threat that their father is going to take them away from me. And I wouldn't feel so desperate all the time. So out of control. And Jack wouldn't have the power to keep twisting the knife. But see, the thing is, I don't know if those things can happen. It could turn out very differently. He could take them away, and things could be worse."

"But they might not be. For a judge to keep you away from the kids, he has to think you're an unfit mother. You're not."

"He'll make things up. His father will pay off the judge." I brought my hands to my temples and gave in to the pain again. "I really feel lousy."

"Sit down," he said. "I'll make you breakfast."

"I honestly don't know if I can eat."

"It's an order," he said. "Now, come on.

Where's your aspirin?"

I told him, and he got me some, made me take them, then found some eggs and started scrambling. They were ready in a few minutes.

He brought my plate to the table, and I took a bite. The food did make me feel a little better, but suddenly I realized how bad I must look to him. Yesterday's makeup was probably smeared under my eyes, and my teeth needed brushing, and under the robe I was still wearing the clothes I'd worn last night.

I was a train wreck.

When I finished eating, I went to change my clothes. I glanced in the mirror when I was in my room and wished I could shrink away. Why Nate would want to come near me when I looked like this was beyond me. Either *he* had bad eyesight and judgment, or he felt incredibly sorry for me.

Despite the throbbing in my head, I quickly changed into jeans and a sweater, brushed my teeth, and washed my face. Forsaking makeup, I went back out to the kitchen.

Nate was pouring me more coffee, and the welcome aroma filled the room.

"Nate, I owe you an apology."

"What for?"

"For last night. I don't even remember anything after we left the restaurant."

He didn't seem surprised. "Do you remember anything *at* the restaurant?"

"Yes, unfortunately. Gerald Stocker." I took a sip of coffee. He'd dumped the spiked cup. "I know I'm drinking too much. I can go all week without a drop, but the minute the kids are gone, I have to drink. And then . . . I can't seem to stop."

"Why do you think you can go all week without anything?"

I looked up at him, my eyes intent on making my point. "Because I have value then. I'm somebody to my kids."

"I know they're part of you. But you had value and were somebody before you ever had them."

I knew he was trying to help, but it didn't work. "You probably visualize me lying around in a drunken stupor while the kids take care of me. It's not like that. I only drink when I'm alone."

"You weren't alone last night."

"No . . ." My reasoning shattered. "It was Jack and his father. I just wanted to numb the pain."

"Are you numb, Brenna?"

I clutched my head again and slowly shook it. "No, I'm anything but numb. And now things are worse. Stocker."

"I'm pretty sure he videotaped it. It might come up in court."

"No!"

"You should be writing things down too. Recording things, like Jack's visit today. That he wouldn't take the breathing machine yesterday, and Noah wheezed all night without it. That he's putting the kids with Rayne's mother today while they're sick and could be with you. Write it down. All of it."

"Yeah. I will."

"And I'm a witness, if you need me. There must be others. What is your lawyer doing to fight for you?"

"He's doing what he can. But I haven't told him all this."

"Then do it today."

"I will."

Nate studied me, his eyes deep, thoughtful, and serious. "Brenna, I read somewhere that depression is sometimes really frozen rage."

"I won't argue with that," I said. "I have a lot of rage."

"I want you to know I've been there. Back when I left home, I didn't have a clue where I was going or what I'd do when I got there. All I knew was that I couldn't go back. I felt so violated because of those rumors

about me starting that fire when I had nothing to do with it. And I was furious at Pop
and disillusioned with the whole town and
all it stood for. Looking back, I can see that
I was in a deep depression for years. I finally
went to therapy, and then to church, and
we dealt with all my rage."

"I don't need therapy," I said. "I need
peace. I need for Jack to be reasonable. I
need my children with me. I need to be able
to shake off all this uncertainty and get on
with my life."

"After the hearing, you can."

"If I win, maybe."

"And if you lose?"

The thought made me sick, and I shook
my head. "I don't know what I'll do, Nate."

"Then I'd say you're just going to have to
make sure you *do* win."

I knew that was his way of telling me not
to drink, but that was a commitment I
didn't feel able to make right now.

"What do you like to do on Saturdays?"
he asked suddenly.

"I don't know. My Saturdays used to be
full of soccer games. But when Jack started
getting the kids every weekend, they had to
drop soccer. He wasn't willing to take
them."

"Write it down," he said. "I saw a sign the

other day for a flea market over in Golden today. What do you say we go there?"

I smiled. "Nate, you don't have to waste your weekends on me. I'll be fine."

His eyes bored into mine. "Brenna, I want to be here."

I stared down at my coffee, unable to meet his eyes. He leaned across the table and touched my chin.

"When I saw you that first night I was back, I saw the source of the best memories of my life. I saw the woman no one else could measure up to in all these years. And I saw a chance to go back and get something in my life right." He took my hand. "Look at me, Brenna."

I did.

"I want to see that peace in your eyes again. If you give me a chance, maybe I can help you get it back."

A big tear rolled down my cheek, and I wiped it away. "Then let's go to the flea market."

BRENNA

Nate kept me out in the sunshine as much as possible that day. When I admired a first edition copy of *The Red Badge of Courage,* he bought it for me.

We had lunch at a picnic table beside a

food truck. "Are you starting to feel better?" he asked.

"Yes, thanks to you. I'm mortified at how I was last night. When you knew me before, I didn't drink at all. Now I'm getting wasted in public."

"You're going through a bad time."

"When I didn't drink before, it was a matter of religion. I felt like it was wrong. The kids I knew who drank weren't Christians. Then as I got older, I saw Christians who did drink socially. They could be strong believers and still drink occasionally. And Jesus changed the water to wine."

"Some say it was grape juice."

"I didn't think that was true, because the waiter told him that people usually gave the good wine at the beginning of an event, so when the guests were drunk, they wouldn't know the difference when the host brought out the bad wine. He wouldn't have said that if they were talking about grape juice. Anyway, I started to drink a little now and then at dinner. It wasn't until my life fell apart that I started to use it to calm and numb myself."

"I get it," he said.

"What about you? I haven't seen you drink at all since you've been here."

He shrugged. "I kind of had the reverse of

what you had. When all that happened with Pop, I didn't want to drink anymore because I didn't want to be like him. I felt branded, you know? So I went out of my way to be the opposite of what he was. When I left town, I worked at odd jobs for a while until I could get into the smokejumpers' program. I realized I could stay on course better when I didn't drink. Then I found a little church I liked and started reading the Bible, and I didn't really need alcohol. It wasn't something I thought about. I just had other things on my mind."

"But you don't mind being around people who are drinking?"

"Not at all. A lot of my teammates need to blow off steam sometimes. I'm okay with that."

He stopped and took a bite of his hamburger. After a moment, he said, "So where would you say your faith is right now? I get the feeling you might be having problems with it."

I bit into a french fry. "I still believe," I said. "I'm still a Christian. But I'm struggling with my understanding of what God does."

"What do you mean?"

"I always thought that if we lived a good life and served and honored him, then he would protect us. Then things turned. Jack cheated, Rayne moved into my life, I had to give up my kids half the time, I had to figure out how to make a living . . . I felt kind of betrayed."

Tears sprang to my eyes as I spoke. "I'm sorry. I get really emotional about this. I think feeling that way about God is sometimes more painful than being betrayed by a husband. I miss my relationship with God."

"Do you feel like he didn't keep up his end of the bargain?"

I thought about that for a long moment. "No, not really. I don't think I feel that way."

"Because part of the bargain of salvation is that you have to take up your cross and follow him."

"Yeah," I said. "I think about that. And I realize he's already done so much. Dying for my sins. It's a fallen world, and we're fallen people. He warned us that in this world we would have trouble."

"But you take it personally?"

His questions were pointed, and they made me think. "Maybe. I just feel like my prayers haven't been answered in a long time. Like there's a brick wall between me and God. My prayers just bounce off the ceiling. People ask me to pray for things, and I do, but I feel like it's a futile effort. I don't know if he's mad at me, or if I have some terrible heart problem that he's trying to prune out of me." I looked down at my fries and picked at them. "I hate the fact that my kids are being hurt. I really need to see that God is answering and working in all this."

"Sometimes we're so distracted that we can't see how he's working."

"Yeah. And he could still answer when we go to court. I haven't given up asking. I guess I'm just resentful that he's been so hard on me."

"But there's nothing to resent if God's not responsible for what's happening. Don't you think Jack is?"

"Yes, but God is powerful. He could be my dread champion, my rear guard, the one who fights for me. But I feel like I'm fighting all alone."

"You're not. You have your lawyer, your family . . . me. And the kids are on your side too."

"I don't want the kids to have to take sides."

"I'm just saying that you don't know what they're saying to their dad, how they're influencing him. God could be working there, and you wouldn't know it. I think you should trust him."

I smiled, so moved by the fact that this man who didn't even know Christ years ago when we were dating was now counseling me, one Christ follower to another. His faith seemed real. It wasn't just for show. I wadded my napkin and put it on my plate. "Thank you, Nate. I needed to hear all this. I'm not open about this with anybody. It's hard to admit my failings and know that I'll be judged."

"I'm not judging you."

"No, you're not."

We walked around the market some more, enjoying our time together more than the things we saw around us. It was natural and calm, and I found my peace coming back. Maybe he was one of the ways God was working in my life.

Hours later, when we were back in his truck, I leaned my head against his shoulder. "This has been a good day, in spite of how it started."

"I told you it would be."

Maybe there *was* hope, I told myself. Maybe I *would* make it through this dark tunnel. I was doing fine without alcohol today. All I needed was a little help. A few distractions. Someone to quell my loneliness. Nate.

We stopped by a grocery store on the way home and bought a couple of steaks to cook at my house. But we were just walking in when my phone chimed. I looked down and saw that I had a voice mail. "I didn't hear my phone ring! How did I miss this?"

"Who's it from?"

"I'm not sure."

"Maybe we were out of range."

I clicked on the voice mail and put it on speaker. The voice was Sophia's, sweet and very soft, as though she didn't want to be caught making the call.

"Mommy," she whispered, "Noah is still real sick, and he's been crying for you all day. We stayed with Mrs. Foster, Rayne's mom, while Daddy played golf, but she was mean and made Noah stay in the bedroom. And now Daddy doesn't do the breathing machine right, and the stuff isn't coming out like it's supposed to. But he won't listen. Mommy, can't you talk him into letting us come home? Please? Only, don't tell him I called, or I'll get in trouble."

Nate got a piece of paper and wrote down what she said.

I clicked on Jack's number to call him back.

"Hello?" It was Rayne's voice, and I braced myself and forced myself to go on.

"I need to speak to Jack, please."

"Who is this?" she asked, though I knew his caller ID had told her.

"Brenna," I said. I could hear Noah crying in the background, coughing intermittently, and when Jack got to the phone, I tried to stay calm.

"What do you want, Brenna?"

"I called to see how Noah is doing."

"He's fine."

"Don't lie to me, Jack. I can hear him coughing. He's sick. Have you given him a treatment?"

"Yes. I've got this under control."

"But maybe you're not doing it right. Sometimes you have to adjust the little knob at the back if the mist isn't coming out."

"How do you know the mist isn't coming out?"

I winced. I was giving Sophia away. "Well, it obviously isn't working if he's coughing like that."

"He's coughing because he's crying. You've spoiled him rotten."

"He's sick, Jack. Maybe his fever has gone up. This doesn't have to be an ego thing. If you love him, you'll want what's best for him."

"He's getting what's best for him, Brenna. You'll see the kids tomorrow."

"But, Jack —"

He hung up before I could finish my sentence, and furious, I flung the phone across the room.

Nate picked it up off the floor and showed me his own phone. "I recorded that."

"You did?"

"Yes. You can too — there are apps you can get to record phone calls like that. Even if you can't use the recording in court, at least it'll refresh your memory so you can tell your attorney and let him bring it up in court."

I couldn't focus. I went into the kitchen and rummaged through my pantry for a bottle of something, anything, that would take the rage away. What had Nate done with my bottles?

He hadn't thrown them away. I found them on the shelf in the pantry. I got one down, opened it.

Nate came in. "Don't do that, Brenna. You can fight this. I'll help you."

"I can't fight him!" Tears streamed down my cheeks. "I've never been able to fight him. My kids can't fight him. Even my lawyer can't fight him!"

"You're wrong!"

"I'm not wrong," I said, pouring the whiskey into a glass and not bothering to mix it with anything. I took a big gulp, shuddering, then gazed up at him, as if daring him to take it away.

"Brenna, put it down."

"I'm a grown woman, Nate, not some sixteen-year-old girl. Don't tell me what I can and can't do!"

"Put the glass down and give me the bottle."

"Or what?"

He stared at me for a long moment, gauging just how serious I was about this. Finally he dropped his hand. "Or I'll leave."

"Then leave!" I shouted, knowing he didn't deserve that. Tears hit my face and I smeared them away. "Take off!"

"Brenna, don't do this. It's been a good day. You said it yourself. Drinking isn't going to help you at all."

"Oh, yes, it will."

"How?"

"It'll make me stop thinking about my baby sitting in that man's house coughing his lungs out. It'll make me forget that my little girl is being held hostage and can't even call me without fearing she'll get caught! It'll make me forget that nothing in this life is fair, that everything stinks, that nothing is going to get better!"

"It won't do any of that, Brenna," he said

quietly. "It never has."

But I simply stood in front of him and finished off the contents in one gulp.

Nate dropped his hands. "I've tried to help you," he said. "But I don't think this is going to end well."

When he went to the door, I only watched him go. He turned back before going out. "Brenna, you're surrendering. I can't watch it."

But I didn't answer.

Looking as if he'd just faced the biggest rejection of his life, Nate left me there, alone with my most vicious enemy. Myself.

CHAPTER 20

NATE

Drew's house was too quiet when I got home, and I lay on my bed and stared up at the ceiling, wondering if I did the right thing.

If I'd stayed and made it pleasant for her while she destroyed herself, I'd be enabling her. And I hated enabling. My mother had done it with my dad for years.

Still, there was no place I'd rather be than with her.

I heard the door open and close, and after a moment, Drew appeared in the doorway. "You're sitting here in the dark. You all right, man?"

"Yeah. I was with Brenna, but things weren't going so well. She had a run-in with her ex, and things kind of went south."

"Uh-oh."

He came in and sat down. "What happened?"

"Her kids. Jack's got them and Noah's sick, and they want to come home. Brenna's all upset. Part of me wants to go to his house with a shotgun — shoot my way in, grab the kids, and take them back to their mother."

"Noble idea, I admit, but it probably wouldn't work. You'd have those pesky police all over you before you could get the kids into the car. The whole kidnapping thing . . ."

"Yeah, but it'd sure feel good. He's taking advantage of her. He knows she's fragile — he made her that way — and he's trying to push her over the edge."

"So why aren't you there keeping her from going over?"

I closed my eyes. "Maybe she's already gone over, and I just can't stand by and watch her hit bottom."

Drew was quiet for a moment, then finally said, "Get up, then. We'll go somewhere."

"Where?"

"To eat something."

"Don't you have to work?"

"Took the night off. Come on, man. I'm hungry, and you can't just stare into space all night."

"What if she calls?"

"What if she doesn't?"

"She may need me."

He grunted. "You'll have your phone. Why'd you leave in the first place?"

"She wasn't in the mood to hang out."

"Well, I am."

I got up, but wasn't really feeling it. "If I go with you, will you shut up and leave me alone?"

"Nope. Love becomes you, brother. You're just aglow with good tidings."

"You didn't answer my question."

"That question being, will I leave you alone? No, I won't do that. That's not in the job description."

"That's what I was afraid of." I forced myself to stand, but suddenly I felt very tired. "All right, I'll go, just to keep you from standing here all night and bugging me to death."

"You know me too well," Drew said with a laugh as we headed out to his truck.

I wasn't able to sleep all night, so the next morning I got up and decided to meet my mother at church. It was where I needed to be.

The building was almost full when I walked into the foyer, and I was amazed at how much the congregation had grown since Bo, the new pastor, had taken over. I stepped into the sanctuary and, standing at the back, looked around for my parents. They were sitting near the back, in the area for the disgraced and those who wanted a low profile, and I smiled at how stiff Pop looked in a suit and tie.

I slipped into the pew beside them, then noticed I was behind Angus, the church gardener. He sat with that simple smile on his face, his mother beside him.

"How are you, Angus?" I whispered, reaching to shake his hand.

Seeing my bandages, Angus didn't want to shake.

His mother smiled at me.

"Hi, Mrs. Johnson. I don't know if you remember me. Nate Beckett."

"Yes, I remember." Her smile suddenly faded. "Sue's boy."

"That's right."

"April ninth," Angus said.

I smiled. "That's my birthday, all right." Looking at his mother, I asked, "How does he do that?"

"I don't know," she said. "It's just one of his gifts."

"Like tending flowerbeds."

"He has lots of gifts," she said. "How did you hurt your hands?"

"I had a run-in with a fire."

234

"Don't play with fire, no sir," Angus said. "Hands get burned."

His mother's laugh sounded forced.

It was then that I noticed the deep scars on his hands, much like the scars left by a bad burn. I hadn't seen them the other day, probably because he was wearing gloves.

"Are those burn scars on your hands, Angus?" I asked.

He looked down at his hands as if he hadn't noticed. His mother stiffened.

"How did he get those?" I asked her.

"Heavens, it was so long ago. He was, uh, playing with a firecracker, and it went off in his hand."

But I'd seen scars from firecrackers before, and these marks didn't look like that.

"Don't play with fire," Angus said again. "Not even to burn clippings. No sirree."

I got quiet and sat back as the organ began to play, and the choir came in wearing their blue robes. I tried to focus on worshiping, but my mind kept wandering to Angus, then to Brenna. By now Brenna was probably dealing with another hangover and hating herself for driving me away last night. I didn't want her to feel that way.

The pastor talked about Elijah, who had just called down a couple of major-league miracles, but when he was finally alone, depression took hold of him and he wanted to die. God provided for him — he sent Elijah to sit under a juniper tree, and he sent an angel to feed him.

I thought of Brenna who had sunk into that kind of depression herself. I prayed that God would send her an angel too, to minister to her needs and pull her out of her pit. Like Elijah, she might not recognize it. Her grievances might distract her from God's work.

When the service was over, I led my parents out of the pew. I waited for Angus and his mother to come out too, but they went the other way and were gone by the time I got to the parking lot.

CHAPTER 21

BRENNA

I woke Sunday morning to an incessant ringing that felt as if it was coming from my brain, but then I realized it was my doorbell. Clutching my throbbing head, I pulled myself out of bed and started barefoot to the front door, still wearing my gown.

Squinting, I opened the door and saw Gerald Stocker and William Hertzog, my former father-in-law, standing there. Stocker was smiling just as he'd been the other night. He held out a stapled set of papers, and William was holding his phone upright. I was pretty sure he was taping.

"What do you want?" I asked.

"I've come as an officer of the court, Brenna, to serve you with these papers," Stocker said.

"What?" I took the papers he thrust at me. "It's Sunday morning."

"You know what day it is, do you?" William asked.

They pushed inside, and I suddenly had the presence of mind to grab my phone off the kitchen counter. I started videotaping. Then I looked down at the papers. "What is this?"

"It's a move to grant temporary custody to my client until the custody hearing," Stocker said. "On the grounds that you're not fit to have the children in your possession, due to alcohol abuse and the company you're keeping."

I skimmed the page with horror and saw Nate Beckett's name. In addition to alleging that I was an alcoholic who couldn't care for my children, it asserted that I'd been bringing a suspected arsonist around them. "These are lies," I said. "You can't do this."

"I'm coming in to pack the rest of the children's clothes," William said. "They won't be coming home tomorrow."

"But I get them back today!" I shouted, standing in his way and not letting him into the hallway. "Jack has to bring them home this afternoon! Where is he? Why didn't he come himself?"

"We agreed it would be more civil if I came. The custody hearing is a week from Tuesday, Brenna. Jack's keeping them until the hearing, and we'll see what the judge says then. I need to get the rest of their clothes."

"No! I am *not* an alcoholic! I only drank when I didn't have the kids with me. I wasn't driving. I didn't break any laws."

"You were stumbling drunk in public. We have witnesses who'll testify that it's a chronic problem."

"This is ridiculous! I go all week without a single drink. This doesn't have anything to do with my parenting! And Nate is not an arsonist! He's never been charged with that."

William shoved me out of the way and headed back to the kids' rooms.

I gripped my phone. "What are you going to do with your videotape, William? Edit out your bullying? Because I'm recording too! This is against the law. You can't barge into my house like this!"

William ignored me and handed his phone to Stocker, who turned the camera on me again as I followed them down the hall.

"You won't get away with this!" I shouted. "My children need me. Noah is sick, and I have proof that Jack isn't taking care of him!"

"Tell it to the judge a week from Tuesday, Brenna." Calmly, William got a large suitcase from the top shelf in Noah's room and began methodically emptying the drawers of my little boy's dresser into the suitcase.

"Do you have Judge Radison in your back pocket? Is that how you set this all up so quickly?"

"I'm only looking out for my grandchildren's welfare."

"No, you're not. You've been trying to find something against me ever since the divorce." I set the phone down and grabbed Noah's clothes out of the suitcase and tried to put them back into the drawers. "You'll take these clothes over my dead body. Get out! You're breaking and entering!"

He got the clothes back out and shoved them into the suitcase again. Outraged, I swung around and grabbed the phone out of Stocker's hand. I turned the video camera off and threw his phone. "Get out of my house or I'll call 911!" I screamed.

"In a minute," William said, dumping the last drawer's contents into the suitcase, then clearing all the clothes out of the closet. "I still have to do Sophia's room."

I followed him into my daughter's room, wishing I had a weapon to force him out, wishing I could do something, anything, to stop him. "Don't you touch her things!" I sobbed. "I won't let you do this!"

He flung me out of his way, and I threw myself at him again, wrestling him for the clothes he was taking out of Sophia's closet. He shoved me harder this time, knocking me to the floor. I scrambled up, turned off my video app, and swiped the phone. "I'm calling the police!"

William was having fun with this. He finished throwing things into the suitcase, then zipped it shut. I dialed 911.

"911, what's your emergency?"

"I have a trespasser in my home," I cried. "Please send the police!"

As I gave my address, William finished packing and made a beeline for the front door. "When they come, show them this emergency order," he said. The two men backed out of the driveway with all my children's clothes, and I couldn't stop them.

Limp with impotent rage, I collapsed onto the floor.

NATE

I glanced toward Brenna's house when I got home. Her car was there, but I didn't see her. I fought the urge to go over to check on her. If she was still in self-destruction mode, I didn't want to be there.

I needed a distraction. My burns were looking better, so I gathered my gear and drove to Simon Plateau Park again. It might have been premature, but I was ready to try running.

I got into my gear and slogged to the entrance. A man was sitting in his car snapping pictures. That was strange, I thought. I could imagine him taking pictures of the lush landscape through an open window, but not through a dirty windshield. I looked back at him and he was taking another picture. I was in his way.

A few hikers were taking pictures next to the sign at the entrance to the hiking trails.

I started my trot then and took off up the mountain. The trail was too easy, so I got off it and ran through the brush. That was how I'd have to do it if I'd jumped from a plane. The brush scraped against my legs, but my pants provided good protection.

I picked up my speed when it got steeper. The burns still pulled, but not as badly as they had before. I could still do this.

I made it up to the top faster than I had in the previous few days. I wanted to run it again, but I was afraid if I overdid it I would set myself back. I would go at this speed and this weight for a couple of days, then try to up the distance.

As I headed back down, I saw that photographer again. Curious, I pulled out my phone, set it to video, and turned it on as I walked toward him. I lifted the phone as if I were reading a text.

He glanced at me as I walked by. I saw his face on my screen. "How ya doing?" I asked.

He muttered something I couldn't hear and turned back to the landscape.

I was drenched with sweat when I got back into the truck, and I grabbed a towel on the seat and wiped my face. My lung capacity seemed to be less than it had been before the burns — I couldn't grab as big a breath. I didn't like the feeling that I wasn't bouncing back to 100 percent faster than I was.

My breathing steadied by the time I got back to Drew's street. I glanced at Brenna's house again as I turned into his driveway. Her drapes were still closed.

Her silence was worrying me. Maybe I should go over after I showered.

My parents' car sat just inside Drew's garage. Pop was probably looking through the files again.

I had just gotten out of the truck when I heard Brenna calling my name. I turned and saw her shooting across the street toward me, leaving her front door open.

I walked toward her. "Brenna, what's wrong?"

"He won't bring the kids back . . . Emergency custody . . . Said I'm unfit . . ."

I glanced behind me. My father had stepped outside and was looking toward us. I prayed he wouldn't come hurt Brenna more than she already was. Ignoring him, I put my hands on her shoulders and looked into her face. " 'Now tell me again, babe. Slowly, so I can understand."

"William Hertzog and his attorney who saw us together served me with papers this morning. They came in with their phones taping me as I ranted and tried to stop them. They got all the kids' clothes. Every last thing. The hearing is more than a week away, and Jack's keeping the children until then. They had an emergency order! I called the police, but William and his attorney were already gone when they got here. I have to go to the station if I want to press charges."

"Have you called your attorney?"

"Yes. He's working on it but says all I can do is wait. The judge on our case is a member of Jack's country club. They don't care that Noah's sick and wants to come home. Sophia and Noah count the hours until they can come home on Sundays, and now he's telling them they can't come home at all? They can't see their mother?"

"What were his grounds, Brenna? Did William say?"

"Of course! It's because of what Stocker saw the other night. Me drunk, and you —"

"Me? They mentioned me?"

She covered her face and shook her head violently. "Their papers say I've been involved with a suspected arsonist! Like we're Bonnie and Clyde. My attorney says that shouldn't be a factor, because you were never charged, and I wasn't drinking with my children . . ."

"Brenna, he must be right. This doesn't make sense."

"But you don't know them! Jack always gets what he wants. He can do anything!" She backed away from me and looked at her house. "Nate, help me."

"How?" I asked gently. "How can I help?"

She spun back to me. "Help me stop drinking! You were right, telling me to stop. What was I thinking? I have to stay focused. I can't be numb. Now the children are the ones having to take the pain."

"You can stop," I said. "You can do it, Brenna."

"Not by myself. Maybe the Hertzogs are right. Maybe I am unfit. I've failed them in so many ways!"

"Brenna, those are lies."

She shook her head. "Don't whitewash my drinking, Nate. You were right last night. I played into his hands. He destroyed our family, and now I'm letting him destroy me! I don't know what to do."

I glanced back toward my father but didn't see him. He must have gone inside. "You know I'll help you," I whispered. "You know I will. We're going back to your house, and we'll make a plan. We can beat this."

She nodded. "All right."

"Just let me go inside and tell my dad I'm leaving."

She nodded. "I'll go back over. I'm so sorry I came here. You didn't sign up for any of this."

"I'm signing up now," I said.

I watched her walk wearily back across the street and go into her house. As I walked toward Drew's side door, I saw that Pop was watching out the window, waiting, his face as mean as I remembered.

I rushed inside and swept past him, and almost ran into my mother.

"Why are you wearing your fire clothes?" she asked me. "Nate, you haven't been working again, have you?"

"No, I was just hiking in the gear, getting in shape. I have to shower," I said. "I need to go across the street to Brenna's. It's kind of an emergency."

"Is there anything I can do?" she asked.

"No. She's upset about her ex. It's pretty important."

"Those Hertzogs are trouble," she said.

Pop just gaped at her, as if she'd betrayed him. "If you keep seeing that woman, Nate, don't come around me again."

"Roy, don't say that!" Mama said. "Oh, Nate . . ."

My face was hard as I stared at my father. "Pop, I'm a grown man and I will see whomever I please. I appreciate the fact that you have hard feelings about her family, but Brenna hasn't done anything to you or to me. She needs my help and I'm giving it to her."

I closed the bathroom door behind me. I showered quickly, then got dressed. My parents were gone when I came out.

When I got to Brenna's, I stepped into her house. Brenna was sitting on the floor looking at papers spread across her coffee table. She looked up as I came in. "Do you think I have a prayer of winning this?" she asked miserably.

"You always have a prayer," I told her. "We both do."

"I'm trying," she said. "But their closets and drawers, they're all empty! I feel so out of control. I should be able to protect them. I'm their mother, and they're probably wondering why I would sit by and allow this. There's no telling what lies Jack's telling them. Or what truths." She clutched her head. "I wish I could storm into his house like they did mine and just grab the kids and take them out. Can you believe they were videotaping me? They were telling me they were keeping my children, and they recorded my reaction so they could prove I was unstable!"

"Any judge will understand your reacting to that."

"This judge . . . Judge Radison. He used to be a member of my father's church. He may be one of those who believes you burned the church down, Nate! He based this decision on my public, drunken display at the restaurant and my association with you."

I was quiet for a moment, letting her words sink in. Was my reappearing in Brenna's life going to do her irreparable harm? Was this judge really going to base his opinion of her on something the grapevine said I had done twelve years earlier? Did the justice system really work that way?

Maybe in the Hertzogs' world, it did.

I had to clear myself. Somehow I had to

lay this whole idea of me being an arsonist to rest. If not for myself, then for her.

We went into the kitchen, and I saw her eyes stray to the pantry where her bottles of booze sat.

As I feared, she grabbed the two bottles there, but instead of opening one, she handed them to me, then reached for another bottle in the back corner. "I have to pour these out."

I didn't say anything.

She went to the sink and poured each bottle out, her chin set in determination. When she was done, she dropped the bottles into the trash, then pulled the garbage bag out. "I have to get rid of this trash. If I put it on the street, I'm afraid they'll steal it. I know that sounds paranoid, but they're trying to find evidence that I'm a lush. They said they had witnesses."

"Who could they be?"

"I don't know. The people who work at the liquor stores? My best friend, Cass, saw me like that. She might have innocently mentioned it to somebody. Others from the restaurant?"

I took the garbage bag. "I'll get rid of it for you."

She let out a harsh breath. "I do have a problem, Nate. You were right last night. I need help. Maybe I'm even an alcoholic."

I pushed her hair back from her wet face. "I'm on your team," I said. "We can fight this."

She nodded, and I slid my fingers through her hair and kissed her forehead. She looked up at me with teary eyes. "You're how God is working, Nate," she whispered. "I do see it."

My throat constricted and I couldn't speak, so I just held her and let her cry.

CHAPTER 22

NATE

A short time later, as I drove back to Brenna's house with the food I'd gone to pick up, I racked my brain for some message of hope to offer her. I knocked lightly when I got back to her house, and she opened the door and motioned me in. She was on speakerphone with her attorney, Bradley Hampton.

"I've read the custody papers carefully," he was saying, "and I think that once we get back before the judge, these allegations aren't going to stand up. But I want you to be honest with me. Tell me about the alcohol."

She raked her fingers through her hair and glanced at me. "I have been drinking," she said in a voice so quiet I could hardly hear her. "I've just been so depressed on the weekends when they're with him. It was the only way I could cope. But after this, I've decided never to drink again. I'm not going near it."

"Well, there's no law against drinking," Hampton said. "Do they have any proof you've abused it? Any DUIs? Any wrecks? Any treatment programs you've entered?"

"No," she said. "I only drank when things were out of control. Like the other night when Noah was sick and Jack wouldn't let me keep him."

"Noah was sick?" he asked.

"Yes," she said. "He's still sick."

I gestured for her to tell him about Sophia's recording.

"I have a tape of Sophia calling Friday night, saying that Jack wasn't doing the treatments right, and Noah was having trouble breathing, and the kids wanted to come home."

"Perfect. I'll need that."

"Jack and his father refused to take the breathing machine when I tried to leave it with him the other day, but when Noah got sick, he wound up coming over early the next morning to get it."

"Perfect," he said. "Got it. Now tell me about your relationship with Nate."

"What about it?" she asked, looking at me.

"Will they say anything has happened while the children were present?"

"No! Not at all. Nothing has happened even when they weren't present. We just started seeing each other a few days ago. Nate isn't what they say. He's a smokejumper. A member of the Rocky Mountain Hotshots. He's a hero, not an arsonist."

"Impressive. Okay, that's good."

"Jack knows the name Nate Beckett, and he knows the judge does too. He thinks that if he throws that name out in connection with me, everyone will remember that Nate's father was convicted of my father's murder."

"Wow," Hampton said. "Okay, that's coming back to me."

"Yeah. Nate is in Carlisle right now because he was injured in a fire. He has second-degree burns."

"Is that right? So when is he going back? Will he be here in case we need him to testify in court?"

I nodded, and she told him yes.

"What about if there are delays? How long will he be here?"

"Delays?" Brenna asked. "There can't be delays. I have to get my kids back!"

"Well, I don't anticipate anything, Brenna. But just in case —"

"Yes, I'll be here," I cut in, calling atten-

253

tion to myself for the first time. "Except for a trip I have to take to Washington in a couple of weeks. I'll make sure I'm here."

Brenna looked at me. "Washington? What for?"

I shrugged. "That award I told you about? Well . . . the president's giving it to me at the White House."

Brenna gasped, and the lawyer said, "Whoa!"

"The *president*?" she asked. "You didn't say anything about the president!"

"What's the award for?" Hampton asked.

"For doing my job," I said. "I got a senator and his family out of their house just ahead of the fire."

"Are you telling me you're the guy who saved Senator Livingston and his family? That was all over the news!"

I hedged. "Well, me and my team."

"No!" he said excitedly. "They said on the news that one firefighter went into that house, risking his life, and got them out. Was it you, Nate?"

"Well, yeah, but they're making it into this really big deal, and any one of us would've done the same thing."

The lawyer began to laugh, and Brenna was smiling too as she turned back to me.

"Boy, oh boy," Hampton said. "Ol' Jack

doesn't know what he's done. He's dragging you into court, Brenna, under the allegation that you've been seeing a guy who's practically a fugitive, when in reality he's a hero about to be recognized by the president of the United States. When we point this out to the judge, he won't believe any of the other allegations either. In fact, he'll be so disgusted he'll probably just throw Jack in jail for good measure."

Brenna laughed tentatively. "Really?"

"Well, no, not really. But it's sure going to help you. It's possible that we'll get your children back the day of court."

"But is there any way I can get them back before then?"

"I'm afraid our hands are tied until next Tuesday, Brenna. But what you can do is try to find out anything you can about Noah's illness. How many treatments they've given him, how sick he is, whether they've taken his temperature, called the doctor. Record those calls."

"Is that legal?"

"Yes. In Colorado, you only need for one party in a phone call to consent to being recorded. That party can be you. The other person doesn't have to be told it's being recorded. If we can get any evidence of neglect or Jack's waiting too long to treat him, that would help. Or any more calls from Sophia. Record and save anything you get, and we'll play them for the judge."

"Meanwhile, my little boy needs his mother."

"Just a few days, Brenna," he said. "It's going to be okay."

I wished I could reassure her, but I wasn't sure anything would ease her mind and heart until she had Sophia and Noah back in her arms.

CHAPTER 23

BRENNA

My lawyer's assurances didn't help me. My children were suffering needlessly, and they wouldn't understand why I wasn't coming to get them. When my cell phone rang, I recognized Rayne's number. I quickly turned on my recording app and swiped on my screen to answer.

"Mommy?"

"Sophia!" I cried. "How are you, honey?"

Her voice still didn't rise above a whisper. "He won't bring us home. He was going to, but then he and Grandpa got in a terrible fight, and now he says we have to stay here. Mommy, please come get us. It's Sunday."

I closed my eyes. "Honey, listen to me. Your daddy got a judge to say he could have you until we go to court. But we can't get in to see him until a week from Tuesday. They won't let me get you until then."

"No!"

"I'm so sorry, honey." I covered my face and tried to steady my voice. "You said he and Grandpa fought? About what?"

"About us!" she said. "Daddy told him Noah needed you because he's so sick, but Grandpa wouldn't listen. Why does Daddy always do what he says?"

My head was suddenly splitting. "Honey, tell me about Noah."

"He's real sick, Mommy! He keeps coughing and throwing up, and now he has a fever, and he's wheezing all the time, and Rayne never wants to clean the machine."

I picked up a pillow and threw it against the wall. It fell without a sound. "Honey, see if you can talk Daddy into taking Noah to the hospital. Tell him they'll know what to do. And try to remind him how much Noah needs his treatments."

"I think Noah's worse because he's so upset. He keeps crying to go home."

I wiped my eyes. "Honey, tell Noah I'm working on it, okay? Tell him we just have to be patient for a few days. Just try to calm him down. It's not that long." But it was an eternity, and I knew it.

Sophia was quiet for a moment, as if she had begun to doubt me. "Daddy's coming," she said finally. "I have to go."

"Okay, honey. I love you."

The phone went dead in my hand, and the rage that always propelled me to drink flashed through me like lightning. My hands were shaking as I checked the recording, titled it, and emailed the voice file to my lawyer.

I didn't sleep that night. I lay awake, wishing for a drink, but when the need got overwhelming, I paced the floor, praying. I hadn't really talked to God in a while, not since the custody battle started and justice became such an imaginary concept.

I finally went to my computer and started writing. My character Lily was between a firing squad and a suicide bomber. I didn't let her wilt. I made her strong, active. I had the firing squad get distracted by the bomber, and she escaped. The victory felt like my own.

By morning, I could smell the smoke from the fires burning just north of town. I wondered how it was impacting Noah.

They couldn't keep me from going to see Noah at school. He was still my child, and I doubted Jack had told them about our emergency order.

But when I went there and asked to see Sophia and Noah, they told me they hadn't come to school that day. I walked back to the car, feeling like Lily between the two enemies. Maybe there really was no escape or reprieve. Only death.

I called Noah's asthma doctor to see if Jack had brought Noah in. He hadn't. He also hadn't visited his pediatrician. And the pharmacist said no prescriptions had been filled. I called the hospital, but he hadn't been admitted.

I went to work, determined to put one foot in front of the other, but Georgi saw how distraught I was and sent me home. As I drove, my craving for a drink swelled up inside me. The welfare of my children seemed to hang in the balance, and without something to calm me, I didn't think I was going to make it.

I drove past the little shopping center where the drugstore sat next to the liquor store and thought of going in and getting something mild. Something just strong enough to take the edge off. Maybe one of those airplane-size bottles. If I could just relax, I could think more clearly.

I pulled into the parking lot and sat in my car for a moment, my hands trembling as I dug through my purse to see if I had any cash. I counted two dollars and some change — not enough to buy what I needed. I could put it on my debit card, but what if Jack could get into my account online? Or

Stocker could subpoena my bank records? I couldn't take the chance of having them see the transaction.

I covered my face, feeling like I would explode into a million pieces if I dropped my hands. I looked up at the cloudless sky.

"What are you doing to me?" I cried out to God. "What do you want me to do? I'm dying! I didn't think you would give us more than we could take! You made me think you loved me, sending Nate after all these years, just when I needed him. But you're letting Jack walk all over me and my kids. You're letting Noah hurt! I can't take that! A week? That's an eternity to Noah, when every breath is a struggle!"

I wept openly, loudly. "Where are you?" I demanded. "Why won't you help me? I need you now!"

I knew my distance from God was my fault. I had let myself drift away. But why had he let me go? Why didn't he fight for me?

I turned on the car and started home. As I drove, I wiped the tears dripping off my chin. As if in answer, that picture of Jesus on the cross flashed into my mind.

He *had* fought for me. He had fought to the death. What else did I want from him?

"I know," I said, as if he were with me in

person, arguing with me. "You don't owe me a thing. But you said that you cared for us. You wept over Lazarus, even though you knew you were going to raise him from the dead. You cried over Jerusalem. But it doesn't feel like you cry over me."

My father's words came storming back through my head. *In tough times, you rely on what you know, not what you feel.*

"But feelings matter," I said to God. "Feelings can drive you off a cliff." I wiped my face, realizing what I was threatening. I pulled my car over and rammed my forehead against the steering wheel. "God, help me. I don't want to feel this way about you."

I wept like a child, hurt and forsaken . . . lost. I needed help. I needed God to pick me up and carry me, holding me in a crushing embrace. At times I did that with Noah, when he was acting his age, when he was upset or angry . . . hungry or sleepy. During those times, he didn't even know I was holding him. But I still did.

Maybe God was holding me, and I was just too caught up in my fit to know it. Maybe his arms were around me right now, crushing me and keeping me from hurting myself. Sending Nate, making sure I didn't have cash . . .

"I'm sorry, Lord," I cried. "I shouldn't

have drifted. I should have stayed connected to you. I should have reached out to you instead of the bottles. But now Noah really, really needs you. Please make the air clean around him. Help him breathe, Lord. Please take care of him."

A shaky sense of peace and trust came over me. I knew if I let myself think too hard, I would lose it.

NATE

On Tuesday, I found Drew in the kitchen, making a sandwich.

"Hey, Drew," I said. "Take a look at this." I pulled up the video on my phone of the photographer I'd seen on the trail and paused it where the man's face was visible. "Do you know this guy?"

Drew took my phone and studied it. "Uh . . . yeah, I think so. He comes into the bar sometimes. I don't know his name though."

"Do you know any of his friends? Who does he talk to?"

Drew tried to think. "I really can't say. I think he usually sits at the bar. Talks to whoever is up there. Why? What's up with him?"

"I don't know. He's been at the park every time I go running in my gear. He may be taking pictures of me."

"That's weird."

"Yeah. I was going to talk to him, but he avoids me if I try to."

"Well, you gotta admit it looks weird. You running up there decked out like you just jumped out of a plane."

"Yeah, I guess."

I put the photographer out of my mind and headed over to my parents'. My father would still be mad that I'd run off to help Brenna. He'd told me not to come around him anymore. Had he meant it?

I thought of the agony on Brenna's face as she took me into the children's rooms to show me what Hertzog had taken. Was that how my mother had felt when I left home twelve years ago? Had she mourned for me? Had she fought the urge to fall completely apart?

And now that I was back, was she mourning again over the thought of me being banished from my father's presence?

I drove to the little blue house on the street where I grew up and pulled into the driveway. For a moment I sat staring at the house, bracing myself for what I would encounter inside.

The front door opened, and my mother stepped out and waved. The look on her face reminded me of Brenna. It was the look of unconditional love between a mother and her child, a look that said I would never be unwelcome, no matter what my father said.

I got out of the truck and walked up the steps. "Hi, Mama."

She reached for me and drew me into a hug, then stepped back and wiped her eyes. 'I'm glad you came back, Nate."

"I don't think Pop will be."

"Talk to him," she said. "You're a man now. You have a lot of pride and so does he, but one of you is going to have to swallow it. And I don't think your father can do it."

I shook my head. "It's not about pride, Mama."

"Maybe not on your part. Your father's out back. He's done a lot of staring off into space today. He's in a real bad mood and doesn't want to talk to anybody."

I stepped into the house and peered out the back door. I saw the old man sitting alone on the porch swing. "I'll go talk to him."

"You do that," she said, then hugged me again.

I walked out onto the back porch, and my father looked up. "I thought I told you to stay away from me."

I took a seat facing my father and set my

elbows on my knees. "I know you did, Pop."

"Then why are you here?"

"I'm not really sure," I said honestly. "Maybe it's just for Mama. But there's a part of me that needs to explain this to you."

"Why?"

"Because we're family."

"That never meant anything to you when I was in prison."

I looked down at my feet. "I agree. Maybe when you took me off the visitors' list, I should have tried harder to get back on it. You know, Pop, I've spent the past twelve years trying to remove myself from this family. Drew and I kept in touch, and so did Mama and I . . . but I didn't like remembering what happened when I was sixteen. I was angry with you."

"Because you believed I did it. And it ruined your little affair with her."

My face reddened. "It was no affair, Pop. We were two kids in love for the first time. Nothing sordid, nothing dirty. But you turned it into a scandal and a tragedy. And I hated you for it."

Pop looked off into the trees skirting the yard. "Well, I'm glad you got that off your chest."

I looked at him, trying to meet his eyes, but Pop wouldn't connect. Still, I saw the pain in his face, the years of loneliness and isolation, the decades of regrets. "I don't hate you anymore. And most important, I don't hate myself. But I'm back here with a second chance, and this time I'm not running away."

"A second chance to do what?"

"A second chance to be a son to you. And a second chance to comfort Brenna during another tragedy in her life. A second chance to be with her, Pop. And there's nothing you can say about her that'll change that. I feel like I got robbed of something real important to me back then. I'm not gonna be robbed again."

"What do you want from me?" Pop asked.

I thought about that for a moment. "Maybe I want to hear you say that your going to prison wasn't my fault. I want you to stop throwing it up to me, like there was anything a sixteen-year-old boy could've done to keep his father from assaulting the preacher. Whether you killed him or not."

But Pop didn't move, and after a while, I knew he wasn't going to budge. He was a hard man, and he did blame me. Nothing about that would ever change.

I stood up. "Well, I tried, Pop."

Pop was silent as I went out the gate, instead of through the house where I'd have

267

to face my hopeful mother. When I drove away, I saw my mother looking out the window, her eyes full of the same pain that Brenna's held.

On my way home, a plume of smoke in the hills where I ran caught my eye. I frowned at the smoke, hoping I was misjudging the distance. Maybe it was a controlled burn somewhere closer.

Just in case, I drove toward it. When I got to the parking lot at Simon Plateau Park, where I always left my car, I grabbed binoculars out of my trunk and ran up on the overlook to see where the smoke was coming from. There it was. Not far from the path where I ran, a line of flames the size of a football field had erupted.

I called 911 and told them about the fire, where it was, and what the best access point was. Then I went back to my car and got my gear out of my truck. I stepped into my jumpsuit and checked all my pockets. The fire department still wasn't here. It was taking too long. Where were they?

Then I remembered that the town of Carlisle still didn't have a regular fire department — only a volunteer unit.

A few guys drove up in a water truck, and I ran over. I recognized some of them.

"Guys, it looks like it started close to the hiking path about a mile up, but your hoses may not reach. It's really going up fast. I can help. Got all my gear here."

Some of the men ran up the hill to check it out while I finished getting my gear on. They decided they might be able to get the truck closer to the fire. Others ran up the path to make sure no one was hiking up there. I followed the truck as they moved it up the hill, and when they got stuck by brush or small trees, I used my Pulaski to chop it back. When they got close enough, they hooked up the hose. The spray seemed wimpy in the face of this wall of flames.

Other firefighters came running uphill in their fire coats as they arrived, but none was equipped as well as I was. "While they're spraying, we have to cut a fire line!" I shouted. "It's spreading fast, and we have to make sure it doesn't come this way. We need chainsaws."

The volunteer chief sent some guys to follow me. They did have axes, but I doubted they knew how wide a stretch to clear. It was going to take a lot more people than this, and a lot of men with chainsaws to cut down trees and help me remove any fuel the fire might try to burn.

I saw the chief on the truck talking into

the radio, and I hoped he was calling for surrounding departments to come and help. Ignoring the stretching of my burned skin, I started doing what I knew how to do, chopping and clearing as well as I could without a chainsaw. If the fire came this way, and if we could cut a wide enough swath to keep the sparks from coming down the slope and starting fires on the town side of the line, we could contain it. The wind was in our favor, pushing it the opposite direction, so maybe we'd be okay.

The water squelched some of the fire, but like a petulant child, the flames just ran in the opposite direction, lighting everything in their path.

More help arrived, including some uniformed from neighboring towns, and others in plain clothes but with their own ragged gear and chainsaws, and soon we had a good team chopping our way through the fire line while other trucks tried to work their way up the slope.

But the fire's path thickened backward, toward the side of the mountain, swelling to the size of two, then three football fields.

When it was clear that we weren't going to be able to fight this on our own, I ran back to the truck. "It's gotten too big. We need to call in some smokejumpers."

"They won't get here in time. They're all tied up with the fires north of us."

"Let me make a call," I said, and I tried to get T-bird on the phone. If they were still in the furnace they wouldn't answer their cell phones, but if they'd gotten out for a bit, maybe they would.

My chief picked up. "Whassup, Nate?"

"Chief, we have a fire that just broke out south of Carlisle, on the Simon Plateau, on Nugget Peak. Three football fields, spreading fast. We have boots on the ground but it's not gonna cut it. We need you guys here." I gave him the exact coordinates, and he took note.

"Okay. We just got a break from the fire up here, but the last thing we need is another one like this one. We'll head that way."

When I got off the phone, the local chief was going through the normal channels to call for jumpers, and still hadn't gotten through. "The Rocky Mountain Hotshots are on their way," I said.

The chief looked like a ton of weight had been taken off his shoulders. I went back to helping with the fire line.

The men sawing the brush and trees weren't clearing it fast enough or cleanly enough, so I went behind them and tried to cut any leftover stumps down to the ground, leaving no fuel for the fire. I took over one of the chainsaws from a man who looked like he needed a break.

Out of the corner of my eye, I saw the chief waving his arms for me. I cut off the chainsaw and heard him yelling from the top of the truck. "Beckett, can you come here?"

I gave the chainsaw back and jogged up to the truck.

"It's jumping!" he shouted. "The wind isn't that strong! How is that happening?"

I took his binoculars and scanned the mountainside. There were three separate, unconnected sections of fire now, a mile or so between them. "That's not from sparks flying," I said. "We've got multiple origin points."

"How? There's no lightning."

I didn't really care how it was happening. I just knew we had to stop it. I checked my watch. My team should be here in the next fifteen minutes. But we were going to need more.

Two of the trucks pulled away, trying to find another way in to fight the other two fires before they exploded and came toward the town. I went back to the line and fought with all my might. As long as the wind didn't turn toward town, we could still do this.

When I finally saw my team's plane coming over the peak, I whooped, and so did the others. The plane circled once as the spotters decided where to drop the men. It slowed and banked left, the side the door was on.

Then my buddies came out two by two, their parachutes opening and easing them to the ground on this side of the flames. I left the other men and ran to the drop-off point to meet my guys.

We went straight to work as they hit the ground, twenty guys in full gear, and the cargo box with all their supplies. We could be out here all night, and it had everything we would need.

"What are you doing here, Cap?" my buddy Bull said when he hit the ground. "You're supposed to be laid up in bed."

"Not when a fire is threatening my town," I said. "Consider me back."

They didn't say another word about it. I could see that the guys were pretty ragged from the fire they'd been fighting, and they may not have slept in days. But they got to work as if this was the first fire all season, grubbing yards and yards of flammable brush in a matter of minutes.

When the plane came back with its Bambi Bucket lowered to dump water over the fire, we cheered again. But it would take a lot more than that to knock back this fire.

BRENNA

My anxiety shot up to record levels as the smell of smoke wafted over the town, threatening even those with healthy lungs. Noah would be in serious trouble. The hills were on fire, and they were pressing toward the town. Mandatory evacuations went into place.

I longed for my children so I could make sure they were safe. I drove to their school and had to park on the street since so many families were picking up children to evacuate. I ran in and went to Noah's classroom, the first one I came to. A glut of parents were in the room, but I didn't see Noah.

I cut through the crowd to his teacher. "Has Noah already been picked up?"

The teacher looked rattled. "Yes, their dad picked them up a while ago."

I ran back to the car and called Jack. He didn't answer his phone, so I got desperate enough to call Rayne. She didn't answer either, so I left a voice mail. "Please let me know where you're taking the children. I want to know they're all right and that they've been evacuated. Don't forget Noah's breathing machine."

Jack's new house had a beautiful view, on the edge of town closest to where the fires were. I tried to drive out there, but the police were setting up a blockade and turned me back

I didn't know what to do, so I drove to the opposite side of town, to my church, which operated as a shelter during times like this. My mother and Georgi were already there when I arrived. They had gone into work mode and were helping as people showed up.

We were filling up the sanctuary first. Any overflow would go into the fellowship hall and the classrooms as needed. I went to those rooms and helped Bo, the preacher, and staff set up chairs.

I hoped Jack would bring the kids here to wait it out, but I figured he would be two towns away in a resort hotel. I wished I knew which one.

I took a break and called Nate's cell. He didn't answer either. Instead of leaving a voice mail, I texted: I hope you're not on the fire line. Praying for you. Be careful!

It was too early in his healing for him to be up on the mountainside fighting the fire, but I knew him well enough to know that it wouldn't matter. Pain or not, he would be there. I also knew he wouldn't stop to look at his phone.

The church filled up fast, and our audio/visual team set up TVs tuned to the local station running news of the fire. An overhead view showed how quickly it had erupted and spread. I shivered as I saw the V-shape of it on the landscape we had grown so used to.

"We've set up every chair we have," Ethel, one of the ladies in charge, said as she joined me to watch the coverage. "The sanctuary is almost full."

"We'll be okay," I said, though I wasn't sure it was true.

The cameras switched to the fire trucks arriving and making their way toward the fires and to the volunteer and uniformed fighters from neighboring towns. I stepped closer as I saw the plane flying over the flames, dropping its load of water.

"The Rocky Mountain Hotshots, a Type 1 crew from the Bureau of Land Management, are on the scene. They parachuted in less than an hour ago and are working on the fire line to hold the flames back before the fire makes its way to the town's structures. Thousands of people have been evacuated." They showed a helicopter view of the traffic jam on the way out of town. I scanned the vehicles, looking for Jack's car. I prayed he'd gotten my children out of here before the traffic backed up. It wouldn't be good for Noah to be stuck on a highway.

I started away to find something else to do when the news cut to another field correspondent interviewing the spokesman for the command center at the fire. "This is a tourist area, and it's possible someone was careless with a cigarette or a campfire, but we do know that there haven't been any lightning strikes or natural reasons for this fire to have started."

They switched back to the anchor, who had her laptop open on the table in front of her. "Larry, it just came to our attention that there's social media gossip about the fire being caused by arson because there were multiple points of origin. Have you heard any of that?"

"Not yet, Sandra, but we'll follow that and get back to you."

I pulled my phone out of my pocket and clicked on Facebook. I scrolled through my feed to see if any of my friends had shared that gossip. I didn't see any.

Cass came in at the back of the sanctuary, and she cut through the crowd of people to me. "I just got here. You okay?" she asked.

"Yeah, fine. I just wish I knew where my kids were."

"I'm sure they're okay. Did you see what's going around on Instagram?"

"No, I've been helping here. What is it?"

She pulled out her phone and clicked on the app and held it up for me to see.

I sucked in a breath as I read. "Local man suspected of arson in Nugget Peak fire." And the picture was of Nate Beckett.

CHAPTER 24

NATE

When our fire line hit a stream running on the side of the fire zone, we decided to start a controlled burn. If the fire started right here inside the firebreak and crept toward the fire that was barreling down the hill, it would smother itself. With no fuel, it would have no place to go.

Between the lake water being scooped into the Bambi Bucket and dumped overhead into the flames, and the work we were doing, it was possible that we could beat this. Our plane pulled up the empty collapsible orange bucket and radioed us that it was ready to use the helitorch, a device under the plane that acted as a flamethrower. We watched as the plane swept over with pinpoint accuracy and the pilot threw the switch, sending a line of flames to the designated area.

From the door of the plane, the spotters

shot out what we called the "Ping-Pong balls." They were small firebombs filled with potassium permanganate and ethylene glycol, with a thirty-second delay. They shot them into the area the helitorch didn't get, making a wider swath of the controlled burn, setting the area between the flames and the firebreak into a mini inferno that did more good than harm. The landscape would be significantly scarred for a while, but at least people would be alive.

"Beckett!" T-bird called. I turned. "Need to talk to you!" he shouted.

That was odd. This was an impossible time to have a conversation. Confused, I left my gear where it was and jogged toward him several yards away. "What's up?" I yelled over the noise of chainsaws, helicopters, and the plane.

"There's something going on down at the parking lot," he shouted. "Cops want to talk to you. I told them you were right in the middle of saving their town, but apparently this is a big deal."

"You're kidding me."

"Just go," he said. "Hopefully you can get back here, even though you weren't supposed to be here until your medical was released."

"I'm doing fine," I shouted. "Is it about that?"

"Doubt it!" he said. "Go!"

I hurried back to the fire line and got my gear. The heat was picking up and getting oppressive. I saw a few fire eruptions right where we wanted them and thought maybe this was going to work.

Hating to leave my team on the field again, I jogged back down the hill toward the entrance where my truck sat. The parking lot was full of fire trucks and equipment, but out on the street were some police cars, which I assumed were directing traffic. I walked toward them and grabbed a cop. "Somebody wanted to talk to me? Nate Beckett?"

"Yeah, come this way," he said.

"Look, I'm really busy out there. They need me. Is this going to take long?"

He didn't answer, but I followed him as he took me to a more authoritative-looking cop at a command post. "Nate Beckett," he called to him.

I reached out to shake his hand, though mine was still gloved and charred. "If this is about my working with burns —"

He interrupted me. "Mr. Beckett, we need you to come to the police station for questioning about the arson on Nugget Peak."

"What?" I yelled. "Do you know the time-line of events here? I saw the smoke. I ran out here and saw the origin of the fire. I called it in."

"That's why we need to talk to you."

"Can't you wait until the emergency is over?"

"No, we can't."

Before I knew it they were ushering me to the backseat of a squad car, putting me in. Cameras were snapping around me, even though my helmet and face guard still covered most of my face.

It was like something out of a bad dream. As the car started up and headed to the police station, I sat back hard against the seat and looked out the window toward the fire. I couldn't tell if the controlled burn was working, but I could see the smoke thickening over the town. I looked toward the houses, trying to gauge how close they were to the flames. An entire neighborhood would go up soon if this didn't work.

I said a quiet prayer. Then I laid my head back and took a few minutes to rest my eyes.

When they'd given me a chance to take off my jumpsuit and wash up in the bath-room, they put me in an interview room and brought me water. Two detectives I didn't know came in and sat down with me.

I had seen this a million times on police videos of interviews, and I knew I was being videotaped and recorded. Fatigue set in like a two-hundred-pound weight on my shoulders, but I told myself to push through this, and then I could get back to the fire.

"So tell us one more time about your runs up on the mountain," one of the detectives said.

"I've told you at least three times already."

"Go over it again. We want to make sure we get everything."

"I've been off of the field because of my burns. I was trying to keep in shape. I have to be able to run uphill with a hundred and ten pounds of gear on. It's as simple as that. The best way to do that is to do it uphill on the mountain instead of in a gym. It kept my legs in shape."

"So when you did that, did you stray off the path? Go down into the brush? Or did you do a straight shot to the top?"

"I'm a smokejumper. We don't normally have paths. I tried to replicate the field as much as I could. So yes, I went off the path."

I closed my eyes and tried to think what more I could tell them to help them understand this. And then it hit me. The man who had been photographing me.

I sat up, suddenly stiffer, and leaned forward on the table. "Is this about that guy who took my picture? The one who's been following me?"

"What guy?"

"I've just been noticing this photographer out there every day. I mean, there've been a lot of tourists and hikers and people from the town who use that area. But there was this guy who kept turning up, taking my picture as he was photographing the landscape. Is he the one who claims I started the fire?"

"Did you ever take your fire-starter equipment with you when you were walking with your gear?"

I gaped at them for a moment. "I don't have fire-starter equipment. Our controlled burns are done from the plane. We don't have those on the ground."

"Did you ever smoke a cigarette out there or start a campfire?"

"Of course not. It looked like a tinderbox. I worried about it every day I was up there. It should have been pruned and cleared. It was an accident waiting to happen. I never would have caused a single spark. But that guy, the one taking my picture, I got a photo of him the other day. I was suspicious and didn't know what was going on with him, so I used my phone and snapped his picture as I was going back to the parking lot. It's not real clear, but you may be able to tell who he is. Can I have my phone to show you?"

The detectives looked at each other, then one of them got up. "I'll go get it and be back."

"It's the last video I took, I'm pretty sure."

The guy came back in a few minutes, slid my phone across the table. I quickly unlocked it and went to my pictures. The very video I was telling them about came up first. "There it is. He was acting like he was photographing the landscape, but then he turned and took my picture. It wasn't the first time. So I just picked up my phone and started videoing him as I walked forward. I don't think he realized I was doing it. Send the picture to yourself if you want."

They took the phone and looked at the guy, then swiped back through the pictures leading up to the last one. I saw one of the detectives send the picture to himself, then he checked his own phone to make sure they had it.

It wasn't until then that I realized I needed help. "Guys, I want to cooperate with you all I can, but if you're going to question me any more, I need a lawyer."

They didn't seem surprised. They took me to a landline phone, and I tried to think. Should I call my dad's lawyer from years ago? Was he even still practicing? The only other attorney I knew was Brenna's divorce attorney.

I asked them to find me the number for Bradley Hampton. Then I dialed his number, hoping he was in his office despite the evacuations.

His phone rang to voice mail, so I left a message. "This is Nate Beckett, Brenna Hertzog's smokejumper friend. I'm being questioned at the police station, and I can tell they think I started the fire up on Nugget Peak. I need a lawyer."

To my surprise, someone miraculously picked up. "Bradley Hampton's office."

I repeated my message, and they gave me his cell number. I quickly dialed it. Hampton said he'd be here in a few minutes.

They put me back in the interview room, and I wished for a shower. My hair reeked of smoke, and although I had washed my face, I felt as if a sticky layer of sweat and soot covered my skin.

True to his word, Bradley arrived a few minutes later, and they brought him to my interview room.

I got to my feet and shook his hand when

he came in.

"Well, this takes the cake. Taking a hero right out of a wildfire to blame him for starting the fire. What's wrong with this picture?"

"We have reason to believe it was arson," one of the detectives said.

"Couldn't he have just stayed ninety miles north and seen all the fire he wanted? In fact, where do you think this man was burned? He saved a senator in the Steamboat Springs Fire. The White House is honoring him as a hero."

The detective's eyebrows shot up and he turned to look at me. "That was you?"

I nodded. "The last thing a smokejumper needs when there are already two wildfires close by is to start another one. It would be insanity."

"Some people are insane."

"Not me," I said.

They left me alone with Bradley, and I showed him the video on my phone.

"So he's been following you?"

"I didn't think so. I only saw him up there when I was working out."

"But did you go the same time every day?"

"No. Just when I could work it in."

"Then he was following you." He expanded the guy's face so he could see it more clearly. "Wait a minute. I think I know who this is."

"You recognize him?"

He grabbed his own phone and stroked around on it. "I think . . ." He googled a few more things, then finally smiled. He turned the phone to me. "This him?"

"Yeah. Who is that?"

"Pete Sanders. He's a local private investigator."

"You think he was following me? But why?"

"No idea. But following you is one thing. Starting a fire is another."

"I think someone probably *did* start that fire. If he was up there, he had just as much opportunity as I had. He could have started it and framed me. But why?"

Bradley got up and went to the door and called the detective. "You guys need to go ahead and arrest him or let him go home."

I didn't like the sound of that. He looked back at me and told me to sit tight, then he closed the door and went to talk to them, taking my phone with him.

Time passed. It bothered me that I had no idea at all what was happening on the field. The fact that we were still in the building was a good sign. I assumed that we would be evacuated if the flames were breaching the town. And where was Brenna? Were her kids all right?

After several minutes, Bradley came back. "Come on," he said. "They're about to evacuate the building and the jail, so the last thing they want to do is process you right now. Especially when they don't have legitimate grounds for an arrest. You're free to go."

Bradley told them to give me back my things, then he tossed me my phone and told me he was leaving to go find out what he could about Pete Sanders before he had to evacuate his office. As I waited for the rest of my gear, I wondered who I could get to drive me home. I didn't want to worry my parents, especially if they were in transit themselves. I called Drew, but he wasn't answering. I wondered if he had heard about the police taking me in. No, if he had, he probably would've been here by now. I checked my phone and saw that I had missed several calls from both him and Brenna while I was in the field.

I called Brenna next. It rang four times before she picked up. "Nate?" She was practically yelling, and I could hear a crowd behind her. "Are you okay? Where are you?"

"I'm at the police station," I shouted. "Can you come get me?"

"What?" she asked. "Did you say the police station?"

"They think I started it."

"I know. It's all over social media."

"They're letting me leave, but I need a ride."

"I'll be there right away. Just a few minutes."

I got off the phone and waited.

Already some of the personnel were leaving, and the guard who was watching me looked irritated that I had slowed him down. He turned on the TV, and I saw the helicopter view of the fire. It looked like the fire line was holding. The fire hadn't progressed any farther than when I'd been there.

They brought back the gear I had taken off, and within minutes, I heard the door clanging open and someone banging on the window. The guard went to talk to the person, then finally he opened the metal door and Brenna burst in.

She came to me and hugged me. "Has the world gone insane?"

"Yep." I followed her out, and as we got into her car, she said, "You're going to need a criminal attorney, Nate."

"I will if this doesn't end. But I gave them the name of a guy who might have done it."

"What guy?"

"Just . . . some guy who was following me."

"What?"

"Never mind. Don't worry about it. You can just take me to Drew's. They don't want me going back to the fire."

"I can't take you home. There's a mandatory evacuation for our part of town. You have to come with me to the shelter."

The thought made me sick. The townspeople might turn on me and revolt. I didn't want to go.

"I'll just sit in your car in the parking lot. I'll listen to the news on my phone."

"No, you won't. You're coming in. You're with me. I can vouch for you."

"I smell like smoke and sweat. I'm filthy."

"So you'll clean up in the bathroom."

I was quiet as she drove there. Finally we parked out on the street. The sun was blocked by the fog of smoke overhead.

"Noah won't be able to breathe," she said. "I don't know where they are. I'm praying that their father got them out of town before all this."

I suspected that he had, if it was true that his father had gotten his thug to start the fire so he could frame me with it. I put all my gear in her trunk, then followed her in.

If things got ugly in here, I would just leave. I would walk home. I wasn't going to make things bad for her.

But she took me to a small Sunday school classroom. My parents were already there, and my mother sprang up and hugged me. Brenna brought me some water, then whispered she was going into another room. She didn't want to be in the room with my dad.

I followed her out and to the room next door, which only had a few people sitting on the floor and listening to their phones. No one seemed to notice me or realize who I was.

Maybe I could keep a low profile if I stayed right here.

As Brenna left the room to help with the others pouring in to find shelter, I went to the men's room, washed my face, and checked under my bandages to see if I'd done any harm to my burns on the field.

I'd split the blistered skin, and there were bloody lines where the puckered skin had pulled so hard it ripped. I desperately needed to change the dressing and take my antibiotics.

As I put the bandages back in place, Angus walked in.

"Angus, how you doing, man?"

"Good," he said, grinning. "April ninth."

"That's my birthday," I said.

"Fire's burning. Somebody did it. Not me."

"No, it wasn't you."

"Don't burn clippings. No sirree."

I kept working on my dressing as he went into a stall. When he came out, I watched him wash his hands. His burns were visible again as he soaped them up.

"Angus, where did you get those burns?"

"At church," Angus said. "And Mama said, 'Don't play with fire, no sirree.'"

I frowned. "Did you get the burns playing with fire?"

"Mama doctored them."

I thought of all those other things he'd said about fire.

"This church is solid . . . . It won't burn up like the other one."

"Why not burn clippings? Have you done it before? At the church?"

Angus looked agitated, and his face distorted.

"What did you do when the church caught fire?" I asked gently. "Do you remember?"

"Ran home," Angus said. "Fast. Won't burn now, though. New church is brick. Bricks don't burn."

"What do you think started the fire at the

293

church?"

"Clippings," Angus said. "It reached out and grabbed the church."

"What did?"

"Fire," he said. "Fire on the clippings, then fire on the church."

"And you started the clippings burning that time?"

"Won't do that no more."

I took a deep breath, knowing I had my answer. Angus had started that fire, and his mother had kept it secret. I followed him out and saw his mother waiting for him in the hallway.

"December 12th," he was saying to someone passing by.

I stopped near his mother. "Mrs. Johnson, can I talk to you for a minute?"

She hesitated, then stepped toward me. "Yes?"

I lowered my voice so no one else would hear. "The police questioned me today because they think I started this fire. Apparently a lot of people think I'm an arsonist."

Angus walked down toward the pastor's office. His mother looked at him, then turned her eyes back to me. "I'm sorry. I just . . . I can't do anything about that."

"I know he started the church fire. He just admitted it to me."

She winced and looked back at him.

"People in town know Angus wouldn't hurt a fly or do anything malicious. Don't you think they'd understand if —"

She stopped me from saying it. "There's too much at stake."

"You bet there is," I said. "More at stake than you know. Besides what's happening to me, Brenna could lose custody of her kids."

"What? How?"

"We've been seeing each other. Her ex-husband is practically claiming I'm a criminal, so the fact that she's brought me around the kids makes her an unfit mother."

Tears sprang to her eyes. "That's ridiculous."

"Yes, it is. Especially when I'm innocent of all this."

She put her hand over her mouth and looked down the hall. Angus was talking to himself as he walked. We couldn't hear him, but he was smiling. Everyone who passed him caught that smile.

"Look, I know this is hard for you. I wouldn't ask you to tell anyone for my sake. I just worry about Brenna. This is really serious."

"I don't want Brenna to lose her kids."

"Her hearing is next Tuesday, if the fire

doesn't get it delayed. The kids are already in his custody temporarily. She doesn't even know where they are right now or whether Noah's asthma is flaring in all this smoke."

I heard footsteps, and Brenna came around the corner. I stiffened. "Just think about it," I whispered.

As Angus's mom went to join her son, I wondered if anything I'd said had made a difference.

CHAPTER 25

BRENNA

My phone rang as Nate and I went to sit down, and I recognized Rayne's number. I swiped it on. "Where are my children?"

"Mommy?"

I caught my breath at the sound of Sophia's voice. "Sophia, where are you, honey?"

"They took us to a hotel," she said, trying to keep her voice low. "But Noah's sick. Daddy took him to the hospital."

I jumped to my feet. "Which hospital, honey?"

"I don't know," she wailed softly. "I asked him if I could call and tell you, but he said no. So I snuck out of my room and got Rayne's phone. She's taking a nap."

"Honey, tell me about Noah. Why did Daddy take him?"

"He couldn't breathe with all the smoke! He was wheezing so bad. And he kept coughing, and he couldn't catch his breath."

Nate set his arm on my back. "All right, sweetheart," I said. "I'll find the hospital and go right now. Don't worry. Noah is going to be all right."

"Mommy, when can I see you?"

"They're telling me I can't see you until court Tuesday, sweetheart. But my lawyer is working on it."

"That's long!"

"Honey, are you all right?"

"No. I want to come home! Does your lawyer think he can change it?"

I hesitated a moment before I answered. "I don't know, baby. Just pray. Pray hard."

When Sophia hung up, I called the Carlisle Hospital and learned they were diverting all their emergency patients to the hospital in Boulder, just south of us.

"When he evacuated, he probably would have taken them to Denver anyway," Nate said. "I bet that's where they are. Let's go while you call. I'll drive."

We ran out to my car, and as we pulled out, I called the ER of each Denver hospital until I finally found out he was at the University of Colorado ER.

"Jack's going to make a scene as it is," I said. "If he sees you with me again, it'll give him even more ammunition for court. I'll probably have to fight my way in just to see Noah."

"Then record it," he said. "Make sure you get everything. If he tries to keep you away from Noah, the video will go a long way in court. I'll wait in the lobby."

"It could be hours."

"That's fine. I can't go home. Have to wait somewhere."

We were at the hospital in thirty minutes, and Nate dropped me off at the door, then parked and went to another section of the hospital to wait. I ran into the emergency room and looked around at the people waiting for help.

There was no sign of Noah.

"Could you tell me if Noah Hertzog was brought in tonight? A five-year-old with brown hair? Asthma?"

"Yes," the nurse said. "He's been taken back. Room 22."

"I'm his mother," I said. "I'd like to see him."

The woman led me out of the waiting room and down the hall, and I could hear Noah wailing as I got closer to his room. I started to run toward the sound of his voice. When I reached his door, I saw him lying on an examining table while a man in scrubs struggled to keep a mask over his mouth.

"How is he?" I demanded as I burst into the room.

Jack spun around, and his father, standing closer to the door, blocked me from getting to Noah. "No way. You're not coming in here."

"Mommy!" Noah cried.

I held my phone up to record the scene. "It's okay, sweetie. Just breathe into the mask."

"I'm taking care of this, Brenna," Jack said.

Noah fought to sit up. "Mommy!"

"I'm here, sweetie," I said. "It's okay. Let the doctors help you."

His grandfather walked toward him, but Noah wrestled the mask off. "No, I want Mommy!"

"You're upsetting him," William shouted. "Get out before you make it worse."

I was in tears as I pushed past Jack and pulled Noah up close to me. His arms tightened around me. "I'm here, baby. Are you okay?" He was crying and wheezing like a seal, and William yelled for a nurse to call security to escort me out. But I ignored him and looked up at the respiratory therapist. "I think he'll accept the mask if I hold it."

"Of course," he said and surrendered it to me. Noah calmed down in my arms and allowed me to put the mask on him.

Jack watched, quiet since Noah was co-operating, but William kept complaining. "Are you going to stand for this, son?"

Jack looked at his dad. "He's okay, Dad. Just . . . Please, let's just wait until he's finished the treatment."

A nurse came in with a tray of medication. "We're about to give him a shot of Adrenalin," she told us, "and we're getting him started on some Prednisone."

I realized my phone was still recording. I set it facedown on the bed next to me. "Deep breaths, baby," I whispered. "Let those tubes just open right up. Breathe . . . out . . ." I felt how he struggled to exhale each breath. His back vibrated with his whistling airway.

He still hiccuped his sobs. "You'll stay?"

"I'm here right now, baby," I said. "We just have to let them give you a shot. It'll hurt for a second, but then it'll help and you'll feel better. Don't you want to feel better?"

He nodded, and I saw how blue-tinted his lips were. This was frightening. Noah let them give him the shot, and slowly, as the treatment continued, I felt his body relax against me. His lips turned pink again.

"There you go, buddy," Jack said as if he

was on our team. I didn't look at him. I didn't want to give him any reason to speak to me and upset Noah again.

William stood at the door now, as if trolling for security to come and escort me out.

As Noah began to breathe easier, he fell asleep in my arms. When the emergency had passed, the doctor, nurse, and orderlies left the room, leaving only me, Jack, and William with Noah.

"How did you know he was here?" Jack asked me, thankfully keeping his voice low.

"Sophia called me," I whispered. "She was worried about her brother."

"I told her I'd take care of it."

"And you were doing a great job," I whispered. "He was screaming himself into shutting down completely. His lips were blue."

"Oh, give me a break," William snapped, louder. "He's doing better because Jack brought him to the hospital and they gave him the medication he needed. Not because of you."

I let that go and checked to make sure my phone was still recording. "Tell me something, Jack," I said quietly. "He's been sick since you got him over a week ago. Why haven't you taken him to the doctor or the hospital before now?"

"Because it wasn't necessary. I had it under control."

"How? Were you giving him the treatments?"

"Yes."

"Were you doing them right?"

He closed his eyes. "How many times has she called you?"

I wasn't going to give him an answer. "Why does that threaten you so much?"

Again, William interrupted. "You give Sophia a false sense of your importance, Brenna. You want them to need you, so you blackmail them emotionally until they think they do."

"And how do I do that?"

He shook his head, waving off the question. "A thousand ways."

"And you don't think that two small children might really need their mother?"

"They have Rayne," Jack said.

I had to pause a moment to restrain my voice so I wouldn't yell. "Rayne's the one who destroyed their family and took away the stability they knew," I bit out. "Not that that lets you off the hook, Jack. The fact is, I'm the one who's been the stable force in their lives. I'm sorry that you grew up without a mother, Jack, so you might not realize how important they are."

"Don't you talk about my mother."

I knew it was tough on him when his mother died when he was in preschool. I didn't want to rub salt into that wound. "I'm just saying that you know what it's like to lose your mother when you're really young. Do you really want your kids to go through that like you did?"

William's face turned red. "Jack lost his mother in a car accident, Brenna. Your kids are losing theirs because she's a promiscuous drunk."

The words cut, and I looked down at my sleeping son, reminding myself that I didn't want to wake him. And I didn't want to cry in front of these men. I lowered my voice to almost a whisper. "What about you, Jack? Do you still have that scotch every day before dinner like you used to? Are the kids there when you do it? And have you cheated on Rayne yet?"

Jack took a threatening step closer to me. "Shut up, Brenna."

"What's the matter, Jack?" I whispered. "You don't like being called a promiscuous drunk?"

The medicine ran out, and I eased the mask off Noah without waking him. He was breathing normally again. "I can't take him home because of the fires," I said. "But I'm coming with you to your hotel. He'll need another treatment in three or four hours. I'll give it to him."

"No way," William said. "You're not coming with us."

I shot the older Hertzog a defiant look. "Jack is his father, not you." I turned back to Jack, pleading with him. "Please, Jack. Let's not upset Noah again. It's more important to keep him calm and let him rest." Jack hesitated, and for a moment I thought he was seeing reason.

But William came to take Noah. "Give him to me."

I tightened my hold on him. "William, be reasonable. You're going to wake him up!"

But William jerked him from my arms.

Noah's eyes came open as he was jolted, and he looked frantically around. "Mommy? I want you!"

"You're going with me, little buddy," Jack told him, taking him from William. "Sophia's at the hotel worried about you."

"I want to go home!" Noah wailed.

"We can't go home because of the fire."

"Mommy's home. My home. Mommy, I want to go with you." I reached over to kiss him. He threw his arms around my neck and clung to me, not letting me go. Jack refused to release him.

"What if I can't breathe again, Mommy? What if I get sick?"

Tears twisted my face. "Jack, please," I said softly. "Just tonight. Think of your son. I'll rent my own room."

"We have papers, Brenna," William said impatiently. "Now, make it easy on him."

When I could see that Jack wasn't going to go against his father, I took a deep breath and said, "Go with Daddy tonight, baby. He has your breathing machine and all your stuff. Daddy will take care of you, and then I'll see you tomorrow, okay?"

Noah's crying crushed my heart. "But I miss you and my bed and my yard. Sophia does too, Mommy."

I tried hard to blink back my tears. "Well, I can't go home now either, because of the fire. I'm having to stay at the church. It's going to be all right. You go with Daddy now. You need to sleep, and Sophia's real worried about you. You have to take care of her. But I'll see you soon."

Noah seemed too tired to cry, so he finally surrendered.

For a moment after they were gone, I stood, unmoving, in the examining room, torn between running after them and letting them think that things were all right.

"Excuse me, ma'am," the nurse said, stepping into the doorway. "Are you the one responsible for the payment?"

"He has insurance," I said. "Didn't his father give it to you?"

"No, we rushed him back as soon as he got here."

I dug into my purse for his insurance card and followed her to take care of the payment.

CHAPTER 26

NATE

By the time we got back to Carlisle, the smoke in the air was clearing. "I think the fires are out," I said. "The controlled burn and fire lines worked."

"How can you tell?"

"There's no new smoke feeding the air. It's not as thick."

"Seems the same to me."

"We'll see." We got back to the shelter as the TV station showed an aerial view of the fire area. Just as I'd said, the fire had been quenched, and the only smoke was from the charred earth.

The crowd cheered, then quieted quickly as the station jumped to a press conference being held in the parking lot where my truck still sat.

My boss, T-Bird, stood at the podium. "As you've probably seen," he said, "the fire has been put out, but that doesn't mean this is over yet. Our team is still working on cleanup, which means that we're making sure all the embers are gone. Most people don't realize that fire can hide underground. Embers can stay alive in the ground for months, even. We're going to be digging through the burn zones to make sure this fire doesn't start back up. We're asking the community to be patient with us for a few more hours. But if all goes well, we'll probably be able to lift the evacuation then."

Another cheer erupted through the building, then a hush fell back over the room as T-Bird went on. "I want to take this opportunity to thank my team, the Rocky Mountain Hotshots, for the great work they do. One of them is Carlisle's own Nate Beckett, who was here recovering from a burn injury sustained in the Steamboat Springs Fire. He saw this fire and called it in. Then he helped us fight it even though he wasn't supposed to be back at work yet. Without him, this fire might have gotten out of control and done serious damage to homes and businesses around the town."

People in the sanctuary started looking around until they found me, and before I knew it, they were applauding me. A crowd quickly formed around me, and people I knew and some I didn't hugged me and thanked me.

I was near tears when Brenna got me through the crowd and to the pastor's quiet office.

When we finally got a chance to look at each other, she put her arms around me and held me tight. "It's going to be all right," she whispered.

"Yes, it is," I said as I held her.

A couple of hours later, the evacuation was lifted and we were able to go home. I waited with Brenna until the last of the shelter-seekers had left the building, then I helped the church members clean up.

When I finally got back to Drew's house, I showered and doctored my wounds. Blood had oozed through my bandages, and it was painful peeling them off. I put ointment on and took my antibiotics, hoping it would help them heal. But I wasn't sure the bleeding didn't require some new kind of intervention.

I hoped that Brenna was napping, so I didn't go to her house right away. Drew was already at the bar, which he opened early to accommodate the extra business he was anticipating due to the day's stress. It baffled me that people would go to Flannigan's rather than home, but I supposed

Drew knew what he was talking about.

I called my parents to see if they'd gotten home all right, and asked Pop if he would come and take me to get my truck. I wondered if he'd seen the press conference on the news. If he had, he didn't mention it.

He looked tired as I got into his truck. "Well, I'm glad they got the fire out," he said.

"You knew they would."

"It doesn't always go like that." He was silent for a moment, then said, "I heard a rumor that you started it."

"Yep, I heard that too."

"Makes a man feel good to hear a thing like that."

"I know the feeling," I said.

He dropped me off at the Simon Plateau parking lot and waited as I got permission to take my truck. The fact that they turned it over to me told me that maybe they believed my story now that T-Bird had vouched for me. Relief hit me like an energy drink.

I didn't hang around, since I wasn't yet out of trouble. Instead, I looked up Pete Sanders, the private investigator who was my arson suspect. Had he really set me up on purpose? If so, why? What could he possibly have to gain?

I looked up his office address and drove there, curious. When I reached his street, I saw a cluster of police cars, and the building was barricaded. A couple of press vans had parked behind the cruisers.

I got out of my truck and walked up to the tape. I scanned the area until I saw a cop I knew. I'd gone to school with Frank Stoddard, so I walked along the edge of the tape toward him.

"Frank! How're you doing, buddy?"

He laughed when he saw me and came to shake my hand. "There's the big hero. I heard what that guy said about you on the news."

"Yeah, thanks. Maybe it'll make people stop thinking of me as an arsonist."

"Give it time, man."

I glanced toward the office, where they were bringing out evidence in paper bags and loading it into a car. "What's going on here?"

He stepped closer so the press wouldn't hear. "The guy's been arrested. They found empty gas cans in the trunk of his car."

That was good, I thought. Evidence of arson.

"They also have video."

"The one I gave them?"

"No. Turns out there are cameras in the

parking lot at Simon Plateau. We got the footage and they were watching for you to see if you took any explosives with you when you hiked. Instead, they saw him at his trunk, loading the gas cans into a hiking pack. Then he took off up the hill."

I frowned and shook my head. "So he was setting me up. But why? I don't even know him."

"We haven't got a motive yet. He's lawyered up, so it might be a while."

He headed back to the house, but then he turned and came back. "Hey, Nate. One other thing might interest you."

"Yeah?"

"I'm not supposed to pass this along, so please keep this to yourself, but you should know that they found something else in this guy's office. Pictures of Pastor Strickland dead in his car."

"What?" I almost couldn't breathe. "Are you kidding me? How? Was he there?"

"Looks like it. And he had a .44 Magnum. They're running ballistics. It could be the missing murder weapon."

My mouth fell open. "My dad spent fourteen years in prison for that. He still swears he didn't do it. He didn't even own a .44 Magnum."

"I know. But if this pans out, at least his

name can be completely cleared."

I said a prayer as I walked back to the truck. But deep in my heart, I knew that God was already working.

BRENNA

After I'd showered, I ran to the store to pick up a few things, then I drove by Jack's house to see if his car was there. It wasn't. The air wasn't quite clean enough for Noah yet, so I hoped they were still in Denver. The fact that I couldn't make sure myself stabbed me like a knife.

The court date was still on since the fire was out. What was I going to do if it didn't come out in my favor? William Hertzog almost always got what he wanted.

Except for that one time . . .

It was so long ago that I had trouble remembering the circumstances, but William had been indicted for his company's waste disposal violations. He hadn't served any jail time, but he had been forced to pay millions in fines.

If that could happen, then not everyone in town was in his pocket. A lot of people were. I prayed that the judge wasn't one of those people. But I had a sick feeling.

Despair turned into a craving, then a need that worked on my brain, until I wondered if there was a bar nearby or an all-night liquor store. I found myself scanning the streets as I drove down the highway, looking for a neon sign . . .

And then I spotted one.

I turned off the interstate and found the frontage road that led to the bar.

Several cars were already in the parking lot even though the evacuation had lifted only an hour or so ago. I sat in my car for a moment.

I turned off the engine and reached for the handle on my car door, but something stopped me.

Trembling at the struggle within myself, I sat still for a moment, a moment in which most of my life passed before my eyes. History and tragedy, love and hate, disappointment and heartbreak, misery and despair.

But along with it came a different picture. The prayers of my friends. The love Nate had brought me. The smiles on my children's innocent faces.

They deserved more than a drunk. All of them, but most of all my children, deserved a clear head and self-control, no matter how bad things got.

I took a deep breath and restarted the car. I wasn't going to drink again, I told myself firmly. I could stop because when I was weak, God was strong. I would lean on him.

I felt as I supposed Noah must have felt as his bronchial passages had cleared. I would breathe all the way home, I thought, and I would breathe through the night. And Tuesday I would breathe throughout court.

And no matter what the outcome, I would be breathing when I left the courthouse. If I could just concentrate on that — on breathing — I would be all right. Because the other things were just too big to think about. They were God-size. And I was too small to conquer them alone.

I got on my phone and did a quick search of AA meetings in my area. There was one at St. Phillip's Episcopal Church in twenty minutes. I started the car and headed to the meeting.

Chapter 27

NATE

By Monday, the suspicions against me had been dropped, and Pete Sanders was in jail. I'd had my burns checked, and the doctor added a couple more weeks to my recovery because of the damage I'd done. I was frustrated about being away from my team, but there was a measure of relief that I could be here longer for Brenna.

Brenna was anxious because her custody hearing was tomorrow, so I took her to lunch at a little deli near her store.

"I'm never going to make it through this." She picked up a french fry, but she didn't bite it. Her lunch hour was almost over, and she'd hardly eaten a thing.

"Yes, you will. You're strong. Look what you've already been through."

She stared at the table. "When Dad died, and I lost you . . . I almost didn't survive it. But this is worse."

She was almost despondent. Court was tomorrow, and she was so nervous she hadn't slept, despite her exhaustion. I wished she could take the afternoon off and relax.

But that was impossible. No mother could relax the day before a judge decided whether she could have her children.

My phone rang, and I looked down at it. "My mother. I'm sorry."

"Take it," she said.

I swiped it on. "Hey, Mama."

"Nate!" Mama was crying. "You're not going to believe what happened. It's a miracle!"

I came to my feet. "What is it? Mama, tell me."

"They charged that man, the one who started the fire . . . They charged him with murder. Pastor Strickland's murder!"

My jaw fell open, and I looked down at Brenna. She was looking up at me.

"How do you know? Did they call you?"

"No, nobody called. It was on the news just now. Channel 7."

"They *said* that Pop was cleared?"

"Yes! They said the governor was right to pardon him! They found evidence in that private eye's office."

The picture of Strickland dead. It had

panned out. I couldn't believe it. I'd deliberately kept it from my parents in case nothing came of it.

"Oh, there's another call coming in. The police. I have to go."

"Mama, I'll be right over."

When I hung up, Brenna looked confused. "What is it, Nate?"

I was shaking. "My father was telling the truth."

"About . . . ?"

"Killing your father. He didn't do it, Brenna. That PI who started the fire . . . *he* did it."

"What? No! That's ridiculous. It's too much of a coincidence."

"Maybe not."

She looked supremely irritated. "What kind of evidence do they have?"

I knew I had to handle this carefully, so I tried to temper my tone. "He had a picture of your father . . . dead in the car."

Her face drained of color. "What?"

"He wasn't on the witness list. He wouldn't have been at the scene. The police got there pretty fast. They wouldn't have let anyone come near him."

"Well . . . maybe he was driving by and tried to help."

"Then why wouldn't he try to revive him

instead of photographing him? Why wasn't he on the list?"

"Then . . . he must have gotten it from the crime scene photographer. Or from the prosecutor."

"Brenna, he had a .44 Magnum. If they're charging him with murder, then ballistics must have shown that it was a match. The murder weapon."

She stared at me for a long moment, and tears filled her eyes again. "I have to go," she said.

"Brenna."

She slid her chair back and got up. "I'll . . . I'll talk to you later."

"Brenna, don't be upset."

"I'm not." She looked back at me, wiping her tears. "I just . . . I don't know what I am."

"Call someone at the police department. Maybe they can shed more light."

"They're not going to publish that picture, are they?"

"No," I said, taking her hands. "No, they wouldn't do that." But I wasn't sure it wouldn't be leaked or be used in court.

"My mom . . . my sister. They can't hear this on the news. Why didn't they call us?"

"They didn't call my parents either. The media must have gotten hold of it somehow before they could — although I think they were trying to call my mother when I hung up. Maybe they called your family too."

"I have to go," she said again. Then she hurried out of the café.

Drew's car was in my parents' driveway when I pulled in. When I got to the door, I could hear laughter inside. Bob Seger was playing — my dad's old favorite — and he was dancing around the living room. I'd never seen him do anything like that.

I stepped inside, grinning, and he spun around. "I told you!" he shouted, laughing. "I told you!"

"You sure did, Pop. Congratulations!"

"Is that what you say when your old man is cleared of murder? Not best wishes? Extreme blessings? Happy acquittal?"

"How about, thank God?"

He laughed out loud again, and Mama came running in. "Yes, thank God! That's it!"

We all circled and danced like children until my parents wore out.

Later, Pop and I went outside on the back porch, and we sat on the creaky swing. "It's something, huh?" he said. "Crazy. All those years."

"I owe you an apology," I said. "I should

have believed you."

"Yeah, you should have."

"It must have been horrible for you. But you're strong. You hung in there. Now you have a future."

"When I was locked up, your mama made me memorize that verse from the Bible. 'For I know the plans I have for you . . .' "

I grinned. " 'Plans to prosper you and not to harm you.' "

He picked up where I'd left off. " 'Plans to give you hope and a future.' "

"Jeremiah 29:11."

"I said it every day of those fourteen years. Hung on to it. Didn't believe it half the time, but I still repeated it over and over. What do you know? It turns out to be true."

"It would be true even if this hadn't happened. But sometimes things just fall into place."

"Sometimes they do."

"I hope you can forgive me, Pop," I said. "A lot of what we do in life is done out of ignorance."

He stared at the yard for a long moment. I wondered if he was thinking again about all those visitation days when I didn't come. All those days I didn't even try.

But I stayed quiet, not sure whether his silence was forgiveness or condemnation.

And I tried not to hold his failure to believe in my own innocence in burning down the church against him. He would never have definitive evidence that I was telling the truth, because I wasn't going to rat out Angus. And his mother would never tell.

Finally, after an awkward few minutes, I changed the subject. "What I'm wondering is, why did that guy take a picture of Strickland? What was that about?"

"He's crazy. That's why. Psychopath. Killing the preacher, of all things."

"But there's something more. I wonder if there was someone behind it. Somebody else who wanted to kill the pastor."

"And frame me."

"Yeah, why us? Same guy frames you, then me. I don't get it. He didn't have anything against you, did he?"

"Not that I know of. But I offended a lot of people in my drinking days."

"Still. Not enough to make someone want to send you to prison for life."

"No, not that. You'd think I'd remember something like that. Or somebody else would. They would have told me."

When we went back into the house, my phone rang, and I stepped outside to answer it. I didn't recognize the number. "Hello?"

"Nate, Bo here. How are you, man?"

Brenna's pastor. "Great. How are you, Pastor?"

"Better than I deserve. Listen, I heard the news about your dad and that arson guy killing Brenna's dad. I just wanted to tell you I'm happy your dad was cleared. Your family deserves it."

I had never had a phone call like this. Something in my heart squeezed, and I drew in a deep breath and wiped my jaw. "Thank you, Pastor. I appreciate that . . . more than you know."

"I'm sincerely sorry for all the grief you've suffered. And I apologize for any of our church members who gave you grief."

"You gotta love humans," I said.

"That's it. They're human."

"They had convincing evidence."

"Anecdotal evidence."

"Right. But I can't really blame them." The call was getting awkward, so I changed the subject. "Listen, I'd appreciate it if you'd pray for Brenna and her family. This is hard for them. They thought they knew what happened all these years, and now to have it all dismantled . . ."

"Yeah, of course. I was going to call her next."

"Another thing she may not tell you. Her

custody court date is tomorrow. She's a wreck."

He was silent for a few seconds. "Hey, what if we put together a little prayer meeting at her house tonight? I could get a few people together."

I breathed a laugh. "Yeah, that would be great. Maybe it would give her some peace. She's convinced she's going to lose."

"Okay, let me make some calls. We'll see you guys at seven. No food, despite what you've heard about our church. Nobody's coming for cheesecake and meatballs. Just prayer."

"Thank you, Pastor."

"Call me Bo. I'm not that comfortable with titles."

"All right, Bo. I'll see you tonight."

Chapter 28

Brenna

I got through the day one minute at a time, though I went through half a dozen boxes of tissues mopping up the tears that assaulted me off and on all day.

My mother and sister had taken the news with a numb kind of stoicism, not crying as I had. Instead, they just stared into space, torturing themselves into imagining again how it had all happened. Nothing made sense. As far as any of us knew, my father didn't even know Pete Sanders.

The rest of the workday was brutal, with Georgi walking around like a zombie and people coming in and out all day, checking on us. We should have closed for the day.

I took a different route home from work, trying to avoid the ever-beckoning liquor store. But when I saw one on the new route home, I pulled into the parking lot. My phone chirped, and I saw a text from Nate.

My pastor was setting up a prayer meeting for me tonight.

I looked at the liquor store and swallowed hard. I couldn't drink now. There was no way I was facing church members drunk. I started my car and pulled back onto the busy street, trying to put as much distance as I could between me and the store. After a few miles, I pulled over again and searched on my phone for more AA meetings in my area. There was one starting soon at a church not far away. I would still have time to go and get home before the pastor and my church friends showed up.

Maybe between the AA meeting and the prayer meeting, I would manage to survive the night.

NATE

The house filled up with longtime members who had worshiped under Pastor Strickland as well as new members who'd been drawn to the church by Bo's programs. Some I recognized from long ago, people who'd looked down on me and accused me, people who'd expected the worst of me. It was starting to look like a lions' den, where the past waited to devour me.

As the prayers began, there was tension in the room. Too many hard feelings, I thought.

Too much blame. Too much unforgiveness.

I was just about to make my excuses and leave for the sake of everyone involved when Bo zeroed right in on the problem. After asking God to forgive us all for our biases, prejudices, and bitterness, he went on to pray earnestly for Brenna.

Then, crowded into the living room and spilling over into the kitchen, they prayed one by one as they felt led. In those prayers, I heard earnest pleas that Brenna's children would be returned to her, that the judge would have discernment, that Jack would love his kids enough to do what was best for them. In my own heart, I pled for forgiveness for my attitude toward him.

By the end of the night, I had a profound sense of hope and acceptance mightier than any I'd ever felt.

And Brenna had a peace I hadn't seen in her since she was sixteen. I only hoped she'd still have it after court tomorrow.

When the last person left and only I remained, Brenna smiled, probably for the first time that day. "I feel better."

I sat down on the couch and reached for her. "Come here."

She turned and I framed her face with my hands. "Tonight was cathartic," I said softly, stroking her skin, washed fresh with her tears. "I learned so many things."

"What did you learn?" she asked.

"I learned that the town of Carlisle has a lot more good than bad in it," I said. "I learned that it's a good place to have a crisis. That good people here will help you through it. I learned that not everyone thinks the worst of me. And I learned about faith — the kind of faith that makes people turn out because they believe that praying together will have results."

"I hope so," she whispered.

"I know it will." My eyes misted over as I gazed at her, a million words swirling through my heart and hanging on the tip of my tongue. "I learned something else, too."

"What, Nate?"

"I learned that when you're in love with someone, it doesn't die. Not even after fourteen years. And it's just as strong a decade later as it was the first time."

Her eyes glistened. "Say it," she whispered. "I need to hear it."

"I love you, Brenna," I said. "I've always loved you. I always will love you."

She breathed a sob and slid her arms around my neck. "I love you too," she whispered against my lips. "I'm so glad you came back. You revived me."

CHAPTER 29

BRENNA

Both Rayne and Jack looked in top form in court Tuesday morning. Rayne was dressed like a librarian, with her hair pulled back in a bun, and Jack played the suffering dad, wearing a lapel pin with his children's pictures on it. Behind them, William Hertzog sat like a doting grandfather.

In my simple navy skirt and blazer, I hoped the bags under my eyes weren't too apparent. I hadn't slept all night. I'd hoped to see the children this morning, but they'd kept them from me. I was told they were in the courthouse somewhere, waiting for the judge to call them.

I hoped Noah was breathing all right. And I hoped Sophia wasn't too upset.

Jack's attorney presented his case first. He began by showing records of my income level and records of Jack's. He supplied records of the hours the children were in day care, then pointed out that Rayne was at home all the time. Then he pulled out the big guns and told of personally seeing me drunk in public recently. They played the torturous video and showed a slideshow of me going in and out of liquor stores.

Jack must have had me followed to get any dirt he could dig up on me.

Then he showed photos of me with Nate and newspaper clippings from years earlier when Nate had been the presumed arsonist who burned down the church and fled from the law.

But the coup de grace was the video of me ranting and raving as Jack's father ransacked the children's drawers. Having laid all that out, Jack's attorney sat and the judge turned it over to my attorney.

"Your Honor, I have two witnesses I'd like to call," Bradley said. "First, Ms. Hertzog's pastor, Bo Levin."

The pastor was sent for, and he came into the room and took his seat at the big table.

"Pastor, could you please tell us how long you've known Ms. Hertzog?"

"About seven years. Since I started serving at my church."

"And in that time, what has been your impression of Brenna?"

"She's a fine woman. She's had a lot of

tragedy in her life, and she's borne up very well. I have a good deal of respect for her."

"And what would you say has been her general mental state in the past few weeks?"

"Well, she's been very depressed. Anyone would be, if their spouse left them for someone else."

I tried not to smile as Jack's attorney made an argument that none of this was relevant to the case.

"This custody battle has been very disturbing to me as well," Bo went on when the judge told him to proceed. "She's been very worried about her children."

"What kind of mother would you say she is?"

"From what I've seen, and I've seen a lot, she's an excellent mother. I wish more mothers could be like her."

"Have you ever known her to be promiscuous in any way?"

The question made my pastor angry, and he shook his head adamantly. "Absolutely not."

Jack's attorney declined to ask him any questions, and I gave him a grateful smile as he got up and left the room. I knew that he, as well as others, would be outside praying for me as they waited to hear the outcome.

"I'd like to call Nate Beckett, Your Honor."

Nate, who'd been waiting in a room somewhere in the courthouse, was brought in. He was dressed in a dark suit and a light blue shirt, with a conservative tie. The shirt brought out the blue in his eyes, and my heart melted. It was amazing how calming Nate's presence was, I thought. Just having him here made me feel that things would be all right.

"Mr. Beckett," Bradley began, "how long have you known Ms. Hertzog?"

"About twenty years, I guess. We went to school together."

"Tell us what you do for a living, Mr. Beckett."

"I'm a smokejumper. I belong to a special team of firefighters — the Rocky Mountain Hotshots."

The judge looked impressed and wrote something down. Bradley looked down at Nate's hands. "I notice your hand is bandaged, Mr. Beckett. Tell us what happened."

Nate considered his injuries. "Well, I was fighting the Steamboat Springs Fire, and I incurred some burn injuries."

The judge's eyebrows shot up.

Bradley went on. "Isn't that the fire that almost killed Senator John Livingston and his family?"

"That's the one."

"It's very fortunate he got out. Tell me, did you have any part in his rescue?"

"Yes," Nate said. "That's how I sustained my injuries."

Bradley picked up a piece of paper and handed it to him. "Could you tell me what this is, Mr. Beckett?"

Nate looked down at it. "It's a formal invitation from the president of the United States requesting that I fly to Washington for a dinner and a ceremony."

"And what is this ceremony for, Mr. Beckett?"

Nate shifted uncomfortably in his chair. "Well, it's about the rescue of the senator."

Bradley took the letter and handed it to the judge, and I glanced at Jack. He was beginning to sweat, but his eyes were riveted on the letter.

"Your Honor, as you can see, this letter is commending Nate Beckett for his heroic actions in saving not only the town of Steamboat Springs but Senator Livingston, his wife, and their children. Mr. Beckett has been invited to fly to Washington to be honored at the White House as an American hero."

The judge's brows furrowed as he read

the letter carefully. "Congratulations, Mr. Beckett. That's quite an honor."

"Thank you, sir."

"A few more questions," Bradley went on. "Mr. Beckett, have you ever spent the night with Ms. Hertzog, with or without her children present?"

"No. Never."

"Thank you. I have no more questions for this witness."

Brenna's attorney sat down, and Gerald Stocker popped up. "Mr. Beckett, have you ever seen Ms. Hertzog drunk?"

Nate hesitated, and my stomach tightened. "Define drunk," he said.

"Have you ever seen her drink?"

"Yes," Nate said. "But I've seen you drink too. In the same restaurant, as a matter of fact."

Stocker bristled. "Have you ever seen her drink too much?"

"How much is too much?"

"Enough to inebriate her."

"I really couldn't say," Nate hedged. "That's all relative, isn't it?"

"How many drinks have you seen her put away in one sitting?"

Again Nate hedged. "This may come as a surprise to you, but I don't normally count how many drinks other people have."

The attorney sighed. "Why don't I just refresh your memory, Mr. Beckett?" He started the video of me drunk in the restaurant. I couldn't watch as it played on the screen in the room.

I looked at the judge. He was frowning again. They had him.

"Tell us about her behavior," Stocker said. "Have you seen any changes in her behavior lately, particularly after she was drinking?"

"She's been very upset lately," Nate said, his voice dropping in timbre. "She's had a lot taken from her. Her husband decided he wanted to trade her in for a younger woman, and now she may wind up losing her kids. She's been sick with worry over what this custody battle is doing to her children, and I'm personally amazed that she's gotten through this as well as she has. A lesser person might have thrown in the towel entirely, and now that I think about it, that might just be what her ex-husband has been hoping she'd do."

Red-faced, Jack gestured to his attorney, and frustrated, Stocker tried again. "Your Honor, do we have to listen to this?"

"No. Don't editorialize, Mr. Beckett."

I glanced at Jack. He wasn't sitting as tall now as he had before, and behind him, his father seemed increasingly agitated.

"Mr. Beckett," Stocker continued. "When did you move away from Carlisle?"

"About twelve years ago," he said.

"What prompted that move?"

"I turned eighteen, and I wanted to be on my own."

"Was there any event in town that prompted your abrupt departure?"

He hesitated. "My father had been accused of killing a man."

"Brenna's father?"

"Yes. The town had a lot of ill will toward my family."

"Did you have anything to do with the Baptist church burning down? Pastor Strickland's church?"

"No, I did not."

"Did the police question you about that?"

"No."

He pulled a newspaper clipping out of his stack. "Did you see this article that came out in the *Carlisle Sun*?"

Nate took the article. "Yes, I think I did."

"Someone quoted in this article suggested that you burned down the church. Isn't that right?"

"I was never a suspect," Nate said. "I told you, I wasn't even questioned."

"How long did you wait to be questioned?"

"What do you mean?"

"I mean, you left town right after the fire. How long was it before you took off?"

"I left the next day, after that article came out."

"Did you say goodbye to your friends?"

"Eventually, on the phone. They knew where I was. And the police could have gotten my contact information if they'd wanted to question me. I could have come back pretty quickly."

"In other words, you left town right after the fire that people suggested you started, to get even for your father's conviction."

Bradley jumped up. "Your Honor, I object to the editorializing from the plaintiff's attorney."

"I agree, Mr. Stocker. The facts, please. You can't get a conviction out of rumors in a newspaper."

Stocker tried again. "You left town right after the fire, didn't you?"

"Yes, but I didn't need to get even. I thought my father did it until last week."

Stocker turned to the judge. "No more questions, Your Honor."

Nate gave me an encouraging look as he left the room, then Bradley stood up again. "Your Honor, I have some recordings I'd like to play for you now. Recordings that, I think, will give you a very clear picture of what my client has been going through and how her children have been suffering as well."

Everyone in the room stiffened as the recordings began to play — four of Sophia's calls to me, and the one I took with William, Jack, and Noah in the hospital.

Finally all was silent, and every eye in the room was on the judge as he thought about all he'd heard. I feared he could hear my heart beating as I waited.

"These matters are very difficult to decide," he said at last, "because I have to be certain that what I'm hearing is the truth. These cases often bring out Oscar-caliber performances in both parties, and it's very difficult to discern who's credible and who's not. Since I have some prior knowledge of each of you, I think I have a clear picture, but one can never know for sure. For this reason, I want to speak to the children in my chambers."

"Your Honor," Stocker said, "my client doesn't want his children traumatized. They're both very young, and being alone in a room with you might frighten them."

The judge frowned at him, then looked at Brenna. "How do you feel about my talking to them, Ms. Hertzog?"

339

I took a deep breath. "I don't think you'll frighten them. Jack just doesn't want you to ask them who they'd like to live with, because he knows what they'll say."

"Oh, for crying out loud," William snapped. "He's worried about his children. She'd throw them to the wolves if she thought it would get her what she wanted."

"William, please." Judge Radison stood up. "I'll be very gentle with them, but I do have to speak to them. After that, I'll make my decision. Court is in recess for thirty minutes."

He left the room, and for a moment after the door closed behind him, everyone sat still and silent.

"Nice try," William said finally. "Recording the whole hospital visit. No wonder you pretended to be so concerned."

"You're not the only one with a smart-phone," I said.

I went to find Nate. We paced in the echo-ing hallway outside the courtroom, waiting and praying. A few yards down, Jack and William paced in front of another bench. Rayne sat on the bench, swiping through her cell phone.

It seemed like an eternity. As I waited, I tried to imagine what questions the judge might ask them.

Has your mother ever been drunk around you?

Does she hurt you?

Does she leave you alone?

My children would be so shocked to hear any of those questions that they might just melt into tears. And if they did, the judge might misinterpret it. *Please, God.*

Suddenly the judge burst out of a door down the hall, holding Noah in his arms. I got to my feet as he hurried toward us. Sophia trailed behind him.

"His inhaler!" he said to Jack. "He's having an asthma attack."

Jack turned to Rayne. "Did you bring it?"

She looked down at her tiny purse. "No, it didn't fit."

"You don't have it?" the judge asked, his voice echoing off the walls.

"I have one!" I cried. "Here, I always carry one." I took it out and he let me take my son. Noah wheezed again the way he had in the hospital, like a seal barking in the ocean. I shook the inhaler, then put it to his lips. "Big breath. Come on."

He cooperated right away, breathing in as I sprayed it. "Again," I said. "Big breath." I sprayed again, and he sucked it into his lungs. I felt his little heartbeat speeding up as his bronchial tubes opened and his breathing calmed. He wrapped his arms around my neck and nuzzled in.

"I was scared, Mommy."

"Scared of what, honey?" I whispered.

"Scared he was going to make me stay with Daddy."

The judge looked rattled as he watched. When he was sure that Noah's emergency had passed, he said, "Let's go back in."

I looked at Sophia and saw the tears on her face. I reached for her, and she hugged me too. "I missed you," she whispered. "Don't let him make us stay."

I couldn't promise her anything. Tears muddled down my face as we walked in. Nate came in behind us. He took a seat a couple of rows behind me.

Judge Radison went back behind his desk, not looking at either of us. He took off his glasses, laid them on the table, then rubbed his eyes. "I just met with those precious children of yours," he said, glancing first at me, then at Jack. "They were very sweet and very articulate, and they clarified a lot for me."

I glanced back at Nate.

"I almost removed myself from this case," the judge said, clasping his hands in front of his face and resting his chin on them. "I was a member of Brenna's father's congregation, as you all know, and I remember Brenna as a child — she looked very much like Sophia. And, Jack, I think I know you very well too. I've known your father for years. The problem, however, is that you know *all* the judges in this county. So I felt comfortable going ahead with this case."

He shoved his glasses back on, then shuffled the papers on his desk. "As I was talking to the children, several things occurred to me. I wondered what your ideas were for raising these children when you first had them. In other words, since you're asking for custody because of her work schedule, among other things, was Brenna a stay-at-home mother while you were married because you both agreed that was best for the children, or was it because she didn't want to work? Well, I thought this over, and I think it's safe to conclude that, since the new Mrs. Hertzog does not work either, perhaps this was as much a decision of Jack's as it was of Brenna's. When you chose to divorce Brenna, however," he said, looking at Jack, "you changed the equation. Brenna had to support herself and her children. Regardless of the ideals she'd had earlier, regardless of the commitments you'd made together, she had to go to work, and she had to put them in child care. Now, it's your contention she should be penalized for that, as though she made a choice to neglect her children. You, on the other hand, contend that your new wife, who is a stay-at-home wife, is more equipped to take care of your children.

"But I'm a little confused. You see, the children haven't spent one weekend with their mother in months. Yet I see you at the golf course, Jack, every single Saturday." Jack bristled and started to speak, but his lawyer stopped him.

"That tells me that these children don't get the benefit of either parent on weekends. And that concerns me."

I held my breath as Judge Radison went on. "However, the allegations of Brenna's alcohol abuse make this case even more complex. Certainly she has been under a great deal of stress. But as a single parent, she's likely to find that stress is a way of life. Is it going to be a pattern for her to turn to alcohol to cope?"

I tried not to fall apart in front of my children.

"She says she isn't going to drink again, ever. And I have no guarantee of that. But she's never had a DUI, never had any legal problems. Despite those embarrassing videos, I have no evidence that she's hurt or neglected her children, or even put them in harm's way. And I have to say, Jack, that when I brought Noah out to you, I was heavily leaning toward leaving their custody with you. But you didn't have his inhaler. That's a matter of life and death for an asthmatic. How could you not have it?"

"Your Honor," Jack said. "We were really stressed when we came here today, and we were getting the kids ready and trying to get out the door."

"Brenna had it. She carries it all the time. There's still smoke in the air, Jack. That concerns me a lot about you."

Jack got quiet. "But it's just one time. One mistake."

"I don't think it's one time. According to Brenna's testimony, it's an ongoing problem. I don't like it."

I didn't dare breathe . . . or move . . . or hope. But I prayed between every phrase.

"A parent with a child who has health needs" — *please, God* — "should have that child's needs foremost" — *help him choose* — "in their mind."

In my peripheral vision I could see Jack sitting more stiffly and William leaning forward as if about to jump out of his seat to intervene.

"I'm giving custody to Brenna, and, Jack,

you can have them on alternate weekends, two weeks in the summer, and on alternating holidays."

I sucked in a breath, not sure I had heard it right.

Sophia wiggled gleefully, but Noah looked at me, confused. "What, Mommy? What?"

"You're going home with me," I whispered, hugging him as blood rushed to my face, almost making me dizzy, and tears overflowed. Behind me, Nate touched my back.

"No!" William said, springing up. "Judge, you're making a mistake."

The judge hit his gavel and got up to leave.

"John, don't walk away! This is wrong. She's a drunk! I showed you!"

Jack spun around. "Dad, stop."

"I'm not going to stop. These are your kids!"

"I said stop! The children shouldn't hear this."

"This is outrageous!" William shouted as the judge left and closed the door. "I'll spend the rest of my life getting even for this! I won't stand for it!"

The bailiff walked toward him. "Are you threatening the judge?"

We all froze, waiting.

"I don't mean him. I mean . . ."

"Her?" Nate asked, baiting him.

"I'm not going to be defeated by that family again. I will spend the rest of my life making sure she doesn't keep those kids."

"Mommy!" Sophia cried.

Jack spoke through his teeth. "I'm telling you to stop! Now! Don't say another word!"

"We will appeal!" William shouted. "It's not over!"

"Get out!" Jack shouted. "I don't want you here."

Rayne protested, "Jack, don't!"

"Now!" Jack said. "Get out or I'll let them take you out."

The bailiffs came closer, and finally William bolted.

When he was sure his father was gone, Jack came toward the kids, and Noah recoiled.

"It's okay, buddy," he said. "I'm not taking you. I just want a hug goodbye. I'll get your stuff home and see you in a couple of weeks, okay?"

Noah nodded and reluctantly gave him a hug. Sophia reached up readily. "Thank you, Daddy."

I looked at Jack, and my heart broke for him. I had never seen him cry before, but now tears rimmed his eyes. And I couldn't help grieving for my children, who had lost something anyway. The days of having their father and mother together were over. It couldn't be easy for them. I would never make them choose again.

Behind Jack, Rayne looked disappointed, but I didn't think it was over the kids. More likely it was because their source of money had just walked out the door. I didn't kid myself. He would be back. And I knew that in her young heart she couldn't be happier — now someone else's children wouldn't be tying her down.

I hugged Bradley and thanked him, and Nate shook his hand. Then we walked out with our heads held high, taking my children home.

CHAPTER 30

NATE

I could have done cartwheels even with my burns as I rode home with Brenna and the children. Once we got there, I didn't want to intrude on their time together, so I went back to Drew's for the afternoon. Brenna's mother and sister were going to Jack's to get the kids' things, and they'd be coming to Brenna's later to welcome Noah and Sophia home. I would see her when things calmed down.

I lay on my bed, basking in the relaxation without the burden of so many problems weighing down on me. Pop was free of his murderous reputation. Brenna was free of the threat of losing her children.

But something nagged at me. What was it that William Hertzog had said before he was escorted out? Something about not letting her family defeat him again.

I heard Drew come in, and I got up and

met him in the kitchen. I'd already told him over the phone how things had turned out, and he was adequately pumped.

"Hey, let me ask you something," I said as we sat on the couch and turned on a Dolphins game. "How well do you know William Hertzog?"

Drew shrugged. "He's a pretty regular customer. Kind of a jerk. Worse when he drinks."

"Today he said something about how he wouldn't let Brenna's family defeat him again. Do you remember any time in the past when they did? I can't think of anything."

"Not that I know of. But I can ask around tonight. Have you asked her?"

"I mean, she heard it. She didn't mention it. There was a lot going on, with the kids and the asthma and the judge. I'm not sure it even registered with her. I didn't want to ask in front of the kids afterward."

"If she doesn't know, her mother probably does."

"Yeah," I said. "But I think I'm going to give her mom a wide berth for a while. I'm not sure she's changed her thinking about our family yet."

But later that afternoon, Brenna called. "Can you come over?" she asked.

I had looked out and seen her sister's car there a few minutes earlier. "Don't you have company?"

"Yeah, my mom and my sister. But they want to talk to you."

"Hmm. Sounds ominous."

"Just come when you can, okay?"

"I'll be there in a few minutes." I hung up and looked at Drew.

"Now's your chance, bro," he said.

I sighed heavily. "I thought all the drama was over for the day." I went back to the bathroom and brushed my teeth and hair, just to make a good impression. Then I crossed the street.

When I stepped into her house, her mother stood up from the dining room table. Georgi was already sitting on the kitchen counter. I greeted them carefully, staying at arm's length.

"I wanted to talk to you," Mrs. Strickland said. "Will you sit down?"

"Sure." I pulled out a chair and sat down. Brenna sat next to me. I could hear the children talking to each other in the bedroom.

"I wanted to thank you for being there for Brenna. You've helped her a lot."

I smiled. "I appreciate that."

"And I owe you an apology. I haven't been

very open to you being back in her life."

I cleared my throat. "That's okay. There's been a lot of water under the bridge."

"Well, it turns out that there isn't any water. There isn't even a bridge. When I first heard about Pete Sanders being the one who shot my husband, I couldn't process it. I've been dead sure it was your father all these years. Never a doubt in my mind."

"I get it," I said. "I felt that way myself, pretty much."

Georgi just sat there, stone-cold, staring at me, as her mother went on. I got the feeling she didn't feel the same way.

"It's taken me some time and a few conversations with the police to understand that it's true. Your father didn't do it. And I can't help wondering how much of everything that's happened since was impacted by that assumption. The way I've thought about you, your family . . ."

Georgi slid off the counter and sauntered toward the table. "What she's saying, Nate, is that we don't think you burned down the church anymore. It may have been Pete Sanders, trying again to frame you."

I didn't answer. I just looked down at a spot on the table.

"All we know is that it wasn't you."

I looked up at her. "I appreciate that."

"You got her to stop drinking," Georgi said.

"I didn't do that," I said. "She did that herself. She was trying to cope. She found other ways."

"He did," Brenna said. "He was a big help. I may not have gotten here without him "

Georgi tried again. "What we're trying to say, Nate, is that you're welcome in our lives. You're good for Brenna. We want her to be happy."

"I want that too," I said, taking Brenna's hand.

Sophia ran in wearing a My Little Pony costume over her clothes. "Mommy, can you zip me?"

"Sure, baby. Come here." Brenna zipped her and straightened the costume, then gave her a kiss.

Noah came out carrying cowboy chaps and wearing a cowboy hat three sizes too big. "Me too!"

Laughter broke up the somber moment, and we all got up and focused on the children.

After a while, when I found myself in the kitchen alone with Mrs. Strickland, I asked her what I needed to know. "Today after court, William Hertzog said he wasn't going to let your family defeat him again. Do you know what he meant by that?"

She stared at me for a moment. "Brenna didn't tell me that."

"She may not have even caught it. But I did. Do you know what he was talking about?"

She sighed. "I think so. It was back when my husband was still here."

"Did they have a run-in or something?"

"No," she said. "I don't think they ever had cross words. But some of our church members worked for Hertzog Industries. After a sermon Richard preached about standing up for what's right, even if it puts you at risk, a group of them came to him privately and told him about some practices at HI that were illegal. It was about waste disposal or something."

"Did he go to the authorities?"

"No, he didn't. But after talking to him, they all decided to become whistleblowers. They went to the district attorney, who impaneled a grand jury. William was indicted."

"Yeah, I heard about that."

"William may have blamed Richard for what happened. There was an article that filled the whole front page of the religion section. 'Local Preacher Takes Down Billionaire.' "

"You're kidding."

"Not at all. It told how Richard's sermon convicted his members so much that they turned on their employer. Now, we knew that God convicted them, not Richard. But it was out there."

"Did he ever threaten you or try to do anything?"

"He may have wanted to. But Richard was killed a year later."

When a shadow of grief fell over her face, I let the conversation end, but something about the timing haunted me. A year later? Could that just be a coincidence? Or did Hertzog have anything to do with Pete Sanders murdering Strickland?

I let it go for the night and didn't mention it to Brenna. She deserved to have a joyful night with her kids. I wouldn't take that away from her for the world.

CHAPTER 31

NATE

The next day, I showed up at the police station at eight sharp and asked to see my friend Frank, who'd told me of the evidence they'd found against Sanders.

"I wanted to ask you," I said, "if any thought had been given to the possibility that Pete Sanders was working for someone else."

"I'm not a detective," he said. "I don't really know a lot that's going on with that case, but I can get the detectives to talk to you. Who do you think it was?"

"I'm not accusing anybody. I don't know. But I think it would be good if they at least investigated William Hertzog."

"Hertzog? Are you kidding?"

"He had something against the preacher. He blamed him for his indictment just a year before Strickland was killed. He wound up with millions of dollars in fines. And according to my dad, William was at the bar the night Strickland was killed."

"So was Pete Sanders. I did hear that."

"No, really? Pop didn't mention him."

"He wasn't sitting at the bar. He was at a table. But he saw the altercation and knew when the preacher drove off."

"So Hertzog could have seen it as the perfect opportunity. Could have sent him after Strickland."

Frank looked at me as the wheels turned in his brain. "Come with me," he said. "Let's talk to the detectives."

I told the detectives on the case what Hertzog had said yesterday and what I'd learned. They said they would follow up. It was all I could do.

I decided to put it out of my mind. I had to get ready to go to Washington. I still had to rent a tux for the dinner. I wasn't even sure who was coming as my guests. Brenna may not want to go — I knew she wouldn't leave the children behind. My mother and Drew were coming, but I still doubted Pop would come.

But despite all I had to do, I couldn't put Hertzog out of my mind. If he'd had Brenna's dad killed, he might be willing to do something drastic to hurt her so that the kids would stay with his son. I couldn't let that happen.

BRENNA

I spent the next day alone with my children, glowing with gratitude. We read and colored and cooked and played and laughed, laughed, and laughed.

Noah fell asleep during his seven-thirty breathing treatment, and I carried him to bed. Then Sophia and I lay on our stomachs on her bed, catching up.

"I told the judge that we loved how you cooked with us and did homework and took care of us, and how you were reading *Charlotte's Web* to us, and I didn't know how it ended. I didn't know why Daddy didn't want us around you at all."

I turned on my side and kissed Sophia's forehead. "You did great. What did Noah say?"

"He said he liked sitting in your lap and having you hold him, and then he said he wanted you, and he started to cry. That made him start wheezing."

I pulled her against me, spooning with her, my chin on the crown of her head. "What did you say were your favorite things to do with Daddy?"

"When he asked us that, I got kinda quiet, because things haven't been that great with

Daddy lately. We're always having to get dressed and go places where we have to sit real still . . . I couldn't think of anything. And then Noah said that his favorite thing to do with Daddy was driving back home to Mommy."

That broke my heart. It was a loss, that adoration of their father. "You know, you do have favorite things with him. Remember how much you like swimming with him? How he dunks and splashes you and puts you on his shoulders?"

She sighed. "We haven't done that in a long time."

"That's because it's September. Remember how you like it when Daddy coaches softball?"

"He probably won't be able to do that this year because of the mayor thing."

"He might. And if he doesn't, there will be other favorite things. You know, your daddy did a real good thing today. He stood up to your grandfather because he does care how you feel. You don't have to be mad at Daddy on my account. I really do want you to have both of us."

"And Rayne?"

I had to think of the right words for Rayne. "Look for good things about her."

"Like . . . ?"

"Like, she hasn't given you a poison apple yet. She hasn't made you clean the fireplace. I mean, those are clear signs of evil step-mothers, and she's not one of them. Right?"

She giggled. "She's not evil. She's just not you."

"Trust me. She doesn't want to be me. But she does like you, and she wants you to like her. Maybe you could help her out a little."

She turned on her back and looked up at me. "Will you sing to me?"

I started to sing a soft lullaby I'd sung to my children since they were babies, and as I did, Sophia's eyes slowly closed.

By the time the song was over, my sweet daughter was sound asleep and tucked into her own bed. As I stood at the door and smiled at my child, a great peace fell over me. God had answered my prayers. He was still listening. He did care.

I turned off the light, then went to check on Noah. He was breathing well, and I knew he'd probably sleep through the night without needing another treatment. But I'd set my alarm to check on him anyway.

I went into the kitchen and cleaned up the supper dishes. When everything was done, I got my phone.

Nate answered on the first ring. "Hello?"

"Hi."

I thought I heard him sigh. "I was sitting here hoping you'd call," he said.

"The kids are asleep now," I said. "We had a wonderful day."

"I'm glad."

"But I miss you," I said. "You want to come over?"

"I'll be there in five minutes." He was here in three, and when I opened the door, he swept me into his arms and kissed me as if he hadn't seen me in weeks.

After a moment, I took his hand and pulled him to the couch. "I wanted you to have time alone with the children," he said, "but I missed you. I've gotten really attached to you lately."

I laughed. "Honestly, I didn't think this day could get any better. But I'm attached to you too. So that works out great." I felt so comfortable gazing into his eyes. "I don't know what I would've done if you hadn't been here for me, Nate. I think I might've died."

"You've had the strength inside you all along. You just needed somebody to remind you it was there."

I smiled back and shook my head. "I still can't believe it's over. The kids are so happy to be home."

"I like seeing you like this." He touched my face with a gentle hand, and his eyes grew serious. "I was thinking about you this afternoon, and the way my mind is locked on you. I can't seem to think about anything else. I'm crazy in love with you."

Tears sprang to my eyes. "I crazy love you, too," I whispered.

He kissed me, and I marveled at how deeply that love pulled me under. I didn't want to come up for air.

But fear crept in, and I pulled back. "You're going to stay around for a while, aren't you? You're not going back to work anytime soon?"

"I've been wanting to talk to you about that."

"What?"

"About the future. About us." He took my hand, laced our fingers, then met my eyes. "I've loved you for so long, Brenna. I know you have a family — maybe all the family you'll ever need. But I would really like to be a part of it."

"Oh, Nate . . ."

"What I'm saying . . . or what I'm asking is . . . Brenna, would you consider marrying me?"

I caught my breath and sat up straight. "Marry you?"

"Wait," he said, stopping me before I could voice the surprise on my face. "Before you answer, let me tell you some things. I've thought a lot about this, about my work and how dangerous it is, and how a woman like you would worry herself sick knowing her husband was off fighting fires that are out of control. And I've realized that, if I had you at home, I wouldn't want to leave anyway. I wouldn't want to take that risk. So I was thinking I could move back here. I could look into working for one of the fire departments in this area — just fight ordinary fires, where I don't have to jump out of airplanes."

"But you love that. How would you fulfill your wild side?"

He grinned. "I've walked on the wild side. I've kind of liked a slower pace these last few days. I want to be your husband, Brenna. I want to help you raise your children and write and be everything that you want. I just want to be with you."

I wanted to shout yes and throw my arms around his neck, and wake up the kids and call my mom and sister . . . "Oh, Nate. It sounds beautiful, but . . ."

His face fell. "But?"

I got up from the couch and turned back to him. "But it's so soon. Part of me wants to say yes right now. But don't you see? I've been using alcohol as a crutch for the past few months, and I don't want to exchange one crutch for another. I don't want to marry you just because I need someone to lean on."

I could see that he didn't know how to feel. "Is that what I am? Someone to lean on?"

"No," I said quickly. "I love you. I mean that. But it would be so easy to lean. I want to know for sure that I'm okay, that I don't need a crutch. I want to be sure that what we have is not a *crisis* love, not just something we both feel out of tragedy and despair. And the children have been through so much. They've had so many adjustments to make in the past few months. They need to get to know you too."

"So it isn't a no?" he whispered.

I smiled. "No, it isn't a no."

"I can deal with a maybe." He stared ahead of him for a moment, clearly thinking. "I know a good way they can get to know me. Bring them to Washington. They'd get a kick out of meeting the president, and we could sightsee, and you could have dinner with me at the White House and be there for the ceremony."

"You really want us to come?"

"More than anything," he said. "It's a big moment, and you're the most precious thing in my life. I want to share it with you."

"All right," I said on the edge of a laugh. "I've never seen the White House up close before."

"So we're going to Washington?"

"I wouldn't miss it," I said.

CHAPTER 32

NATE

I hadn't slept much in a couple of days because I'd spent my nights at Drew's living room window, watching Brenna's house in case the elder Hertzog made a move. He wouldn't want to harm his grandchildren, so I doubted he would have anyone set fire to the house. Besides, his hired gun/arsonist friend was in jail. But the threat against Brenna was still there. And I had no doubt that he had other friends who would do his bidding.

As I watched her house, I searched my computer for newspaper articles about the Hertzog indictment years before. There were quotes from him about the preacher who'd started an avalanche of whistleblowers. He definitely had an ax to grind.

Then I found the article the religion section had done about Brenna's dad and his influence on the people who'd brought

Hertzog down. I tried to imagine it all from Hertzog's point of view . . . reading the article and feeling that this one man had come close to dismantling an entire company.

I found the names of the whistleblowers and wrote them down on a legal pad.

A car drove past, and I leaned forward, waiting to see if it slowed at Brenna's. It was just a neighbor who turned into a driveway and pulled into a garage.

I did a computer search of the newspaper for everything I could find about the whistleblowers. There had been six of them, counting the three leaders who had gone to the DA to initiate the investigation. I didn't get a hit unrelated to the company until I typed in the third name. Haley Summers.

An obituary came up. I frowned and clicked on it.

The woman had died at forty-two of "natural causes," according to the obituary. The mother of three had been healthy right up until she was struck with a fatal illness.

I looked at the date. A few months before Strickland's death . . . months after Hertzog's indictment. Could that be a coincidence?

It was too late at night to call the family to ask about her death. I would call in the morning.

I searched for obituaries for each whistle-blower name and found one other hit.

Joe Holloway had died a year after the indictment. He'd been traveling to his daughter's house in Denver when he hit black ice and slid off the road. He was killed instantly.

No way.

I was beginning to sweat. I saw headlights again and closed my computer. I stood as the car approached. It passed without slowing.

By morning, I was aching all over and struggling to stay awake, but when I saw Brenna load her kids into the car to go to school and work, I finally left the window.

I slept for a couple of hours, and when my alarm went off, I showered and headed to the police station with my laptop.

I found Frank at his desk, getting ready to leave on patrol. "Hey, you got a minute?"

"Sure," he said. "What's up, man?"

"I came up here to talk to the detectives on the Sanders case. I think I have something they might be interested in."

"Yeah? I don't think they're in right now. You know how it is. They sleep in and claim they're out interviewing people. I guess if they get the job done, nobody cares."

"That gives me a warm, secure feeling."

"What you got? I could call them if it's important."

I showed him what I'd discovered. "Two of the three main whistleblowers from Hertzog Industries died within a year of Hertzog's indictment. That doesn't seem like a coincidence to me."

"Are you sure?"

"I can send you the links to the obituaries."

"You have them on your phone?"

"Yes." I went to my browser. The second obit was already open. I handed him my phone, and he read it.

When he was finished, he said, "Just a minute. Let me look for this third one." He turned back to his computer and used a police database to search for that name. As he worked, he pointed me to the coffeepot, and I poured a cup of black coffee and came back to his desk. He was still reading when I sat down. "This guy moved. Last known address was here in Carlisle, but I can't find any record of him after that."

"At least he's not dead."

Frank leaned across the desk and lowered his voice. "The thing is, before they left the office last night, the detectives mentioned that they'd been over Pete Sanders's financial records and found six-figure deposits into a shell company account traced to him. One of the deposits was made the day after Strickland's death."

"You're kidding."

"And the other day when the fire was started, there was another deposit to the same account. I wonder if the dots connect back to Hertzog."

"Maybe you'd better call the detectives."

"Yeah, I'll get them in. You have time to wait?"

"All day," I said.

My information gave the detectives a jumpstart on their investigation. It didn't take long for them to trace the deposits back to Hertzog, and not much longer for them to get a search warrant. Just after lunchtime, they headed out to search Hertzog's house.

I couldn't make myself stay away. I drove over there and stood at the edge of the property, watching the police bring out evidence from the grandest estate in town. One of the detectives was coming out of the gates to the driveway when he saw me.

He grinned. "You had to see it for yourself, huh?"

"I hope it's okay."

"As long as you didn't bring a camera

crew. You'll never believe what we found in his study."

"What?"

"That picture Sanders had of Strickland dead, and similar pictures of the two dead whistleblowers. Only the killer could have had those shots."

I stared at him, stunned. "That's the closest thing you could have to a smoking gun. What are you going to do about it?"

"Stick around," he said with a wink. "You'll see."

I stood there for an hour or more, then, as if a switch had been flipped, everyone started moving faster. Cops hurried out of the house and opened the back door of a patrol car, and then immediately they walked Hertzog out in handcuffs.

The old man didn't look so bold now. He looked stooped and broken, insulted and livid. But he was alone. No one was coming to his aid.

I knew he would lawyer up and declare his innocence, and he might even be able to buy his way out. And after this battle, Hertzog would know that he'd never get away with touching her. That was all I cared about.

As the police locked him in the backseat and the cruiser drove away to take him to where he belonged, I went back to my car.

I could sleep now, and Brenna could live her life.

Prayers had been answered again.

CHAPTER 33

BRENNA

We all flew into Washington the day before the ceremony. The trip was filled with wonder and excitement for Sophia and Noah, who'd never flown before. For me, the trip was a chance to be with the man I loved. My mother came with us to watch the kids while we went to the White House dinner.

I had been to many AA and Celebrate Recovery meetings in the past couple of weeks, and I brought a list of meetings in the vicinity of my hotel in case I needed to go to one.

The night of the dinner, the White House sent a limo for us and drove us to the famous double doors at the West Wing, where we were greeted as if Nate were royalty. They seated us at a place of honor, along with the handful of others who'd be receiving awards, and I blossomed with pride as I saw the respect with which the president, as well as some of his cabinet members, his press staff, and others, greeted Nate. He was a true American hero, they said. A man who personified the American spirit. A man who was a role model for young men across the country.

As we rode back to the hotel in the limousine afterward, I snuggled up to Nate.

"So what did you think?" he asked, smiling.

I laughed. "I think I'm very lucky."

"Lucky? Why?"

"Because you're in love with me when you could have anyone else in the world."

"What would I want with anyone else?" He studied me for a moment. "How are you? Okay?"

I brushed his hair back off his forehead. "I know it hasn't been that long since court, but I'm feeling so much stronger. My head is so clear. I don't feel like a basket case anymore."

"No one ever thought you were a basket case."

"Well, I did. And you rescued me. You really did. You were there for me through it all, even though you had absolutely no obligation to me. You could've just left it all alone."

"How could I have done that? The moment I saw you that night I came back to town, I knew I'd never stopped loving you. I would've done anything I could to help you."

"You were my hero," I whispered. "I know how that senator feels."

I kissed him, and after a moment I pressed my forehead against his. "Ask me again, Nate."

He knew instantly what I meant, and he looked into my eyes for the assurance he needed. "Will you marry me, Brenna?"

"Yes," I said softly. "Yes, I'll marry you."

He closed his eyes and pulled me close. Life was turning out as it should, I thought with a poignant jolt of surprise. He laughed aloud as he held me and yelled up to the driver. "She said yes, Mike!"

"To what, sir?"

"To marrying me!"

I saw the driver grinning in the rearview mirror. "Congratulations. I thought you two were already married. You look like you belong together."

"We do!" I told him.

As we rode back to the hotel, Nate's smile faded, and his gaze strayed out the window. "What's wrong?" I asked.

He sighed and smiled again. "Nothing. I

was just thinking . . . I really want my father to be at the wedding. I want his approval, if I can get it. I'm marrying you with or without it, but it sure would be nice if I could reach some kind of peace with him."

"I understand," I said. "Your father and I . . . Well, things will probably always be awkward between us. But after what happened at the hearing . . . well, I believe in miracles. And I'll try my best to bridge the gap between us."

NATE

Jumping into an inferno was child's play compared to getting ready to be on national TV. My nerves were making me sweat in my new suit, and my mouth was dry.

Brenna knocked on my hotel room door. I opened it, and she stood there in her jeans, smiling up at me. "Look at you," she said. "You *look* like a hero who's getting an award. I wish I could go early too."

"I don't know if I can do this."

"Of course you can. We'll all be in the Rose Garden when you come out. Or is it on the Rose Garden? At? I wish I'd paid more attention when I've seen that place on the news."

"I think those of us who are White House–savvy say *in.*"

By the time she walked with me down to my limo, my nerves had calmed. She had that effect on me. She and the children would be transported to the White House later, where they'd be shown to special seats at the front of the crowd.

The morning went by in a whirl and with a lot of hoopla that made me uncomfortable and ramped my nerves back up to record level. It was nonsense, I thought, being labeled a hero and doing interviews over and over about what I'd done in that fire. I was being touted as something superhuman, when all I'd done was my job. And I hadn't done it alone.

By the time the ceremony was about to start, I found myself standing inside the White House with the other honorees — one who'd rescued a woman from a burning car, a teenager who'd saved three drowning children, an old man who dove into a river to rescue a man who'd jumped. Those people might be heroes, I thought, but not me. As I looked out the french doors at the cameras and the hundreds of people in the Rose Garden, I felt as if it was all some sick joke, and behind me someone had hung a big sign saying *He's Falling for It. He Thinks This Is Real.* I had a lot of nerve standing here as if I was somebody, I thought as I began to sweat.

The band on the side of the platform launched into a medley of patriotic tunes, and the honorees were ushered outside to take our seats on the platform with the president. Also present were the victims or parents of victims who'd been rescued, each of whom would make a speech about the heroics they'd witnessed and what it had meant to them. I listened in awe as their feats were recounted and wished again that I'd never agreed to be here.

When it was Senator Livingston's turn to talk, I stared down at my feet, hot and uncomfortable, wishing I could escape from this scrutiny. I felt like a bug caught for a collection, then pinned by its wings to a page where everyone could study it. Would my family's issues be plastered across the tabloids and discussed in the next news cycle?

Senator Livingston eloquently told of how I had single-handedly fought through the flames to get to his house, how I'd carried out both of his children and ushered out him and his wife, how even the dog had gotten out unharmed.

"Nate Beckett is a man I will point to when my daughter asks me what kind of man she should marry. He's the man I will use as an example when my son asks what kind of man he should be. I'll remind them of the man who ran through walls of flames to rescue a sleeping family. I'll remind them of the burns on his hands and legs as a result, the burns that I see as badges of courage, testimonies to the fact that this man is an American of the purest sort, the kind of brave heart this country was founded on. The kind of man who charges in, willing to lay down his life for another, willing to suffer so others won't have to. I owe my life, the lives of my beloved children and precious wife, to the courage of Nate Beckett."

The crowd erupted in a roar of applause and cheering as I was escorted to the podium. Everyone came to their feet as the president gave me the plaque that named me an American hero.

Smiling, trying to blink back the emotion so apparent on my face, I shook the hand of the senator, then the hand of the president, and when the senator reached out to hug me, dozens of cameras clicked. Stepping back, the senator took one of my hands, and the president the other, and they held them up in a victorious V— a picture that would be on the front page of every newspaper across the country that evening.

"America loves its heroes, son," the president said. "We don't have that many to go around." I looked out at the crowd, astonished that the throng of people remained standing, clapping and cheering for me as if I really was somebody, as if I really had done something. Tears filled my eyes as I scanned the front row and saw Brenna, beaming and crying, and Sophia and Noah jumping up and down in joyous celebration, and Drew standing there with tears in his eyes.

And then I saw my father, standing between my mother and Drew, applauding with all his might.

He had come, I thought. My father had come.

"That's my boy," Pop mouthed as he applauded.

I got choked up then and barely held it together as I went back to my seat.

My father was proud of me.

After the ceremony, I made my way off the stage, amid cameras flashing and media vying for my attention, but I pushed through them and took Brenna in my arms. She was still teary-eyed.

"I'm so proud of you," she said.

Noah slapped my hand. "It's like you're a

superhero. My mommy is marrying a super-hero!"

Laughing, I picked him up and hugged him. As I put him down, I looked for my father. The crowd had broken up, and clusters of people stood between us. "When did my father get here?"

"Not long ago. He was almost late. But Drew got him a seat up here with us. He does love you, Nate. While we waited for you, he was bursting with pride."

"Did he speak to you?"

"Not directly," she said, "but he wasn't rude. And your mother hugged all of us. He's trying, Nate. He really is."

I let Brenna go and caught sight of my brother. He hugged me roughly and studied the plaque I carried. My mother cut through the crowd and threw her arms around me.

"Thanks for coming, Mama."

"I was always going to come," she said. "Nothing could have stopped me."

As we hugged, I met Pop's eyes. Awkwardly, he reached out to shake my hand.

"I didn't expect to see you here, Pop."

His eyes were misty. "I couldn't stay away when my boy's being honored," he said in a soft, raspy voice. "I'm proud of you, son. Real proud."

Tears came to my eyes again as I savored

the words I'd waited a lifetime to hear, and finally I let Pop's hand go and pulled him into a hug.

For a moment, my father was stiff, uncomfortable with the physical display of affection, but finally he relaxed, and his arms closed around me.

I pulled back. "I'm marrying her, Pop, but it sure would be nice if you could offer us your blessing. I'd love to have you stand up for me."

Tears filled his eyes again, and wilting with the astonishing blow of love I had offered him, he covered his face. "You want me to be your best man?"

"Will you do it?"

He turned his face away, struggling with the emotion tearing at him. Finally he met my eyes. "How can I say no?"

And as I turned back to my mother and told her the news, the family embraced Brenna, congratulating and hugging her, welcoming her into a family that was complex, confused, and conflicted . . . but still a family nonetheless. It was the family I had.

And for the first time in my life, it was good enough.

ACKNOWLEDGMENTS

It takes a village to get a book from my computer into the stores, and I'm always aware that this is something I can't do on my own. A lot of my writer friends have defected from their publishers in order to be independent, self-published authors, which is a viable option these days. But I've chosen to stay with my publisher because of the team who works on every aspect of my book from editing to proofreading, to cover design and marketing.

First, I'd like to thank Amanda Bostic, the fiction publisher at Thomas Nelson (an imprint of HarperCollins Christian Publishing). She has been so patient with me in the last few years when I've had personal challenges and has made me feel valuable at every turn. Amanda has allowed me to continue working with Dave Lambert, the editor I've worked with since 1995, even though he's freelancing now. It makes a huge difference to have someone weighing in on my books who knows my whole body of work, understands how I think and what I'm trying to do, and always challenges me to take my books to the next level. Amanda also allows me to continue working with Ellen Tarver, who does a copyedit after I've done my revision for Dave. I couldn't continue publishing books without these people making sure I've written my way through several more drafts.

Once they've finished with their part, my book goes to the team at Harper, who get the manuscript into book form, create the cover, and introduce it to the world. I depend on Jodi Hughes, Paul Fisher, Allison Carter, Matt Bray, Savannah Summers, and Kristen Andrews to do all those things that make it successful. They are a top-notch team who make every writer feel like the only one.

I'm also grateful for Natasha Kern, my agent, who looks out for me and takes care of my career, even when I'm distracted by other things. I don't know what I'd do without her empathy and insight.

And finally, I'm overflowing with thanks for my husband, Ken Blackstock, who has been my rock in helping me raise our grandson and has given me so much acceptance, grace, and support that it moves me to tears. He models God's love to me every day and is a great example to me. He's the answer to prayers I prayed many years ago.

God has been so good to me to give me this group of people to help me through my life. Without them, I would have stopped writing long ago.

DISCUSSION QUESTIONS

1. Which character in this story did you most relate to or most empathize with? Why?
2. Nate and Brenna are still being impacted by the past, even all these years later. Would you have done anything differently in their shoes?
3. Are we all products of the past? Do you believe we should strive to overcome our pasts? Or is there another way to think about it?
4. How does forgiveness play a role in this story? Who do you think had the most difficult time offering forgiveness? Who was most impacted by forgiveness?
5. What are Nate's and Brenna's core flaws? How have these impacted their lives?
6. When Brenna's world seems to be falling apart, she turns to alcohol. If you were her best friend, what advice would you give her?

7. Jack's father believes his money allows him to control the events around him, but that did not ultimately turn out to be true. How have you seen money play a role — positively or negatively — in happiness? What about in pride?

8. What traits made Nate a good smoke jumper? Do those same traits serve him well in his relationships with Brenna and her children?

9. What themes from this story stood out to you? Do you know why those particular ones resonated with you?

10. If you were writing an epilogue for *Smoke Screen,* what future would you envision for Nate and Brenna?

ABOUT THE AUTHOR

Terri Blackstock has sold over seven million books worldwide and is a *New York Times* and *USA TODAY* best-selling author. She is the award-winning author of *Intervention, Vicious Cycle,* and *Downfall,* as well as such series as Cape Refuge, Newpointe 911, the SunCoast Chronicles, and the Restoration series.

terriblackstock.com
Facebook: tblackstock
Twitter: @terriblackstock